AN AMERICAN
OUTLAW

JOHN STONEHOUSE

Cover Design by Books Covered
Interior Layout by Polgarus Studio

ISBN -13: 9781497463684

ACKNOWLEDGEMENTS

Thomas Stofer, for sticking with it to the end. Marion Donaldson, Sam Copeland, Jennifer McVeigh, Susannah Godman, Ian Drury, JT Lindroos and Stuart Bache.

Author's Note

Anyone familiar with the geography and topography of West Texas will realize I have taken more than a few liberties; and while many of the places in the book do exist, they have been altered according to the demands of the story, and should, therefore, be regarded as entirely fictitious.

For B & T
mes plus belles étoiles

CHAPTER 1

Terlingua, TX.

My name is Gilman James. I come from Lafayette, Louisiana. So much happened to me, I have to tell somebody, to get it all out of my system. Nothing seems real anymore.

I know you don't know me. If you ever *do* hear about me, it probably means I'm dead.

My family came from Missouri, originally, before Louisiana. You might've heard of my Great-Great-Grandaddy. His name was Jesse.

It was like this.

About ten o' clock one morning I'm walking onto this gas station forecourt, out of the hot sun, into the shade. They had a big red and white Coca-Cola machine right by the door—to make you buy one.

Soon as I looked at it the lights went out on it. And it stopped buzzing.

At the same time, this skinny old guy's walking out of the gas station store looking at three quarters in the open palm

1

of his hand. He puts them in the Coca-Cola machine but it just spits them back out again.

He stares at his money lying there; rejected. Then he sees it ain't even working.

By this time I'm standing next to him, about to go on inside.

He looked up at me, straight in the face.

I nodded.

He says, "God-*dammit.*"

Whatever happened to Texas Friendly?

I says, "How's it going?"

"Don't put no money in there, Mister," he said. Then he shouted out, "Lem. Say, *Lem.* Looks like we got another God-damn *power*-outage…"

And that was the start of it. Right there.

Terlingua. I never will forget the name.

The far southwest of Texas. Ex-mining town. Silver. Minerals and shit. It had two motels, plus a combination gas station, store and diner—all rolled into one.

I was only supposed to be there one night. I still think about that, sometimes.

The old guy with the quarters turned around and went back inside the store.

I followed. He never even held the door for me.

Inside, there's this big guy working the counter.

"I know," he says, "we're all out. It just hit in here, too."

The old guy's shouting. "What the hell's the *matter* with these people, Lem? That's the third damn time this month."

"What are you going to do?" the guy says.

I wanted breakfast. I was hungry; it was gone ten already.

I says to the counter guy, "I get some breakfast? In the diner? Still an' all?"

"You can go ahead and take whatever we cooked already." He pointed to the hot-plates, over on the side. "But you heard what we's saying? We're powered out. Kitchen's closed."

The quarters guy says, "How long you figure we'll be out, Lem?"

"Can't say yet. I got to call it in. It'll be something, though."

Now the skinny old bastard starts hollerin', "What in hell are they doing? I mean, God dammit, what's *wrong* with these people?"

I went over to where the food was at; to get away from him pissing vinegar. I loaded up with sausage and eggs.

The counter guy calls over to me. "I guess that coffee's still hot in there, too…"

"Uh, got it," I says, "thanks." I felt like I could've worked that one out, though. I think he just did it so he could ignore that fuckin' little dillweed with the quarters. He was still going at it.

Anyhow, least one of them was friendly. That *is* what Texas is supposed to mean.

I took a sixteen-ounce cup of coffee and a Bavarian creme doughnut, along with the sausage and eggs. I sat by the window. Ate, while a guy rigged a diesel generator outside. There was black smoke pouring out of it. Noisy, too.

The air in the diner was already getting hot—without A/C. Texas is going to do that in July.

It was so far south it was nearly Mexico, maybe ten miles to the Rio Grande. Out the window, the terrain was familiar ground; straight-up desert—to a former-Marine.

I was going to just eat breakfast and get back on the road. I had to be some place. That afternoon I was robbing the bank up at Alpine.

It wasn't just me; there were three of us. Me, Michael Tyler, Steven Childress.

We all split up when we crossed the state line from Louisiana into east Texas. We was all driving trucks, I guess we looked about like anybody else around there. I had my old Ford F150. Candy-apple red. Beat up, covered in dirt.

We did all the scouting, all the reconn, two weeks back. I always liked reconn. It's never a waste of time. We picked a bunch of places we could stay, once we all split up. I got Terlingua—the southern watch. It had everything you'd need.

I'd never robbed a bank before. I'd seen some action—the Marine Corps; in Iraq. But the truth is, I had a bad feeling about that bank. Maybe I never inherited the family genes. The stealin' ones, that is. When it comes to tearin' shit up—I got the blood on that. Jesse was a hell of a fighter in the war against the North. The Civil War.

I ate breakfast. And thought about the town of Alpine where the bank was at. Eighty miles north, up the road.

Two days back, I'd committed my first crime—my home town, Lafayette. We pulled a warehouse heist, at the airport.

Burnt our bridges with the regular world.

The door of the diner opened. A hard-looking Mexican woman walks in. Stone-wash jeans. Red high-heel shoes. She had a scowl on her face like a two-year-old.

"Hey," she says, "how come I can't pump no gas out there?"

"Ma'am, there's a power outage. Half the county's out. Can't pump no gas till they fix it."

I bit so hard into my doughnut the Bavarian creme burst out all over my pants.

The Mexican woman looks around with her mouth wide open. She looks out the window by me. "How 'bout that generator you runnin' back there?"

"That thing's running these here refrigerators, ma'am, that's all. I can't pump no gas on it."

I just sat looking at the two of them.

The Mexican woman's shaking her head. "Damn. How long you figure we're going to be out?"

"I called the power company—just got off of the phone to 'em. They're saying five, maybe six hours."

Now I was staring.

She said, "They gotta be kidding, right?"

"No, ma'am. First they got to find the break. Can't fix it till they find it. Could take longer, at that."

"I just drove twenty miles to get here." She starts in sucking on her cheeks. "What am I supposed to do, turn around and go home? I got to call before it's even worth I come out here?"

"Don't be counting on that, ma'am—oftentimes, there's

a power outage, they got to shut the phone line down also. Something 'bout the sub-station can't work right. Or the *ex*change. Something…"

She stomped back out to the black Dodge Ram on the forecourt. I just sat staring out the window at the pumps.

I needed gas. Sweat started running down my back. I needed gas. Period.

The night before, driving in, the truck got to running low—but there was nowhere to stop on the road. Nothing but desert and empty highway. I figured it didn't matter—knowing Terlingua had a gas station, knowing it from the scout. But the time I rolled in it was shut already, closed for the night.

Alpine was eighty miles north. No way I was going to make it.

It was already eleven o' clock. If the power stayed out as long as they said, I wasn't going to make it. *Jesus.*

I went to pay for breakfast.

The guy makes my change. I says, "There some place else I can get gas around here? I guess I need to get back on the road a ways."

He thought about it. "Nearest place'd be Presidio. Out on one-seventy. El camino rio."

"How far is that?"

"Fifty something."

"Fifty?"

He shrugged. "That's all there is."

I took my change.

6

"It ain't nothing but a ranch road," the guy says. "Rock hounds like it, I guess."

I left the diner. Walked back to the motel I spent the night before—The Old Mission Motel.

Red dirt was blowing across the road. Down there it's more like sand than dirt. I tried to remember what they call it; I'm always thinking shit like that. My Company Commander used to look at me sideways, sometimes. Said I got an *in*quiring mind. Guess I do wish my education wouldn't have got so screwed. Maybe things could've been different.

I still had the motel room, paid 'em two nights so I could use it the rest of the day.

I didn't know whether to call Michael, or Steven. We were all split up around the town of Alpine to cut the odds of being seen. Like spokes on a wheel, Steven said. I thought it was more like points on a compass. It was, really.

I had the southern watch—Michael was east in Fort Stockton—Steven up in Pecos, the northern point.

I didn't want to make any call, not till I could think of a solution. We were supposed to meet up at three, at Alpine. If the power stayed out I'd never make it, with no gas. But would it stay out? And how about the phones?

I had a cell in my bag. No good. Too far out in the desert, no signal.

I found Presidio, where the other gas station was at, on my Department of Transportation map. Forget it. I'd have to hitch a ride. Both ways. Somebody would remember. A guy hitching a ride a hundred miles for gas? It would've been like a story around there.

I folded the map. Put it away in my bag. I put it on top of my M9 Beretta, to hide it.

It was hot in the motel room. Coming on midday. They had a pool out front—you could see the gas station from there. I had some old cargo shorts in my bag. I put them on and went outside.

Not many people came by that gas station in Terlingua. From the pool, I kept checking the big Exxon sign, to see if the lights flashed on up inside it. But nothing happened.

It was quiet. A dog-still afternoon. Hot like a furnace. A dry wind swayed the top of a green ocotillo by the chain fence. Red sand was blowing in the pool. People don't go that far south in summer. That was part of why Michael and me chose it. The only people passing through were rock hounds hunting cinnabar, and migrant workers headed back to Mexico. Seeds drifting on the wind.

And me. Waiting on robbing that bank.

Alpine was up in the Highlands—they got Highlands in Texas, I never knew before I went there on scout.

It was a college town; people came there from all over, from overseas—wherever. They had a bunch of money coming in 'cause of all the students, Steven said. Steven was the third man in our team of three. Little brother of Nate—about the best friend I ever had.

But Nate was dead.

Steven went to college in Alpine. He met a girl there; stuck around after. It all went south with the girl, but by then he'd got himself a job—at the bank; the Farmer's Bank—

around the same time Nate and me and Michael deployed third tour USMC. To Iraq.

A lot happened since then.

I stuck my head under the water, dived to the bottom of the pool. Felt the cold pressure, emptying my mind.

I came back up, lay floating, watching yellow blades against the turquoise liner.

A black outline of a man appears. The edge of the pool. Big guy, Comanche. He drops in the water, fully clothed, just to cool down.

Don't know where he came from. He never said two words. He folded his arms across his chest, standing in his boots, the water up to his neck. Like some red skinned cross between a wolf and a shark.

I stared at the sky overhead. Flat, hard. Radiating heat. When I looked back a minute later, the man was gone.

I still didn't try to call Michael, nor Steven. Not yet. There'd be time. If I didn't show, they'd wait; bail. That was the deal—we all agreed.

But they'd fix the power.

I thought of back home, Lafayette, the night we first talked—saying out loud, about taking; stealing, robbing a warehouse. A bank. Everything else. Nate was newly dead then. The three of us raw—Steven and Michael and me. We were drinking beer out on the porch at Michael's place, by the freeway. All the time we were talking, I could hear traffic in the background. Cars and trucks, running down Evangeline. The world heedless, turning on.

I pulled myself out of the pool. Sat at the water's edge.

Thought again of the other gas station; Presidio.

Maybe the truck could make it? On the map, the road out had seemed short enough. Even as I thought of it, something else hit me—a feeling something wasn't right. *The gun in my bag*—in the motel room. When I'd put the map away, on top of it, something had caught my eye.

I sat a second more. Then jumped to my feet, ran back in the motel room and locked the door.

I ripped open the bag. Pulled the gun out from under the map. Stared at it.

The last number machine-stamped on the frame was a seven. A seven, not a one. Wrong serial number. I had *Nate's* gun.

Christ. Steven must have mine.

I picked up the phone to call Steven. The line was dead. Yeah. It fucking had to be. I sat on the bed, thinking.

I checked my watch. Almost one. I felt my heart rate quicken, ran a hand through my wet hair.

They wouldn't go, they'd pull it, like we said. Anybody didn't show, we'd scratch. Re-arrange the hit the next day.

I dressed quick, grabbed my keys, ran out, ran to the truck. I climbed in, drove around back of the motel—away from the road, where no one would see.

It was too late, no way I'd make it. If we were bugging out, less anybody saw of me, the fewer eyes the better—like I learned in the Corps.

I'd stay out of sight. Wait on the power. Blow as soon as it hooked back up.

I locked the truck. Left it well out of sight behind a couple of rusted dumpsters.

From the scout, I knew there was a clap-board store a mile up the hill. I could walk up, buy something to eat, something to drink, stay away from the diner.

I set out to walk up the highway keeping back from the road, among the scrub and rock. At the top of the long hill I tried the cell again, holding it in the palm of my hand; willing it to work.

Nothing. Miles it'd been, a whole day before, since I'd last had any signal.

But they'd wait.

Inside the store, it was dark, deserted, no power, no working lights. The sound of some guy in back running around yelling, all his stock starting to melt.

I picked out what I needed. Left money by the counter.

I headed on back down the hill. Thinking on Steven, and my gun.

An M9 Beretta—service-issue. My gun. Nobody ever had it, except for me.

At The Old Mission, everything was deserted. One room only rented—my room. A clerk showed up in the morning at check-out time, then again in the evening, for any new arrivals. The place was empty, Terlingua an outpost. No-one came there, that was the reason we chose it.

I waited on the pumps. On that Exxon sign to light up. No way of moving. Nobody I could call.

A feeling started to grip my stomach.

In back of the diner the generator ran on, kicking black

smoke—to vanish in the hot wind. Every once in a while, a car pulled in off the highway, into the gas station. And pulled back out a minute later, seeing it closed.

If there was anybody living within twenty miles, they must've known the place was shut down. Nobody came.

I thought of Michael and Steven.

If they'd pulled it, if they'd bailed—how come nobody came to look for me?

Maybe not Steven. But Michael would.

By late afternoon, I watched the big guy from the diner start to close it up. Him and some short-order cook. The big guy, Lem, tanked the generator from a ten gallon can and climbed into a Bronco.

The cook got into a panel van.

The pair of them hit the highway. I watched them both disappear.

I went around back of The Old Mission to sit in my truck. Watching the light start to change. To fade into evening.

I pulled the gun from my bag, the gun that Steven had been carrying—Nate had owned it, in the service. It was exactly alike with mine. Marine-issue M9 semi-auto. Identical, but for the numbers stamped along the frame.

Two pistols that'd kept him and me alive.

I climbed down from the cab. Stood watching the empty highway.

Dusk was closing in all around now. I went around back of my truck, climbed over the side and lay in the truck bed, against the hard metal. Sweat running in my hair.

I tried not to think. Of Nate. I tried not to think of a desert, thousands of miles from there. Of the flashes in my head, if I closed my eyes.

All I could do was wait.

There was just the wind. Grit sticking to my wet fingers. A blackening sky.

No sign of any life, no light across the land.

Where were they?

CHAPTER 2

I'm still laying in back of the truck when the power snapped back on.

I felt a rush, gripped the steel sides of the truck—hauled myself to my knees, trying to shake the confusion. There were lights burning from out of the dark everywhere—like a battlefield. But it wasn't Iraq. I couldn't be there.

I sprang out of the truck. Stumbled. Ran across the dirt to my motel room.

The door was wide open. All the lights on, the A/C unit—the TV. Unreal. My eyes blinking, trying to focus. Hands feeling along the wall, for switches, to turn out the lights.

By the bed, a clock. A red display of numbers—*five-thirty a.m.*

By the clock the phone. I grabbed it. Clamped it against my ear. Already dialing a number for Michael.

No sound's coming out of it. It's dead. Not connected. I stabbed at the cradle, chopping it up and down.

On the wall above the bed is a TV. Set to the local news

station—a loop, running through the early hours, A/C drowning out the sound. I saw the flash of an image. Brick building, two-story. Nausea flooding my stomach.

I scrambled for the remote, turned up the sound. Knowing it was Alpine—even before they said the name.

One man shot dead. Another escaped the scene.

Police issuing an alert—for *Gilman Francis James*. Of Lafayette, Louisiana. Owner of a red Ford F150. Louisiana plate.

I woke up so fast with all that adrenaline flooding my bloodstream.

How long does it take to put up a manhunt? How long to cut the roads?

I didn't know that morning. Thank God, is all I can say.

'Cause it was just getting started.

Chapter 3

Steven must be dead.

It was my gun he'd been carrying; my numbers on it, it had to be Steven—if they were looking for me.

I snapped off the TV. Stared at the condensation on the window by the A/C unit. Listening to it rattle and blow.

Michael must've got out, somehow.

I drank some water from the faucet. Put my head under its cold stream.

I had to find him. Wherever he was.

I checked the room fast—nothing of mine left inside there.

I ran out, ran the fifty yards to the gas station. The pumps dead. The big Exxon sign unlit.

Inside the diner, ceiling lights showed, but nothing else.

I ran around the back. Any vehicle. Anything would do. Beyond the building, the ground was deserted. There was nothing.

Past the dumpsters, behind the Old Mission, I could see

my truck. Low sun starting to creep over the mountains.

I sprinted back to the truck, scrambled into the cab, grabbed Nate's pistol, checked the map. Due north was Alpine. East, the road gave out in the hills. Only place to go was west—toward Presidio. Get out of Terlingua. I'd get as far as I could. Then dump the truck. Find something; improvise.

I fired up the truck. Pulled out of the lot. Took the turn onto 170, the sun rising behind me.

I felt for my cell, set it with the pistol on the empty seat beside me. Steered onto a two-lane into desert of flat scrub. Jag of red mountain on the skyline.

Steven was dead. Steven or Michael. I knew it must be Steven. Gone. Like Nate, like his brother.

I thought of their mother—back on east Vermilion. Thought of Michael, that I grew up with, his place on south Refinery, where he finished up—dumped couches, abandoned shacks. Thinking on why that was. Why I blamed myself. And always would.

I came up a rise in the road. Shale bank at the side of the highway. Where the road topped out, the ground opened into a wide plain.

A truck was headed towards me. White pick-up. Side-lights on.

I held my speed, right hand floating from the wheel—till I could feel the M9.

The pick-up drew level. One guy in it, wearing a Western hat.

It passed behind. I held steady, watched the rear-view till

he topped the rise and disappeared the other side.

Ahead, the road stretched west, the land empty, mountains rising in the south. White cloud hanging over Mexico. Across the border—the only other way out.

To the north, on a bluff of rock, an outline showed against the sky; some kind of mast. A repeater mast. It could be.

I checked the rear-view. Grabbed the cell off the seat. Held it in front of the wheel.

At the right-hand edge of the road, a dirt track ran north towards the mast. I slowed up, steered off, holding the phone out in front of me. Weak signal showing. Keying in the number for Michael.

It's ringing. I pressed the phone to my ear. Held my breath.

It picks up.

I stamped on the brakes. "Michael?"

"Gil?" he says. He sounded hoarse. Close to panic.

The truck skidded to a stop in the dirt. "Tell me where you are?"

"Marfa."

I snatched the map off the empty passenger seat. Found the place. My finger tracing it, due north across the desert.

"Don't come here," he says. "Police are everywhere. Steven went crazy…"

"Are you hurt?"

He didn't answer.

I heard him cough, the sound muffled into his hand.

"Steven's dead," I said. "Isn't he? Tell me what happened…"

"He went in," Michael's voice rising. "He just went right in. On his own."

I shook my head.

"I tried to get him out…" He was silent.

I says, "You were supposed to wait."

"Why didn't you come?"

"I'm coming now."

"No, man."

"Steven had my gun. I've got his. I got no alibi…"

He didn't answer.

"They're looking for me. It's too late," I says. "You know that."

All I could hear was him breathing; labored.

"Where are you?"

"Christ. Some motel."

"Are you hurt?"

Nothing but silence on the end of the line.

"Stay put," I told him. "I'll get you."

"Jesus Christ, Gil."

"Are you shot?"

"Yeah," he says, "I'm shot."

"Put the phone down. Stay where you are."

"Don't come here."

"Keep off the phone. I get to Marfa, I'll find you, I'll call again…"

"Fuckin' don't."

"Michael," I says, "I'm hanging up." I clicked off the call.

He was shot—but still alive.

He'd stay alive, I told myself.

robbery like this in a long time, not in rural West Texas. We've got serious crime, including robbery, down to one quarter the national average…"

"Well, this one's hot off the shovel," says Whicher.

"It's hot?"

"Department of Public Safety, via the Governor's Office. I think you might have something with that theory of yours. Somebody put a rocket up my boss' ass. Guess where it ends up next?"

"Copy that."

"You want to run me what happened?"

The lieutenant sits up in his chair. "Yesterday afternoon around three pm there's a shooting incident at a supermarket."

"A supermarket?"

"Win-Dixie, downtown. Some guy shooting up the ceiling, generally pissing off the folks in the express aisle."

"We talking about a diversion?"

"It sure looks that way. Nothing got stolen," the lieutenant says. "But first word of a shooter, the dispatcher sent all available units. Everybody we had was tied up there."

"Okay."

"Straight after, it looks like they headed across town to the Farmer's Bank…"

"How long before it got hit?"

"Less than ten minutes. Two of them tried to hold it up. Say, you want to take a ride down there?"

"You got people there?"

"Sure."

"That guy y'all shot? He still dead?"

"Uh. Yes," says the lieutenant.

"Let's stay here."

"Right." The lieutenant clears his throat. "Well, sir, the bank staff hit the alarm, but we had all units out at the first incident. There was a little confusion, to be honest—two major incidents; the dispatcher's screen lighting up."

"No great Monday…"

"We pulled half the units, sent them to the bank. I guess we got our people there faster than they thought we would. Or else something delayed them."

Whicher frowns.

"The guy shot dead was attempting to leave the bank. The one that actually made it out is believed injured. One of my officers thinks he hit him."

"How come he still made it out?"

"I have a patrol sergeant reckons he was using tactical movement."

Whicher leans his head a fraction to the side.

"My sergeant's a former infantry specialist. Said the guy was moving and shooting like a trained soldier."

Whicher stares at the lieutenant's desk. He crosses a boot over the knee of his suit. "You want to know my end of the deal?"

"Yes, sir."

"I get into work this morning there's a new guy top of the 15."

"The 15?"

"US Marshals Service 15 most wanted. Know something else? That's fast. In with a bullet."

"Well, marshal, ATF identified the gun from the bank as a military designation Beretta 9mm. Marine Corps side-arm. Registered to a Gilman James. We got his name, we got an address, law enforcement hit the place in Louisiana. Nobody there."

The lieutenant takes a sheet of printed paper from a pile on his desk. He pushes it toward the marshal.

Whicher scans it. The copy of a ticket on a Ford F150. "This his. Y'all looking for it?"

"That's the vehicle registered to him. At the address in Lafayette…"

"Anybody seen him there—in Louisiana?"

"Neighbors haven't seen him for days."

"Any record? Ever been on the yard?"

"No, sir."

"Honorable discharge?"

The lieutenant shakes his head. "We've got nothing on him."

"This link ATF are making? This airport robbery—in Lafayette?"

"They think there's evidence it's the same guys hit both there and here."

"What evidence?"

"ATF recovered an empty Beretta magazine at that airport. A magazine and a bunch of spent rounds. They say they're Marine Corps issue. Like we got here at the bank."

"The same gun?"

"No, sir, not the same. Two distinct weapons. They don't yet have a full ID on the gun used at the airport in Lafayette.

But two Marine Corps weapons?"

Whicher leans back in his seat.

"According to ATF," the lieutenant says, "that's a highly unusual confluence. Statistically speaking."

"No shit."

Whicher scowls. Runs a hand across his jawbone.

"You know why I get this?"

"This case?"

"Yeah. Tell you why. I'm a criminal investigator."

"Yes, sir, marshal."

"No, I mean, the pay grade's 25 per cent higher."

The lieutenant puts his pen down on the desk. "Okay."

"That's what's going on. You're going to learn that. Thing of it is, I'm pretty good at it, like to get my man."

"Everybody's pulling for that."

"You have some serious resource, but we've got one big ass problem—West Texas. Nobody's seen this guy, nobody knows where he's at, nobody knows nothin'. That about it?"

"He'll break cover some place."

"You think the guy that escaped from the bank is Gilman James, lieutenant?"

"I don't know. My sergeant said the guy was blond. The record we saw on James says he's dark."

"You think there's two of 'em out there?"

"My guess would be two."

"Know what I don't like?"

"What's that, marshal."

"If this is some bunch of ex-service boys, they get working on something, they get a head of steam, somebody's going to end up cooked. It ain't like Joe Hood. They start shooting, they ain't going to miss."

"So, how do you want to approach it?"

"Fight fire with fire."

CHAPTER 5

The Solitario, TX.

The fuel gauge was low—way low, the needle down. And sweat running off my skin like water.

Odometer in the dash made it less than thirty miles since Terlingua. I steered the truck across the raw scrub, tires kicking up a cloud of dust.

The dirt track from the highway had disappeared. It'd reached an old farmstead—and just stopped.

I'd checked the place, but it was abandoned—an old stone-built house, nothing more than a ruin. Barns, tin shacks, their sides hanging off. There'd been nothing I could use, nothing to take, no sign of any life.

I'd picked a way forward in the truck since then, searching out any path north, any kind of route. Crossing drifts of deep sand, working, sweating not to get an axle stuck. Climbing banks of gravel and shale under the hammering sun.

The truck was ready to quit. I knew. Running on fumes.

Ahead, the land was scrub covered mountain, and bare caliche. Tracts of Spanish bayonet, clumps of tangle-head and sotol.

I glanced at the map on the seat. I reckoned it still another thirty miles, maybe more, to Michael, up in Marfa.

The cell on the passenger seat was stone dead—no signal. Nate's M9 beside it, butting up against the seat back.

I thought of my own gun. That Steven died with. They must've had to prize it from his hand.

I pushed the image from my mind.

When I left the Corps, I requested to keep my side-arm. Nate'd done the same. We bought 'em—both bought our pistols; a mark, what it was, on a day in Iraq. A day we couldn't ever forget.

9mm Beretta. A symbol. A weapon of last resort.

Marine carries a pistol, it's not a fighting gun, but for self-defense. Bringing that thing on a robbery was my way of making sure I'd never use it. I never would have.

Steven wanted to carry Nate's. What was I going to tell him?

I stared out the windshield at the ground ahead, rising sharp.

That day in Iraq changed our lives. Nothing would ever be the same.

Steven had to carry his brother's gun.

I flicked a gear down. Steered a way up a pile of loose rock and scree. Engine whining, the truck slipping and baulking, tires spitting stones. Then it cut on me. It died, caught again—and lurched forward.

I hit the brake.

I glanced behind, to the foot of the slope below, the motor hunting.

There was an overhang of rock—a stand of evergreen sumac.

I stuck her into neutral. Rolled back down. Nothing to do but try to hide the truck as best I could under the thin-grown trees. The motor cut a last time. I switched off and pulled out the keys.

Waves of heat blasted off the desert scrub. I jumped out, climbed in back, unlocked the tool chest, sun biting into my skin.

Inside the tool chest were two full water bottles—desert habit I never break. There was a back pack—I ripped it open, stuffed in the water bottles, extra clothing, a jacket.

From the cab I took Nate's gun, the cell phone, my road map.

Nothing else for it. On foot I could make myself a son-of-a-bitch to find. I reckoned Marfa at thirty to forty miles north. How long it'd take to reach would depend on the lie of the land. I'd have to pace it.

I scrambled my way up the pile of scree. At the top, I took a bearing north, the best I could.

I could see I'd have to deviate plenty, it was bad ground, covered in dense spine of cactus and creosote bush.

I felt the sweat lifting from my skin. Made myself walk slow and easy. I set out across a dried up arroyo full of loose rock and stone.

Tried not to think on the temperature rising.

⅄

Late afternoon. A deep canyon. Squatting in the shade of a north facing wall.

The wind moved through on a low moan. Across the rock floor were potholes, some with rainwater still in 'em. I cupped my hands, got some in me. I drunk worse.

Two hours. Two hours tracking through a canyon, running east the whole time—east, instead of north. But no way around it, in the sapping heat.

Marfa was too far, now. No way of making it, before nightfall. Michael was up there, somewhere. Some motel. With a gunshot wound. But I couldn't see well enough—not near enough, I'd never find my way.

I'd have to overnight. There'd be places; ruined places the silver miners built a hundred years and more ago. Some just a few broken walls, others with roofs and timber still intact. I'd find food. Chihuahuan desert I knew there were jack-rabbits, every kind of bird, roadrunner, javelina. More life, more water than any regular desert I'd seen.

I sat against the canyon wall, waiting on the temperature to drop. Took Nate's gun apart, cleaned it with a strip of cloth.

I broke it down, six main pieces. Put it on back together. Touched all fifteen rounds in the magazine.

I thought of Jesse.

I know he used to hide out in Texas—in the war.

What I know of Jesse and Frank James, their daddy was a preacher, the Second Great Awakening. But he was dead long before the first shot.

They came home from the war with nothing.

Jesse took a ball in the lung, the last days of fighting—not expected to live. Union forces put him on a boat up the Missouri River, to Rulo, Nebraska. To die, with his momma. Exiles in their own land.

Our side came down from his daughter—if it all was true.

She had three sons, one of 'em my Grandaddy, it was said.

My own mother was illegit—the fifties. Raised by the Daughters of Charity. *'Father unknown'* marked on her birth certificate. Mother a Creole dancing girl, in New Orleans.

She was given up to Saint Elizabeth's. Somebody at the orphanage gave her the name of James. And told her—that her line went on back. I don't know.

Mostly, I figured it for a story. To make her feel like somebody. Much good it did.

I put away the gun. Behind the mountains to the west, the sun was almost gone, the sting of heat drawn from the day. I needed to move.

I kept the pistol loaded; ready in my jacket. Pack tight across my back. Around my lower legs I wrapped extra clothing, a shirt on one leg, tee-shirt on the other. Once the sun went down, there'd be a bunch of snake and scorpion. Tarantula, too.

I walked heavy, kicking stones and dirt with my feet to run 'em off.

I stopped often, looking for movement; listening for any sound.

Out of habit, I made a couple of random direction changes and threw in a fish-hook, where you sort of swing around back on yourself—in case there was anyone behind me. There was no-one.

By now, I could feel the hunger starting to kick in. I could've used a couple of ration packs. At least I had enough water.

I worked my way across a high plateau full of salt grass and cane cholla.

At the edge of a boulder field, in a shallow-sided valley, the stone walls of a miner's house stood bare.

A section of the roof was gone. I didn't figure anyone could be in there. I slipped loose the Beretta, just the same.

I got low to my haunches, watching. The ground gave no sign. It looked like nobody used it. I started to move in slow, in the gathering dark.

Close up, it looked abandoned. An empty doorway, the walls bare stone, no glass in any of its windows.

I picked my way inside, across a beaten-earth floor. Loose rubble of plaster underfoot. I stared at the sky through the broken roof. Listened to the wind moving in the salt grass.

I put away Nate's M9 in my jacket. Thought of my own house. Lafayette. Each room; seeing it in my mind, like I was walking through there. Only sound, the heat ticking on the roof. Dust moving in the sunlight. Weeds and a bunch of oil stains in the yard.

My mother died, the place had come to me. There was no-one else. I slept at the house only if I visited on furlough, I was always gone.

The last months, since leaving the service, I'd stayed there, but it was no home. I joined the Corps at twenty. Never came back. My only real family was Nate and Michael. I'd known 'em both since second grade.

I left the house and took a walk around.

A line of broken fence posts stretched out to a break of honey mesquite; seedpods hanging from the branches. Jack rabbits ate 'em. I cut some sapling wood, stripped it to fine lengths. Tied it together; to set a bunch of traps—I wanted to eat in the morning.

I worked my way back to the house. Stashed the back pack in an old window. I took off the jacket. Laid it, with the M9, in a dark corner behind a pile of rocks.

I drank a little water. Warm. I drunk some warm water in my time—out of canteens, metal cups, plastic bags.

I caught some rest. Saved energy. Knowing I wasn't about to sleep. Thinking on Michael. On Nate. His little brother, Steven. Dead and gone.

I listened to the night sounds. Cicada and the wind against those empty stones.

Restless, I left the house again to check on the traps.

I traced a wide circle through the valley floor. Moon low at the south, the mountain sides sharp against the blackened sky.

Before first light, I'd get moving. Make up the ground, before the worst of the heat.

The wind started to pick up, scattering sand across the bone dry ground. I caught a boot in a snag of bush muhly.

I stopped. Stood rigid.

A sound.

Something on the wind.

It was gone again, as soon as I'd heard it.

I looked for light.

There was nothing.

The nearest place would be miles away. Forty? Maybe more.

Nothing could be out there, it was just the wind. I turned back toward the house, straining to listen above the beat of cicadas.

There was a muffled sound, now. Like an animal—a dog.

I felt the hairs rise on my arm.

If it was a dog, it was shut up inside of something. A vehicle—it could be in a vehicle.

Nate's gun was in my jacket; at the house.

I ran, smashed a path through the scrub, jumped a broken wall—hit the ground.

I picked myself up, scrambled to the back wall of the house, to an opening, stepped in a room—no idea which.

There was the faintest scent suddenly in the air.

"*Hold it.* Hold still…"

A woman's voice. From somewhere out of the dark.

I couldn't see nothing.

I could see *something*. Through a rotted-out timber hole in the wall, the barrel of a twelve-gauge was pointing at me

"Who the hell are you? What're you doing?"

I stared at the wall where her voice came from; the only sound that dog going crazy, locked up somewhere, in a car.

"You're trespassing on private property," she said. "This here's my Granddaddy's house…"

What kind of horseshit luck you got to take all inside of one day?

⅄

I tried not to act like any kind of a threat to her, considering.

She held that twelve-gauge rock steady.

I'd have to talk my way out of it. Try to, anyhow.

If I couldn't, I'd have to hurt her or she'd have to shoot me. What else was there?

"I was out hiking the trail, ma'am. Just figured on stopping for the night…"

The dog kept on barking. It stopped to listen every few seconds.

"Didn't know this here all belonged to nobody," I says.

I waited for her to speak again. She let me.

The wind stirred in the long grass growing outside the house.

"You're hiking the Mesa de Anguila? In summer? You're pretty far off of the trail."

"I was looking for water," I said. Any hiker would be in July. "Supposed to be a tinaja around here someplace. According to the trail book."

The barrel of the twelve-gauge moved a fraction through the gap in the wall. "There's nothing around here."

She let the silence judge me while she thought it over. Dog sure wasn't buying any.

"I was just fixing to get some sleep," I said. "Head on out again, first light."

The shotgun stayed on me; dumb and black.

"These old houses," I says, "most of 'em got a spring some place about. I figured I could maybe find something in the morning."

She snapped on a flashlight. Shone the beam square in my face.

I squinted into it; blinded.

"Look," I said, "I can just move right on out. Find someplace else to camp—seeing how I'm on private property, an' all."

She didn't answer. The sound of cicadas beat in the night air. That dog howled out again and again.

She must have followed my thoughts. "He knew there was somebody out here," she said. "He knew."

"Ma'am?"

"My dog. He always knows if there's trespassin'."

"Sure sounds like it."

"He don't care for it, neither."

She shone the flashlight in my face again. Held it there.

I tried to look like I didn't mind it, nothing to hide. But I couldn't see now. She figure on that?

I could hear her moving. The flashlight snapped off.

I was blind and disoriented. I heard her feet on the ground, near me now. In front of me. But I couldn't see a damn thing. I didn't try to move.

"Thirsty man, huh?"

She was just a few feet in front of me. Wearing some kind of scent.

I tried to focus on her. My eyes adjusting, slowly. The moon made shadows off the roof timbers. Lines and shapes across the dirt floor.

I could see her as a kind of silhouette. I could see she was tall. Long limbs, slender, sort of dark.

I heard her feel for something, inside her clothes.

There was a flare of orange light as she struck a match and lit up a cigarette. I could see a mass of long, dark hair. She swept a hand through it, brushing it back off her face. She held her head to one side as she cupped the flame.

In the match-glow, I could see dark eyes, strong eyebrows. High cheekbones, full lips. Real pretty girl. She was Mexican or Spanish looking. Latin. The all-white of the cigarette stood out against her sun-brown skin. She had silver jewelry on her fingers and around her wrists. And I could see the shotgun balanced in the crook of her arm.

I didn't try to talk.

She smoked her cigarette. Thought whatever the hell it was she was thinking.

I slumped down on the edge of a fallen wall, adrenaline sinking out of me.

She pulled hard on the cigarette. Blew her smoke out extra heavy. "Somebody send you out here?"

"Ma'am?"

"Did Leon send you?"

I ran a hand through my hair. "I don't know anybody around here. I'm just…"

"Hiking the trail," she cut in. "Right."

I glanced at the shotgun. She was holding it loose in her right hand. I thought about how fast I'd need to be to get it.

"You don't have much gear," she says. "For a hiker."

She ground her cigarette out into sparks. Swung the shotgun from her waist. Leveled it at me.

I raised my hands. "Take it easy…"

She says; "I'm getting my dog."

She stepped out of the house. Disappeared toward the sound of the barking.

I jumped up, straining my eyes to see, trying to feel my way through the darkened room.

Where was it?

I heard a car door creak open. She was saying something, now, talking to her dog.

There was no sign of the gun.

I looked for anything laying around that I could use. A length of timber for the dog, if she turned it loose; her I could put down with my feet and hands, depending on the shotgun.

She have it in her to shoot somebody?

I didn't want to hurt her, but I had to get clear. There was no time, I could hear her, hear the dog running.

And something's rising up inside me, a feeling from another place, another life—something I try to shut out, and never let back in.

Tightness. Gripping my chest, like a steel band, ripping at me. Images flashing in my mind.

And the dog.

The sound of the dog. It's stopped, somewhere in front of me.

She snaps the flashlight beam full in my face. White-burn. Like tracer. Everything else black, red, out of balance.

Anger's starting to flood in me, weight moving forward, hands outstretched.

My head hit something. Pain like a hammer blow.

Everything burst in a shower of light and flame.

And I'm falling. Dead weight in the pitch black.

Then nothing.

Chapter 6

Alpine.

Outside the City of Alpine Morgue, Marshal John Whicher takes a last gulp at a carry-out cup of coffee. He drains it, crumples it in a big hand and tosses the screwed up remains in the trash. He checks his watch. Inside, waiting in a cold room, is Steven Childress. Age twenty eight.

In the last twenty-four hours, the details on Childress's short life show he's a former Alpine resident. Ex-employee at the Farmer's Bank. No criminal record. No previous. Some kid; dreaming of pulling off an inside job. ATF theory about a hard-core military connection, some bunch of vets turned rogue—where was the evidence?

A Marine-issue gun. Circumstantial. Who knew how it got there?

The marshal squints into the low sun of a new day—it slants from the roof of a mid-rise office block. *Last thing anybody needs is a serial spree.*

From the street, Police Lieutenant Rodgers' Crown Vic

pulls in. The lieutenant parks in the empty slot beside Whicher's Silverado. He steps from the squad car, hurries across the asphalt lot.

"Sorry if I'm late, marshal."

"Don't worry. I'm early."

The young lieutenant pushes open the door to the City Morgue. Inside, in a sparse reception room, a middle-aged woman in a business suit waits behind a desk.

"Good morning," she looks up solemnly. "Gentlemen."

Whicher takes off the Resistol hat.

"Morning, Ann," Rodgers removes his own cap. "Can we go straight in?"

"Room Four. Dr. Wendell."

Whicher follows the lieutenant down a corridor to a wide set of double doors, hardly noticing the smell of disinfectant, the lighting, the sombre weight that hangs in the air.

Beyond the double doors is a cold room, white-tiled. A man in his sixties working at a steel desk in one corner.

"Dr. Wendell," says the lieutenant, "this is Deputy Marshal John Whicher."

The doctor looks up from his desk. Lab coat over a shirt and tie. Black-rimmed spectacles in his thinning hair.

In the middle of the room is a gurney. On it, a body, covered with a sheet; a head of dark hair showing from under it.

Doctor Wendell crosses the room, on a bad hip, Whicher notices. He draws down the sheet on the corpse. Places his spectacles on the bridge of his nose.

"Steven Wade Childress. Cause of death, multiple gunshot wounds."

The doctor slips a ball point pen from the pocket of his lab coat. "The fatal shot almost certainly entered here," he indicates with the pen, "underneath the right eye, causing extensive cavitation, penetration of the brain. Exiting wound here—the left parietal bone, at the back of the skull…"

Whicher glances at Lieutenant Rodgers. "You didn't tell me your boys practically blew the guy's head off."

"The severity of the facial injury is the reason I wanted you to take a look, Marshal."

"How's that?"

"We've got witness reports now, from the supermarket shooting."

"That diversion?"

The lieutenant nods. "The descriptions of the shooter are pretty close to this guy. Right age, right build."

"Okay."

"But I wanted you to see for yourself. We don't know for sure if it was Steven Childress up there shooting, or if it could've been this other guy, Gilman James."

"What about the ballistics fingerprint? You get one yet?"

"The shooter picked up the empty shell cases."

Whicher frowns; "You're sure on that?"

"It's in the witness reports. Plus the scene techs couldn't find them."

"What about the rounds?"

The lieutenant runs a hand over his buzz-cut hair. "The two rounds fired at the supermarket went straight through a suspended ceiling, passed through a cinder-block wall and ended up hitting the steel joists holding up the roof."

"They're both trashed?"

"They look like a couple of beans my dog stepped on. Lab says there's no way to tell if they could've come from the gun we've got at the bank."

The lieutenant reaches to his shirt pocket.

"Anyway, marshal, I brought along this picture…"

He brings out a photocopied head-and-shoulders shot.

Whicher looks at it. He's seen it before. The picture shows a man similar to the corpse on the gurney. Dark hair, dark skin.

The lieutenant holds the picture close to the face of the corpse.

They're close enough. Close enough to be confused for one another. Especially by a witness taking cover in a supermarket aisle.

Lieutenant Rodgers turns to Doctor Wendell. "What do you think of this? If a witness was describing Childress, could it have actually been this guy?" He taps on the picture of Gilman James.

The doctor peers through his glasses. "There are similarities."

"Yeah," says Whicher, "we can see that." He studies the picture again. "Hey Doc, we're not asking for an official identification. What's your best guess?"

"Nothing that'd stand up in court."

"I think they're describing Childress," the lieutenant cuts in. He gestures to Doctor Wendell. "Alright. You can cover him up now."

Whicher folds his arms across his chest. The doctor raises the sheet back up. Wheels the body from the room.

"Why did you want me to see this?"

"We can't say for sure," says the lieutenant, "if Steven Childress was the shooter at the supermarket. Maybe he wasn't. I think he was. But either way, you've seen for yourself—it's inconclusive."

"Right." Whicher thinks of the shooter—stopping to pick up the empty shell cases.

"But we have to assume three men were involved in raiding the bank."

The marshal nods. "If we can't prove it was two…"

Chapter 7

Black Mesa, Terlingua.

I opened my eyes. The first thing I seen was the inside of a barn roof. Rough timber frame, old shingle. Smell of horses. Horse and grain.

My face was running with sweat, hair soaking. Heart racing, my breath coming short.

I lay still, breathing shallow. Gripped—close to panic. I'd had the dream again.

I felt like I could smell the rank air in the black sewer, beneath the road in Fallujah, feel its damp living stench. M9 Beretta slippery in my hand. Four of us, deafened—after the noise of the first shots.

Moments, crouching. Trying to hear again. Nate and me. Behind us, a corporal and a private from my second fire team. Were any more coming in—after the first two? They were up ahead, somewhere. We'd have to walk over their still-warm corpses.

I sat up, pressed a hand against my eyes. I was in a barn.

Somewhere. Not there.

Overhead, the roof seemed to rush at me. I rolled on my side, tried to sit up, pain surging through the back of my head.

I put my face in my hands. Tried to black out everything.

"*Hey…*"

A woman's voice. Calling out somewhere behind me. I thought of Nate's wife; Orla.

I turned. To a silhouette of a girl. At the barn's open door.

"You finally woke up?"

The girl at the ruined miner's house; the night before.

The girl with the shotgun.

I tried to sit, mouth dry. Unsure of anything.

"You don't remember?" she said.

I propped myself on my arms. Shook my head slow. Put a hand up, felt the swelling at the side of my skull.

She stepped into the barn interior, her long dark hair loose—over a green hunter's jacket.

"You knocked yourself cold," she said.

She pushed her hair back, out of her face.

"Up at my Grandaddy's place. That ruin you were in?"

"Yeah," I croaked. "That it?"

She moved closer.

I tried not to stare.

"You were hiking," she said. "Looking for water. You camped down. I found you there."

I breathed slow. Smelled the horse sweat. Stale air.

"You tripped," she said. "In the dark—all that loose

stone up there. You hit your head—against a wall."

I put my hand against the swelling on my head. I thought about standing—my legs were heavy; numb.

"You just about broke your skull open."

She stopped short. Eyed me, wary.

"I couldn't just leave you."

I felt my tongue, like leather inside my mouth.

"You could've lain there all night. All day, too."

I nodded.

"You would've died of thirst."

She took a pace back. Shoved her hands into her pockets.

"I dragged you back to my truck. Brought you here. Let you sleep in the barn. I was just about to call a doctor…"

"Don't do that."

She watched a moment.

"You look a mess."

I took a couple of shallow breaths, tried to focus my mind.

She walked to the shadows, at the edge of the barn.

"I left this," she says.

She picked up a bottle of water. Carried it to me. Unscrewed the top.

I took it from her. Poured some in me.

"My name's Tennille."

"Gil." I said it without thinking.

She stared at me. "You sure my husband didn't send you?"

I took a long drink. Felt the water swell my belly. Put the bottle on the ground.

"I don't know him." I rolled to my side. Pushed myself upright. "I don't know anybody around here."

She watched me, dark eyes intense, close on hostile.

"I brought your backpack. I put it in the corner—over there."

I stood. Hands gripping the tops of my legs. Thinking on Nate's gun.

"Take your time," she says. She stepped in closer. Eyed my head. "I'm going on up to the house. I'll bring you something."

She turned and walked from the barn, into the glare of light.

I staggered across the dirt-beat floor to my backpack—hands fumbling on the zipper.

I pushed my fingers inside the pack, feeling for metal, pushing all the way down. It wasn't in there. I held one arm against the barn side, to hold myself upright. *The jacket*. The gun was in the jacket. I left it somewhere at the miner's house.

I stood; legs rigid, trying to think.

She couldn't have found it.

But I had to get out. I should've been long gone. I should've been with Michael, up in Marfa.

I rummaged through the bag again, found the cell phone, head swimming.

I tried the cell—no signal. I walked unsteady out the barn.

I was in a fenced lot. Thin desert grass. The baked earth marked up with hooves.

The battery on the phone was practically out, left on all night, searching out a signal.

The girl was nowhere now, I couldn't see her. Above the barn, the ground rose to a ridge of bedrock, the house must be over the ridge, somewhere out of sight.

I stumbled around the sloping lot, like a drunk across the uneven ground. Headed downhill towards a bank of snakeweed, by a concrete stock tank.

There had to be a signal, somewhere. I stared at the cell's screen, willing there to be one.

From where I'd been, in the ruins of that miner's house, I'd reckoned it at thirty to forty miles up to Marfa. I thought of trying to cover the desert ground on foot, like before. My body ached, my head was a mess. I'd never make it.

I stared at the hills rising in the south—in Mexico. The land stretching out, wave after wave of scorching desert.

Michael was hurt. Maybe they'd found him? I checked the phone a last time—still nothing. I switched it off.

I thought of the girl, Tennille—whoever she was. She couldn't know what'd happened; about me, about Alpine, she'd have called it in.

To the south and east, the desert was open ground, long sight-lines, twenty miles and more.

To the north the land rose up, cutting the horizon in bluffs of rock. No sign of life, no road anywhere, no buildings. Where were we?

From lower down the slope, beyond a bank of scrub, I could see dust rising. A thin line of tan against the sky.

For a minute, I watched it, a column of dust. I thought

of making for the barn—maybe fifty yards behind me up the slope. In the still air there was something; some faint sound. I thought of hooves. Feet hammering against the dirt.

I stared past the concrete stock tank. A horse was crashing through the bank of scrub, charging straight for a mess of wire.

It hit the wire—reared up on its hind legs, bucking and kicking, eyes wide. Instead of staying still, it turns in a frenzy, twisting and writhing, the wire cutting into it, dark blood already on its flanks.

I ran, closed the space, reached the horse, threw my arms around its neck. Blind panic in the air. Dust swirling, choking. Like some evil magic.

It turns, swivels, lifting me off my feet.

Somebody's shouting; "*Stay there…*"

A girl's voice.

The horse is slowing.

My arms gripping tight about its neck. Face buried in its mane.

It's not kicking, not rearing any more. And I realize, as the horse stops, its feet still.

I'm in a dirt field. In Texas.

I loosened my grip. Took a half-step back.

The girl's beside me, Tennille, a pair of cutters in her hand.

She pushes her fingers against the horse's flesh, where the wire's ripping, blood running underneath. She slips the cutters in, fast, moving from one wire to the next. Horse blood dripping down her arm.

"Keep your hand in her mane. Don't let go."

I held tight. Legs weak, fighting for breath.

She moved around the horse's body, cutting it free.

"Try to lead her out. You've got her…"

I staggered out from the wire, to where the ground was clear. Pushing at the horse, heading her up the field, holding on.

We reached the barn, its doors wide.

Tennille ran inside.

She grabbed a head collar, ran back out and pushed it over the horse's head. She tied the rope to a hitching post.

I slackened my grip. Eased my hand from the mane. Coarse black hair sticking to my fingers.

"I saw her coming, from the house," she says. "She must've bolted."

She knotted the end of the rope tight.

I stepped away. Walked backwards. Crashed down on a grain sack. Now that I stopped, my head felt about to burst.

"Gil?" she says.

She ran her bloody hands across the horse, checking the cuts.

"Is that what you said your name was?"

I nodded. Sweat pouring off of me, like water.

She turned from the horse. Fixed me with this look. "What you did…"

I watched her from the grain sack. Rubbed a hand across my face.

She stared—held my eye with hers.

For a second, something softened. Then she broke off.

I just sat breathless. Trying to come down. My mind half in another place, another desert. A different life.

She finished checking over the horse, talking to it, soft sounding.

"This one belongs to one of my neighbors," she said.

After a minute, she turns to me, "Come up to the house."

I felt the dry ache in my mouth, my throat. Sick feeling. Dazed. I shook my head. Felt it reeling.

"Come up," she says. "Anyhow. There's no way you can leave…"

⅄

Her house was on a ridge above the horse barn. Adobe-style; render walls the color of fired earth.

I stared at a sign driven into the hard ground—branded letters on it, *Labrea Ranch*.

In front of the house, she had a garden—a bunch of cacti set in gravel; strawberry pitaya, rainbow. She had chimes, hanging feathers, beads; plants in wood boxes. Stones snaked out in patterns on the path.

Heat was already building in the morning air.

I took a look around.

To the side of the house was a truck. Battered 350 Crew Cab. Ten years old. Black and red.

Maybe I could take it.

Around the front and rear, the house had a raised porch; shaded, with tables and chairs. There was a cycle, it was resting against the wall of an outbuilding. A kid's cycle. Pink. Paint faded from the sun.

I thought of the horse. She'd loosed it, soon as it had calmed. She'd put it in a fenced off lot down the sloping field.

I watched the dog she must've had with her the night before—running around now, nose to the ground.

I thought about what to say to her. All I could think was her standing there—in the barn, by that horse. Way she looked at me.

I walked on around the back of the house.

At the far corner, the wall was burned. Render blackened by flame. The roof was damaged. And on the ground lay charred wood, the burnt remains of a lean-to.

I thought of fire. Out there, it'd get ugly fast.

I saw the door open.

She came out, on the back porch. She'd changed, she was wearing this print-dress. White with dabs of purple-blue. She had a pot of coffee.

I walked towards her. Climbed the porch steps. She pulled out a chair.

I sat.

The dabs on her dress were flowers. Texas bluebonnets, I think.

"I made a call," she says. "About the horse."

She poured the coffee.

"You got somebody coming out?" I tried to make it sound casual.

She looked at me.

"Somebody coming up?" I says. "To fetch her?"

She pushed a cup across the table to me. "Maybe later."

I put a hand against the bruise on my head. Felt the swelling under the skin.

"Where're you from?" she says.

I thought about it. I'd never see her again. "Louisiana."

"What brings you here? Down in Texas?"

I watched the line of distant hills—lit up in the sun. "Like to take off," I says, "time to time."

"In the wilderness?"

"Something like that."

She turned the mess of silver bracelets at her wrist.

"Supposed to be mountain lions," I says. "Up in the hills. Never seen one. Kind of hoping I might."

She took a sip on her cup of coffee. "Wild cats can be dangerous."

"You ride around like that a lot?" I says. "Out in the desert."

"What's that mean?"

"I don't know. On your own…"

In her hand, she held a brushed-steel Zippo. She flicked it open with her thumb. Flicked it closed.

"I don't scare easy."

Her dog sidled up the steps of the porch, to sit down by her feet.

"What happened to your house?" I says. "Fire back there."

She turned the silver bracelets. Eyes hooded. "An accident."

I watched the sun on the hills. Color changing by the second. I drank the coffee, felt the heat hit my empty stomach. Turning my gut.

A wave of nausea swept over me. "You think I could use the bathroom?"

"Through the house. Down the hall."

I pushed myself out of the chair, to my feet.

"Last but one room," she says, "at the left."

I tried not to stagger, walking in to the house.

Inside, the air was cool. A central corridor. Rooms leading off at either side. I walked to the last room but one. Took a right.

It was a bedroom, a child's room. Neat-folded clothes laid out on a chair.

A girl's room—line of soft toys across the top of the bed.

I shook my head. *Left*, she told me, at the end. I backed out—feeling like I shouldn't have seen it. Closed the door. Found the bathroom opposite.

I stared at myself in the mirror above the sink. Sweat and dust in lines on my skin.

I ran water from the faucet, threw some over my face. Its cold sting sharp against my scalp. I put my fingers in my hair, tried to feel around the swelling on my head.

I had to get out, get to Michael. No way I'd make it out on foot, the way I was. I could take her truck. Make up lost ground. But where were we?

I steadied myself. Pushed open the bathroom door.

I walked back slow, out to the porch.

I wasn't about to hurt her. All I needed was to get the hell away.

She was smoking on a cigarette, now. One hand resting on top of her dog.

"We on our own here?"

"Why?" Her chin juts a fraction.

"Kid's bike," I says. "I saw a kid's bike out front."

She took a hit on the cigarette. Shook her head. But something passed behind her eyes. I saw it. A flash of something.

"You can't stay here," she says.

Whatever she liked of me saving that horse, she was done, now.

"I run you someplace?"

I took a pull on my cup of coffee. Didn't answer. Bought a second, tried to think.

The world turned on a knife edge; I'd seen it enough times in the Corps.

"I've got a car. Up in Marfa."

She watched me from across the table. Turning the silver bracelets.

"Is it far?" I says. "From here?"

She nodded. "Around an hour."

"I got a ride down. I was going to trek up. Tell the truth, I'm a little lost."

I could tell she wasn't buying it. But she wanted me gone.

I threw her a look. "You take me out to the highway?"

She sat back a fraction. Took another hit off her smoke.

It was worth a shot. No idea where I was.

She flicked the top of the Zippo. "If you want…"

She could take me to the highway. Better that than me trying to take her truck.

From the highway, I'd improvise; find a way. Get to Marfa.

I'd think of something. At least I'd be moving. The time I lost laying in her barn, I'd have to gamble, with Michael hurt.

She ran a hand over her dog. He twitched, laying at her feet.

She drained her cup.

"You want to get your stuff from the barn?" She stood. Went on back in the house, the dog following behind her, black tail flicking.

I listened through the open kitchen window as she ran some water in the sink, a radio playing low.

I called through the window. "Alright then. I'll just be a minute…"

Maybe she heard. I couldn't tell.

Above the sound of the radio.

Chapter 8

Alpine.

At the Alpine Police Department, Marshal Whicher stares at a computer screen—US Marine Corps files, the entries brief, regimented. He scans the text, notices key words struck out at regular intervals; names of places, individuals, dates. All removed.

He thinks of the doctor, in the cold room at the morgue. The kid on the gurney. Steven Childress.

Lieutenant Rodgers enters the office.

"Marshal, I've got something one of our civilian support staff just turned up…"

Whicher pauses over the keyboard.

"It's a misdemeanor report," the lieutenant says. "Written up on Childress. Earlier this year."

The marshal pushes the swivel chair away from the desk.

"A misdemeanor?"

The lieutenant reads from the print-out in his hand.

"Arrested. Not charged. Making a public nuisance. Outside the bank."

"*This* bank?"

"Yes, sir. And get this—Childress' place of residence at the time is given not as Alpine, but Lafayette, Louisiana."

Whicher stares at the younger man.

"Right where that airport robbery took place. Gilman James' home town."

"Yeah, yeah, I got that."

Rodgers offers him the print-out. "This thing didn't come up first time we searched the record. It was too minor to show up."

The marshal takes it. Black mood descending.

Neither man speaks for a minute.

"You know the people at the bank. The manager?"

"I know him."

"Reckon you could find out what happened?"

"I have to head out, I can call him from the road."

"Where you headed?"

"We've got new search teams arriving in. There's extra road surveillance, I need to check in, get everybody briefed. Do you want to ride along?"

"No, but keep your radio on."

"I'll do that." The lieutenant glances at Whicher. "If you need to speak to Dr. Wendell, I left his number for the morgue. It's on the desk there."

"Gilman James, I need to speak to…"

"There's no word from Lafayette police. They're on alert if he turns up."

The marshal shakes his head.

Lieutenant Rodgers puts on his cap. "I'll call the manager of the bank from the car." He steps from the room. Pulls the door closed.

Whicher reads the brief lines of the report on Childress. Then turns to the computer screen, the USMC file on Gilman James.

Records show James left the service after ten years plus. Active tours; the Marine Expeditionary Force from 2003—multiple tours in the Al Anbar Province, Western Iraq, from 2004. Assaults on the cities of Fallujah, Ramadi, Al Qa-im. Counter insurgency. Liberation of enemy controlled strongholds. Whicher leans back from the desk.

No disciplinaries. Regular promotion—to the rank of Staff Sergeant. And then Whicher stops at a line on the screen.

There's a nomination. Candidacy; for the Navy Cross.

He reads the line again. Sits in the air-conditioned office. Eyes momentarily blank.

The CO. Somewhere there must be a CO.

Talk to him, get a heads-up.

Whicher scans the record, finds the last commanding officer. Rifle platoon, a particular company. A name. He writes it on a lined notepad. Then types into the USMC search directory.

A Marine lieutenant. Recently promoted captain. Then invalided out of the service, severely wounded in combat. In Iraq.

The record shows initial treatment at Ibn Sina, then

critical care in Landstuhl, Germany. Followed by repatriation to National Naval Medical Center, Bethesda, MD.

Whicher writes fast in the notepad. Where's the guy now?

The entry closes with a list of different centers; private clinics, therapy units. An injured man—likely still a patient somewhere, there'd be a wall of silence.

The Office of the US Marshals Service enforced the law. In the end. No matter what. Brick by brick, you had to take down each wall.

🙶

Whicher dials the fifth number written on his notepad. He rolls a pencil on the desk. Staring at Lieutenant Rodgers' elk-skin pen holder.

The phone rings three times. It picks up.

"Brooke AMC." A female voice.

Whicher pins the phone against his neck.

"Is that Brooke Army Medical Center? San Antonio?"

"Yes, sir. How may I help?"

"Ma'am, my name is John Whicher—Deputy US Marshal; Western Division."

He reaches for a second sheet of paper, full of hand-written notes.

"I'm trying to trace the whereabouts of an injured serviceman. I've been making inquiries at several of the main treatment centers for returning US service personnel."

"Well, we're certainly one of the main treatment centers,

marshal. But we're not at liberty to discuss individual cases…"

"I know that, ma'am."

"Especially not on the telephone."

"I understand," says Whicher. "Ma'am, is there somebody I could speak with about this? It's in relation to a serious crime investigation."

"Involving a wounded man?"

Whicher catches the tone in the woman's voice.

"Indirectly." He lifts the notepad off the desk. "If I ran a name at you, do you think you might at least be able to confirm if the person is at your facility? Receiving treatment?"

A pause on the line. "I'd have to ask my superior on that."

"Well. I tell you what. How about I give you the name? And then, I'll give you a number where you can reach me— at the police department, here in Alpine."

Another pause.

"Well. Alright, sir. I suppose I can ask…"

"Okay. You got a pen? Okay. It's a captain in the US Marine Corps…"

"Oh. Well, marshal, they're mainly Army here."

"You don't have any Marines?"

"We do. But that'd be Doctor Zemetti. He handles the inter-service cases. I can speak with him."

"Ma'am, I'd appreciate that. I'd be obliged."

"What's the name of this captain?"

"Heywood Black."

"Alright, sir. I'll be sure and speak with Doctor Zemetti."

"I appreciate your help, ma'am."

Whicher hangs up. And reaches for another sheet of paper.

CHAPTER 9

Black Mesa, Terlingua.

The door of the barn blew loose in the hot wind. The timber prop toppling in the dirt. I grabbed my back pack, swung it over my shoulder. Turned to climb the ridge, get back up to the house.

I stepped around the side of the barn.

Tennille's standing, watching me. Stock still. The green hunter's jacket over her print dress.

Staring straight down the barrel of her twelve-gauge.

She jerked the shotgun.

"Put your hands in the air."

"What the hell are you doing?"

I took a step back, saw the look in her eye. Cold fury.

I raised my hands above my shoulders.

"I'll tell you what," she says, "Mr. Gilman Francis James—out of Lafayette, Louisiana. You're wanted for armed robbery. It just came on my radio…."

I blew my cheeks out. Stared at her.

She swung the shotgun to one side. Fired into the air. The noise echoing out across the scorched ground.

"I'm not afraid to use this…"

"I see that."

"Start walking. Up to the house."

She leveled the twelve-gauge. My mind raced to think of something. Anything.

She circled wide and dropped behind me.

I walked slow up the dirt slope, toward the adobe house.

"Get in that truck," she said.

I glanced at the 350 parked up.

"Get inside. You're driving. We're headed down the hill."

I craned my neck, trying to see her. "Listen…"

"Just get in."

I walked to the truck. Opened up the driver's door. Swung the pack off my shoulder. Turned to look at her.

"Throw your pack on the back seat." Her eyes narrow.

I slung it inside, got behind the wheel.

The keys were hanging in the ignition.

"Start it up," she says.

I fired the engine.

"I'm going to ride up in back—but I'll blow you through the windshield you pull the slightest move."

"Where are we going?"

"Alpine. Police department."

I stuck the truck into gear.

I steered towards a track leading out, down the hill. Fighting the feeling, rising up inside. I caught her eye in the rear-view. Anger in the set of her jaw.

"Don't look at me. You son of a bitch."

She raised the shotgun above the seat back—to where I could see it.

"I took you in. I should have left you to die in the desert."

⁂

Alpine.

Whicher snatches up the ringing phone from the desk.

"Whicher."

"Marshal? It's Lieutenant Rodgers. I've got news…"

"Okay, lieutenant."

"Everything alright back there?"

"Yeah. I'm waiting on another call…"

"Alright, I'll make it quick. I just got done speaking with the manager of the bank. About that misdemeanor report—on Steven Childress?"

"Yeah, go ahead."

"He told me they'd had to let him go. On account of he was only working there short-term. Some fixed term contract. But Childress took it bad. And then, not long after, he was arrested outside, protesting."

"About what?"

"Iraq. Wounded vets."

Whicher frowns.

"Childress seemed to think the town should be doing more to support them. That the bank should."

The marshal writes a note in the pad on his desk.

"You still there?" the lieutenant says.

"Yeah."

"Okay. Well, look, I'm over liaising with the Brewster County sheriff's department, now. The sheriff put together a pretty good plan to cover all routes in and out of the area. He was hoping to meet with you, go over the plan of containment. You're not too tied up?"

"It can wait."

"Also, there's an ATF agent, down from Houston. He was wanting to talk with you."

"That a fact?"

"I suggested we all meet on the highway, south of town. Sheriff's got the road blocked, there. They're checking all vehicles. Thought you might want to see it."

"Alright, good. Y'all got plenty of fire power down there?"

"Yes, sir, Marshal."

"Keep it the hell ready…"

ᛉ

Butcherknife Hill.

I steered the black and red 350 down an incline, the highway just below us.

"We get to that highway," she says, "make a left. Head north."

Through the open window of the truck, the terrain was like a moonscape. No place to hide. I steered on, trying to play for time.

Down on the highway, a big sedan was moving, headed toward us, a cloud of red dust trailing in its wake. One guy in it, driving. Black Stetson pushed down on his head.

I swung the truck out on the road. Drove silent, staring through the open window at the blur of pale scrub rushing by.

"I'm not a bank robber. Not like you think…"

"I heard what I heard."

I risked a look at her, in the rear-view.

A line of sweat ran down the side of her face.

"You ever hear of Walter Reed?"

"Who?"

"It's a place. Walter Reed. In D.C."

I thought of Nate. The time he spent in that hospital. Orla, his widow. Two kids, boy and a girl.

Whatever happened, I wasn't going in. No matter what.

I didn't plan on hurting her. I wasn't about to rot in any jail.

There had to be some way to get to Michael. Some other way.

Ahead, the highway twisted north. I watched the heat shimmer through the dust streaked windshield.

"I'll give you fifty thousand dollars…"

Nothing, from the back of the crew cab.

"I keep driving. We get to Marfa, I get out. I'll give you the money."

I glanced in the rear-view. Saw her eyes meet mine.

She says, "I'll shoot you dead."

She raised the shotgun across the seat back.

"They wouldn't charge you…"

"I swear to God…"

"I said; they wouldn't *charge* you."

"What the hell's that supposed to mean?"

"If you did. If you shot me."

There's a long silence.

"I'm wanted. For armed robbery. You were trying to turn me in. I went for you…"

There's nothing but the growl of the engine. The sound of the truck tires, humming against the road.

"You got the perfect alibi. Anybody stops us, you're trying to turn me in…"

"Are you crazy? Are you even listening?"

"Who are they going to believe, me or you?"

My mind raced. Every second that passed we were heading in closer to Alpine.

"How hard," she says, "did you hit your God damn head last night?"

I thought of Michael with a bullet in him.

Either I was making it, or she'd have to cut me in half with her shotgun.

I tried to swallow, my mouth so dry I could hardly spit.

"*Stop the truck*," she shouts.

"*What?*"

"You heard me. Stop the God damn truck."

I braked hard. Skidded to a standstill. Breath coming shallow in my chest.

"Get out," she says.

I put a hand on the door lever. Pushed it slow, stepped

out, my skin crawling in the blast of desert heat.

She got out from the back seat.

I stood with my hands half-way raised.

She grabbed my pack off the seat. Threw it across the road. Pushed the butt of the shotgun into her shoulder.

"Open it."

I stared down the empty highway.

To the south, it was deserted. To the north, it curved right, behind a bank of mesquite. Any car could come, any vehicle; me standing there—her holding a shotgun.

"Empty the bag," she says.

I squatted. Unzipped it, slowly.

"I even think you're about to pull something," she said, "I swear, I'll kill you."

I opened the back pack; drew loose the top.

"Empty it," she said. "Right there. On the highway."

The cell phone clattered on the asphalt. I tipped out the few clothes; the half-drunk bottles of water. They rolled away. I shook out everything. Held the pack empty.

"What fifty thousand?" she calls out.

"Not me," I says.

She moved her hand on the fore-stock of the twelve gauge.

"The guy I'm meeting with," I says, "in Marfa…"

"You're full of shit."

"Three days back we robbed a cash shipment. An airport. In Lafayette."

She stared at me. Her face a mask.

"All you got to do is keep that shotgun on me. Get us to Marfa."

"Maybe you don't believe I'd shoot you?"

The sun caught the rib of the shotgun barrel.

"I believe it."

Her jaw was set hard. She shook her head.

I listened for the sound of anything approaching from the north.

"Get the hell back in the truck…"

Alpine.

A hot wind is blowing sand along the blacktop. From a dirt lot, by a low-roofed shack, Whicher leans against the hood of the Silverado.

His eyes drift toward a ridge of mountains rising in the west.

To the north, white sides of one-floor houses glint among the mesa dropseed.

He scans the vehicles formed up in a defensive line. No way through.

Two Border Patrol SUVs are parked across the road from the south. Officers in combat fatigues. M4 carbines resting on the roofs of their vehicles.

A state trooper cruiser blocks the center of the highway. Driver waiting by his vehicle to stop all incoming cars.

In the dirt lot behind Whicher is a black pick-up and an unmarked sedan. Brewster County sheriff in the pick-up. ATF special agent in the sedan.

The marshal removes the jacket of his gray suit. He

pushes the tan Resistol a notch forward, the wide brim shading his eyes.

Underneath the jacket, he wears a shoulder holster. He takes out a .357 Magnum Revolver. Six inch barrel. Finished in stainless steel.

He places it on the roof of the Silverado. Leans in, hands clasped. Thinks of Gilman James.

Fight fire with fire.

Behind him, a car door opens. A man walks towards him, across the dirt lot.

"How's it going, cowboy?"

Whicher turns his head to the side. Conceals the scowl that's formed up on his face.

Beside him stands a man in his early forties. Dark hair combed back. Olive skin, Wayfarer sunglasses, leisure shirt.

"Drew Cornell. Special Agent. Bureau of Alcohol, Tobacco, Firearms and Explosives."

"Deputy US Marshal John Whicher."

"You're the criminal investigator?"

"For my sins."

Whicher offers the man a rough hand. Shakes hard.

Agent Cornell steps up towards the Silverado. He leans against the truck, uninvited.

"US Marshals office, huh?"

He points a finger and thumb at Whicher's pistol.

"The fuck is that thing?"

"Ruger. Revolver."

"I know what it is. I mean what the hell you carry it for?"

Whicher stares at the man. "Excuse me?"

"You carry a large-frame revolver? This day and age?"

The marshal unbuckles a second gun belt at his waist. He swings it, together with the polymer holster, up onto the roof of the truck.

"I got this little plastic thing, too."

"Glock 22. So what's with the six-shooter?"

"You're not from around here, are you?"

"Houston. The 5th Ward."

Whicher throws a squint at the ATF agent. "These little plastic guns jam up on a feller." He nods at the Glock. "With the heat. The sand and grit an' all."

Cornell shakes his head. "Like steppin' into yesteryear."

Whicher chews on his lip. "How come they bus your ass down here?"

"Special request. But there's a lot of chiefs, it looks like, to me. Not enough Indians."

"ATF feeling the squeeze?"

"We can't all have jurisdiction, marshal. ATF have the best record of any DOJ agency in the country…"

"So?"

"So when they put us in charge? It's 'cause we punch our weight."

Whicher turns his eyes to the mountains. Thinks of punching.

"Alpine Police told me you wanted to talk to me?"

"Right."

"You run a trace on the gun from the bank?"

"The guy that got popped was carrying a mil-spec semi-auto. M9. Belonging to a Gilman James. You know we got the best trace system…"

"Yeah, yeah, we know."

"Take it easy, cowboy," says Cornell.

Whicher turns to face him. "Son. Don't call me cowboy."

Agent Cornell stares back behind the black Wayfarers.

"Alright, marshal," he says. "No offense."

But in his crooked smile, there's nothing but.

"Gilman James is a former Marine," says Whicher.

"You look him up?"

Whicher nods. "Combat vet…"

"Yep. And no sheet."

"I don't like it."

"Come out to Houston. This guy's a pussycat compared to some of the shitbags we're kickin'."

"No," Whicher shakes his head. "No, he ain't."

"Well," says Cornell, "you're lead investigator. Any case, it's the other robbery I wanted to talk to you about—at Lafayette; the airport. You know we found a Marine-issue magazine? Plus some spent shells?"

"That's the link…"

"Right," says Cornell. "You know the statistical likelihood of that? Of identifying traceable, service-issue firearms, used in successive robberies. Four days apart?"

"I'm guessing low."

"They're linked. But here's the thing. We had a hard time getting a distinct ID—on the magazine and the shells at Lafayette."

"But?"

"Now we think we've got one."

"An ID?"

"Yeah, marshal. And here, it gets weird."

Whicher looks at the ATF agent from under the brim of his hat. "How's that?"

"That gun was used in a suicide. Less than three weeks ago."

"Can't be."

"Yeah," says Cornell. "A suicide."

"That's how it turned up?"

Cornell nods.

"What's the name of the suicide?"

"Nathaniel Childress."

"*Childress?*"

"Yes, sir."

"As in Childress. Steven Childress? Like the dead guy?"

"Uh-huh," says Agent Cornell. "I thought you'd want to know…"

"You thought right."

Del Norte Mountains.

Ten more miles—it couldn't be more.

This Ford Super Duty comes around a bend in the road. Suddenly it's flashing its headlights on and off.

It closes with us—then it's honking on its horn.

It blows by. The driver shouting something out the window.

Something up ahead, it must be.

Tennille pushed the shotgun barrel at me from the back seat of the crew cab—its muzzle digging hard against my ribs.

I met her eyes, in the rear-view.

"Don't even think about stopping."

Ten more miles.

Only minutes left.

Ahead, what—a roadblock, some kind of checkpoint?

"You need money?"

She didn't answer.

"How come you had to take a look—inside that bag?"

I glanced again in the rear-view. Saw her eyes flick up, then away.

"This guy in Marfa. He has money…"

I could feel her—wound up, two feet apart, in the truck.

She says; "What makes you think I believe you?"

"How come the radio's putting out an alert? A guy with nothing?"

She didn't answer.

"Fifty thousand dollars."

"Just drive. Jesus Christ."

I searched the ground stretching from the edge of the highway. Flat scrub. Low hills in the distance. No cover in a hundred yards.

"You got nothing to lose," I says. "You got a mind, you can turn me in, do whatever the hell you want."

I felt the dryness in my throat. There was nowhere to run.

"You drive this truck into Alpine, or I'll shoot you dead."

If I stopped the truck—then what?

It'd take something for her to pull the trigger. A space as small as that cab.

"You need money?"

"Shut up. I'm turning you in," she says, "you hear me?"

"Get me to Marfa…"

"Shut your damn mouth."

"All you got to do is get me there…"

"I swear to God. I'll pull this trigger. I'll blow you clean through the windshield."

My heart's racing. Maybe this was it. A girl I never would've met, that I didn't know a thing about. My life in her hands.

I'd only known her hours; I tried to think back. Anything she'd said. Why'd she want to see inside the bag?

She had to know.

I thought of the ruined miner's house. The way she found me. She said something; accused me. Something. About a husband. Then again—at the house. What was the name? She'd said a name. *Lee? Leo?* "Leon…"

"What?"

Her eyes met mine in the mirror.

"You thought he sent me—you said so."

We came up a rise in the road. The faintest outlines through the heat haze. Buildings, in the distance, outlying the town, up ahead.

"Whatever trouble you're in, fifty thousand maybe get you out of it."

"*Christ*," she shouts out.

"Up ahead, there's going to be cops. You know it. On the junction into town."

My hands were wet against the steering wheel. Electricity at my skin.

Last chance.

Put it all on her.

If I stopped the truck, what would she do?

Pull the trigger? Choke?

If we went on, I knew it was over. If I stepped out—if I put it all on her.

To shoot a man dead on a highway.

Watch a shotgun blast rip him apart.

Blood flying, like a slaughterhouse. I'd seen it before, that kind of pressure. Could she raise the stock? Push it in her shoulder?

"You're holding…"

No answer.

"You make the choice. I'm going to stop. I'm going to get out."

"I'll shoot you dead…"

"I'm getting out, I'll cut the junction—on the road. On foot. I'll meet you in there. In the town"

Nothing from the back of the cab.

"You give me ten minutes, I'm not there you call the cops."

Nothing.

"Tell 'em what you want. That I forced you to give me a ride. That you were bringing me in—I broke out…"

I felt the shotgun.

She held it up, against my cheekbone.

I braced my body. Foot lifting from the throttle pedal.

"What are you doing? Don't slow down…"

The engine note's dropping.

"Speed up," she says, "don't slow down."

"Ask yourself—what have you got to lose?"

There's nothing but the hum of the motor. Pitching down. The sound of the big tires, rolling against the road.

My right foot's loose against the floor now. No gas. Nothing feeding the motor.

I felt the shotgun barrel cutting against my cheek.

"What have you got to lose—against what you have to gain…"

CHAPTER 10

Alpine.

Whicher rubs a big hand across his jaw. Still thinking on a pistol from a suicide.

From the back of the dirt lot, doors are opening on the black pick-up truck—the Brewster County sheriff getting out.

The sheriff's a bull-necked guy, late fifties.

"Good God Almighty," he calls out, "look at what the first bank robbery in fifteen years done for the county. I ain't never seen so many cops."

ATF agent Cornell snaps off a call on his cell phone.

The sheriff's accompanied by a younger deputy, around thirty, pitted skin. He walks with a map held in front of him, at arm's length.

"Mind if we use that big old Chevy hood of yours?" the sheriff says. "Make us a fine campaign table, marshal."

"You go right ahead."

Whicher checks the older man's badge on his shirt front. *Sheriff Emory.*

The deputy lays out the map.

"Gentlemen," says the sheriff. "Somewhere in this damn thing is where they're at. We know for sure one man escaped the robbery. Likely injured. Do we have a second guy?"

Cornell looks at the sheriff. "You think there's two men out there?"

"We don't know. But let me run a couple of numbers past y'all."

Cornell leans in over the map. Edges of his mouth down-turned. The Wayfarers slip a notch down the bridge of his nose.

"For them as ain't familiar," Sheriff Emory glances at Cornell, then at Whicher, in turn. "Marshal, I know some of this you know…"

"Let's hear it, anyhow."

"Alright." The sheriff pumps his bull-neck. Stabs a thick finger at the map on the hood. "I give y'all West Texas. The Far West, at that." He looks from Cornell to Whicher. "The Trans-Pecos area. Thirty thousand square miles of desert and mountain and honest-to-God wilderness."

"Holy crap," says Cornell.

"My county, Brewster County, covers an area over six thousand square miles. That's just *my* watch."

"Mite large," says Whicher.

"Bigger than the state of Connecticut." The sheriff folds his arms across his shirt front. "Anyhow. I ain't looking for braggin' rights. Big as it is, it all don't mean shit; except for one thing—I don't have the manpower of a state."

"I heard that," says the marshal.

"All in," the sheriff says, "it's one hell of a place for a man to go missing."

Cornell looks at him. "What are we doing about it?"

"Let's get to that." The sheriff circles an area on the map. "This section is our part. The southern Trans-Pecos. Any further south, you're in Mexico. But we figure they're in here somewhere. Y'all look at the road network, there ain't much of it. There's four main strategic points, four towns, each one a crossroad." The sheriff moves his hand from west to east along the map. "Marfa," he points, "twenty five miles west. Then Fort Davis—us here at Alpine—and Marathon to the east. "

Whicher studies the map. The scant roads in and out. "What's happening with those other towns?"

"I been on the radio. The sheriffs of Jeff Davis and Presidio have 'em locked down between them. Plus Border Patrol has a station up at Marfa, that don't hurt…"

Cornell pushes the Wayfarers back up. "You figure that's it? That's how you're going to find him? Or them. Whichever it is."

"They ain't walking out of here," says the sheriff, "that's for damn sure."

Whicher nods. "Has to be in a vehicle."

"So, we stop everything that comes in off the road."

Agent Cornell touches a finger to the side of his temple. "Just supposing they were to get out? Where would they go next?"

"The whole damn idea's to keep 'em in here."

Whicher glances at Cornell from under the shade of his

hat brim. "Something on your mind?"

"Nathaniel Childress," says Cornell.

The sheriff looks at him. "Who in hell's that?"

"Brother of Steven Childress—the shooter at the bank. Older brother. Recent suicide." Cornell takes off his sunglasses. "You're going to like this marshal."

"Why's that?"

"He was US Marine Corps. Alongside Gilman James. Invalided out…"

Whicher picks the Ruger revolver off of the Chevy roof. He slips it back in the shoulder holster, closes the thumb-break and pulls the Glock off the roof—gun belt uncoiling, like a snake.

He straps it around the waist of his gray suit pants. "You want to know what gives me the shits…"

He starts walking fast, boots clipping across the highway—Sheriff Emory and Agent Cornell pulled along in his wake.

"If these guys come in out of the hills—they can do some serious damage. I got me a feeling—and it's not a good one."

The two men follow Whicher across the highway. Down the southern approach, toward a white Border Patrol SUV—angled across the road.

"Officer," says the marshal.

The uniformed man turns his head, rifle still resting on the roof.

"I take a look down that scope?"

"Yes, sir. Not a problem." He holds out the M4 Carbine.

Whicher looks into the telescopic sight, down the flat

highway. Waves of heat shimmer in the magnified lens. On an empty, dust-blown road. With a ridge of mountain framing the horizon. He lines the reticle on a withered fence post. "What's the range on this?"

"Lethal range is five hundred meters. Wing 'em at six."

"Good. Alright. How many vehicles have you stopped so far today?"

"Hundred plus."

"That's it?"

"That's a bunch, for here, marshal."

"Keep a damn good watch on 'em coming. Be ready to open fire. You hear me?"

"I'll be ready, sir."

⚔

Highway 118, outside of Alpine.

I stood on the road. Tennille held the shotgun at me, through the open door.

She hadn't fired. Not yet.

I stepped away from the truck a pace. Heart racing.

She kept the shotgun on me. She climbed out from the back seat. Stood by her truck.

I backed away, slow. I wasn't running.

She raised the shotgun up to her shoulder. Locked eyes on mine.

There was just the sound of the engine, idling.

Tennille staring down the sights.

Holding my breath.

Put it all on her.

"I'm walking. You can shoot me right here. Or you can meet me in Alpine."

The black muzzle never wavered.

I thought of my life. Ending. On that road. In the desert, in the blinding sun. Lives I'd seen end that way. Strange sense. At the death.

She glared at me. The stock of the gun tight in at her shoulder.

"Before you reach town. Half a mile from here. There's a dirt track."

She took a step sideways—towards the open driver's door.

"It's off the highway. You'll see it coming in at the left." She dropped the shotgun to her waist. "Find the track. Head up it. Then make a right."

I looked at her.

"Cross the rail tracks. Get on Main. Holland Avenue, it's called."

She bent into the driver's seat; shotgun still pointing at me.

"There's a grocery store. 11th and Holland. You've got fifteen minutes."

I watched, as she sat half in the truck. One foot still on the road.

"You got an alibi."

"I'm not planning on needing one." She grabbed the door. Slammed it. And hit the gas.

I stood where I was, my breath coming shallow.

She disappeared from sight, down the road.

I walked fast. My gut twisting. *Were we really doing this?*

I made myself walk, not run.

Yard after yard along the highway.

Praying no car would come. The middle of nowhere—a lone man don't look right. If I had to run, I'd run. But not yet.

I could see the road widen out up ahead. A line that could be an overgrown track coming in from the left.

If it was the track, it looked dis-used. Blocked from the highway by a bank of earth.

What were the odds seeing her again? Or finding a bunch of cops waiting on me.

I checked both ways on the highway. Nothing coming. I kept on, the wind picking up, clumps of bunchgrass flicking around the edge of my vision.

I reached the edge of the track. Started down it. Past a couple of empty-looking barns, rusted fencing, the ground hard, bleached by sun. Anybody saw me; a stranger, I'd stand out, the same as any place.

I thought of Jesse. Jesse must've known a hundred places like it.

If any cop was stationed to cut off the track, it was going to be tight. We weren't going to be doing any talking.

I could see the rooftops of buildings in the distance, now. If I only had a gun.

Jesse's day, they carried as many as they could—Navy Colts, the most part; they took time to load. You carried a bunch, shot 'em all, got the hell out. They say he had his first job loading pistols, age of sixteen, in the war. Blew the top of his finger clean off. But he never went unarmed—that time to the end of his life.

There were more buildings, now. The track giving way to regular road. Couple of one-story houses. An old garage. A hoist. Bunch of scrap iron rotting out front.

Ahead, there was another road leading off right. To the edge of town.

6th Street, the panel read. It led north, towards the buildings. Up there was going to be Main.

I walked fast. Parallel with the highway. The wind lifting dust up in the air.

Everything was deserted. The only sound a loose gate, banging and blowing. I forced myself not to run down the empty lane. Reached Eleventh Street.

11th & Holland. A grocery store. That was what she'd said.

I could still run.

But not yet.

I started to walk towards a yellow panel marked with a black cross—a rail road line. She'd said to cross it.

I could see cars moving, up on the highway. All the buildings to the north side. Nothing this side, just a slat-board barn, no doors, gaping black.

It was open ground—but I had to go across.

I stepped out, where the rail line ran to the distance. Heat radiating off the steel tracks. Smell of hot tar and oil.

Past the tracks, I came close to a sidewalk. It was running the length of the main drag, the roadway part hid behind a strip of trees. Thin Cypress. A narrow screen. I kept myself well behind it.

A girl like her—what could make her so desperate?

Fifty thousand dollars.

I'd give her the money, no lie.

I reached a gap in the screen of Cypress trees. Drew breath. Gave it a second. Stepped out.

Above the sidewalk, a sign read; *Holland Avenue.*

Holland and 11th.

Fifteen minutes. All I had to do was find a grocery store. Find her. Inside the time.

⋏

Approaching from the south, a dusty truck starts to slow. Red and black Ford F350.

Whicher sees it as it rolls in.

A state trooper stands in the center of the highway—in front of his vehicle. He holds out his hand; the signal to stop.

Something about the truck makes Whicher start to walk forward toward it.

He strides down the baking highway. Draws level with the Border Patrol officers still staring down the scopes of their carbines.

"It's a woman, marshal," the left-hand shooter says.

"That so?"

"Real pretty-looking girl. I've got her right in my cross-hairs."

Whicher carries on walking.

The truck pulls up. It stops, beside the trooper.

The girl inside rolls the window.

She pushes a strand of long dark hair behind her ear. She's in her mid-twenties. Hispanic. Attractive.

She's smiling at the trooper. Expecting a reaction.

Whicher tips his hat forward, against the glare of sun.

"You don't mind officer," he says, "I'd like to speak to the driver."

The trooper turns, checks. Steps aside.

"Ma'am, if you wouldn't mind switching off the motor a moment?"

She looks out at him. A slight frown on her brow.

"My name's Whicher. John Whicher."

She reaches to the keys in the ignition.

He flashes his badge. "I'm a Deputy US Marshal. Like to ask you a couple of questions."

She turns off the motor. "Marshal?"

He notices the perspiration on her forehead. Tension in her eyebrows.

"Whereabouts you headed?"

"Into Alpine."

"You come far?"

"Fifty miles or so," she says.

"From the south?"

She nods.

"You see many vehicles out there?" Whicher looks at her.

"Vehicles?"

"We're looking for a red truck. Ford F150. Louisiana plate."

"I don't think so," she says. "I don't remember one."

There's something about her. Beyond the disconcerting good-looks. Something; self-possessed.

Whicher reaches in his pocket. Pulls out a printed picture and description of Gilman James.

"Have you seen anybody that looked like this?"

He watches her study it. A little blank.

"No. I don't think so."

"You don't think?"

"Well, I'd remember."

"You came up from the south, you say?"

She hesitates. "Uh-huh," she nods.

Why'd she hesitate?

"You didn't see anything unusual? Anything different? Out of the ordinary."

"No." She looks at him. Eyes a fraction wider. "That's a lot of cops," she says. She points a finger from the steering wheel.

"Right. We're after taking this guy in."

Her gaze shifts from one vehicle to the next. State trooper cruisers. Border Patrol SUVs. "Is he some kind of head-case?"

"How's that?"

"This man that you're looking for?"

Whicher looks in at her, sitting up straight behind the wheel. "Why's that, ma'am?"

She touches the silver bracelets at her wrist. "I don't know."

"It's in connection with a robbery at the bank. Here in Alpine."

"I live alone," she says, "in the hills. You know?"

"Ma'am?"

"It's not some nut, then?"

"No ma'am. It's nothing like that."

She gives the faintest nod.

"You hear about it?"

"Excuse me?"

"The robbery?"

She hesitates. A second time.

"Yes," she says. "I think so. Yes."

Whicher stares in through the truck's open window. Why'd she hesitate? Not once.

But two times.

CHAPTER 11

11ᵗʰ & Holland Avenue, Alpine.

I found it. A white building. Flat roof, hand painted sign on the wall. It was two blocks up—not exactly where she'd said.

Her truck was nowhere. I scanned the street.

There was no other store. It had to be the one.

I walked fast back down to Holland. Ducked under a porch roof.

The highway had been deserted when I'd crossed it; I'd had to stop myself from running. All it took was one thing out of place.

But I could watch for her on the highway, if I was careful.

I got myself in behind a boarded-up feed store; stole a look east, up the road. A farm truck blew by. I ducked in.

When I looked back again, I could see there was a truck parked—a hundred yards further up.

It looked like her.

Alongside the truck there was a man in uniform. A state

trooper. Leaning in the window.

I checked the ground behind the feed store. One-floor houses, container yards, empty concrete lots. If I took off, it was wide open; no place to hide.

I glanced back—the trooper was reaching for something, now; inside his shirt pocket.

I double-checked for a partner. Twenty yards further back, behind Tennille's truck, his cruiser was parked at the side of the road. No-one inside it, that I could see.

He was on his own, his back toward me—she hadn't seen me.

But now he was stepping away from the truck. The door was opening; she was stepping out.

He was handing her something. She took it, flicked her hair to one side.

The she turned and walked away.

I was staring, now.

The trooper hitched his belt and pants. He started walking toward the cruiser.

I ran behind the feed store; up Twelfth Street, parallel with Eleventh.

I saw her reach the grocery store. Glance up and down the street. Then head inside.

There was barely a car, no people anywhere.

If she was setting me up, where was everybody?

I took a breath. Stepped out. Across Eleventh.

I reached the store.

I pushed open the door, stepped inside.

Tennille was at the far end of an aisle, filling up a plastic basket—there was nobody else inside there, that I could see. The counter was empty.

"Hey," I called.

She turned, saw me. "They're everywhere," she said. "Wait for me outside."

I just stared at her.

"Go," she breathed.

I turned around. Walked out. Scanned the street.

At the end, on Main, the state trooper's walking by the intersection with the highway.

I backed around the side of the grocery store. Waited by the garbage cans, stinking in the mid-day heat.

From the corner of the store, I could just about watch the highway. A car was turning in off it, rolling up the street. It drove up, and then by me. German Shepherd watching me from the passenger seat.

I heard the door. Tennille coming out.

She was carrying a paper grocery bag.

I called out; "Over here..."

She turned her head a fraction. "Stay there," she says. "We're going out the back way."

She walked toward the intersection.

She's about to turn and head toward her truck, when the trooper stepped back in view—from the opposite sidewalk. She checked her step. Nodded toward him. Lifted her hand to the side of her face. Little finger and her thumb extended. Like a telephone sign.

Then she turned the corner. She was out of sight. The trooper still waiting.

I was rooted; no way I could move.

A minute passed.

I was staring down the street, at the highway. The front end of her truck swung past the intersection. She turned in slow, around the corner.

She drove up the street, pulled the truck over, stepped out.

"You're driving," she said.

She wrenched open the rear door of the crew cab. Jumped in back.

I stepped out from behind the grocery store. Climbed in, behind the wheel.

She was holding out a piece of paper in her hand.

I glanced at it; saw my face staring back at me.

I took the square of paper; studied the photograph—it was an out of date driver's license, taken back when I was still in the service. Hair cropped close in to the scalp. Look on my face like I'm in a bad mood. What people tell me.

When I looked up she was holding the shotgun on me. Beneath the line of the window.

"Call your friend," she says.

"Are we doing this?"

"Get him out of Marfa. We can't go there. There's too many cops."

"Then how's he going to make it out?"

"You see his picture anywhere on that piece of paper?"

"So?"

"They're not looking for him."

"You don't know that."

"Use a payphone. There's a post office. Three blocks from here."

I checked the street. Pulled out from the kerbside. Drove away from the highway, past a bunch of houses on fenced lots.

"They stop you?" I says, "they talk to you?"

"They had a roadblock. On the entry into town. I guess you got that right."

I nodded. "What'd you tell 'em?"

"That I was headed into Alpine."

"They buy it?"

I scanned the dirt blown streets to either side. Brick barns at the end of a grit track.

"Some marshal was there," she said. "He gave me that picture. Turn the next left—by the church."

I turned past the white-sided building.

"How about that trooper? How come he stopped you? I saw. He gave you something."

"His phone number."

"You serious?"

"Yeah."

"He looking for a soul-mate?"

"I doubt that."

I drove down the street. Saw the post office. Out front, a payphone on the wall.

"Tell your friend," she says, "ten miles out of Marfa, you pass a ranch entrance. FD Ranch. You see a track. It runs south, off the road."

"Okay."

"Tell him to follow it up in the hills. To Paisano Pass."

I pulled the truck over. Jumped out, walked fast.

I grabbed a hold of the payphone, stuck in fifty cents. I dialed the number. Michael's cell. It's ringing.

Overhead, the sky's darkening. Weather rolling in from the south.

The phone picked up. "Michael, it's Gil."

A moment's silence. "Where the hell are you?" His voice was a rasp.

"In Alpine."

I heard the catch in his breath.

"Just, listen," I says. "There's no time. Are you still in Marfa?"

"Yeah." His voice weak.

"Can you drive?"

I listened to the sound of his breathing.

"I need you to drive ten miles. East. Toward here."

He coughs.

"Can you?"

"Shit…"

"Take the highway. But watch for cops."

"Gil," he breathed The line hummed.

"Pass a ranch. FD Ranch. Make a right. Up a track—into the hills. Paisano Pass…"

There was nothing. Just the hum on the line.

"I'll be waiting," I says.

"This is going to hell…"

"Can you get there?"

He'd already clicked off the call.

I stood by the roadside, in the wind. Tennille watching me from the truck cab.

Dark eyed.

Shotgun below the window.

⋏

I kept my hands light on the steering wheel. Held the truck loose on the bone hard ground.

For thirty minutes Tennille had led us down tracks, out the back way from Alpine. We crossed US 90 five miles out of town.

We were headed toward a flat pass, bouncing over the caliche between hills—blunt mountain rising in the west.

I glanced at her in the rear-view.

"You really plan keeping a shotgun on me the whole way?"

"My rules."

"How much further?"

"A mile and a half."

I slowed the truck as the ground worsened. Brush hissing beneath the chassis.

We were climbing two, maybe three hundred feet. Into a high valley, hidden from the road. We passed a board sign; for a Baptist Camp. I read the words painted on it.

I will lift up mine eyes to the hills

From whence comes my help

Psalms 12 1:1

I looked at her in the mirror. Waited till her eyes met mine. Saw the flush at her face, in her dark skin.

"You still got an alibi."

"I'm not planning on needing one…"

I steered on, to where the pass flattened out—watching the sky, bruised-up sky.

Across the scrub grass a blue Toyota pick-up wound its way in the lee of a square-topped mountain. Michael's truck. He must've been waiting. Seen us, driving up.

I stopped. Killed the motor. Put my arm on the handle of the door.

"Stay the hell where you are. Don't move. I'll tell you when."

"I need to show him who it is. He don't know this truck…"

"I don't care. Wait till he's closer."

The pick-up came on slow. Sun glaring in a streak off the windshield. I couldn't make him out.

Tennille says, "Don't screw this up now."

I turned in my seat. Stared at her. "I told you—I'll give you the money."

She sat back. Flicked the barrel of the twelve gauge up an inch.

I turned around again, to look at Michael.

The swelling on the side of my skull ached. I put a hand in my hair.

"If I never would've knocked my goddamn head…"

I took my hand away. At least there was no blood.

"I thought you were sent," she says.

"What?"

"It doesn't matter…"

"What do you mean, *sent?*"

She was silent a moment. Then she said, "You didn't trip, last night."

I watched Michael. Still approaching.

"The only thing you knocked your head against—was the butt end of this."

I twisted in my seat to look at her.

"I thought Leon sent you. The bastard I married…"

"*You* hit me?"

She nodded. "Just shut up."

"You knocked me out?"

I turned back to looking at Michael.

"What did you think I was going to do?"

She didn't answer.

Michael's pick-up was thirty yards out. He'd slowed to a crawl.

"He do that a lot?" I says. "Your old man? Send people out? Up to your place?"

"It's not the first time."

The pick-up was twenty yards out now. And closing.

From the back seat of the crew cab, Tennille said, "He wants our daughter."

I twisted again, to look at her.

"You pull any shit…"

"I'm not pulling anything. Take it easy."

"Turn around. Keep your eyes on your friend out there."

Michael had stopped. Ten yards from us. He hadn't got out.

"You got a husband that sends people. To get your daughter."

"Or me," she says.

I met her eyes in the mirror. Saw her jaw tighten.

"You saw that fire? The back of my house. You remember? You saw it was burned?"

I thought of the damaged roof. Black render falling off the wall.

"He did that," she said.

"You got a husband set your house on fire?"

"You can get out, now. But do it slow."

I put a hand on the lever. Pushed open the driver's door.

"What's he want with you?"

"He wants me dead."

I stood in the glare of desert.

Tennille got out.

The window started to roll on Michael's truck.

"Hey," I called over.

His face was in the open window of the pick-up truck. He was staring at Tennille—behind my shoulder. "Who the hell is that?"

I started to walk towards him. Tennille in step behind me.

I felt the muzzle of the shotgun in my back.

Michael was pale. His blond hair matted. A film of sweat on his face. His blue eyes winced as he tried to straighten himself at the wheel. "Who's the girl?" he said. He wasn't smiling.

Tennille stepped from behind my shoulder. She raised the shotgun. "I'm the reason your friend here made it this far."

Michael stared at her. Then at me.

"They know," I said. "They're looking for the truck; my truck."

She said, "We made a deal. Fifty thousand dollars."

He pushed the matted blond hair off his forehead. "The fuck is she talking about?"

"Just give her the money. Let her have it."

Michael raised his chin.

"We'll make it all back," I said. "This ain't finished."

He shook his head, slowly.

Tennille stepped forward. She raised the shotgun. "I'll shoot the pair of you, right here."

"Honey," said Michael. "It don't matter if you do."

I said, "What's that mean?"

"The money," he said. "From Lafayette? It was in Steven's car."

Tennille stepped in closer, "What is this bullshit?"

I said, "Steven had all the *money*?"

"It's gone, man…"

Michael slumped back in the driver's seat. Head hanging.

Tennille fired a round in the air. It boomed off the mountain.

She stepped back. Pumped another shell. "I'm giving you thirty seconds."

"Go ahead," said Michael.

"*Wait*," I said.

"Thirty seconds…" she spat. "You son of a bitch." Eyes narrow, like a wild-cat.

The door of Michael's pick-up opened.

Tennille whipped the barrel from me—to him.

He put one leg, one boot out of the truck.

She had the shotgun pressed tight into her shoulder.

As Michael collapsed. Face down. Onto the dirt.

CHAPTER 12

ANBAR PROVINCE, WESTERN IRAQ.

Five years earlier.

A *patrol Route reconnaissance. The city of Fallujah; insurgent zone.*
Two rifle squads. Twenty six men, all told.

There were no dogs.

I saw it. I should have known.

I was overall leader; first shirt. Nate Childress was second in command. My squad was on security. Nate leading the reconn element. A car man. Intel on suspicious vehicles. We moved out in fire teams of four. Scouts at the front, rear and flanks.

The middle of the day. A suburb of a city. An hour into that patrol, the streets were deserted. Nate kept the reconn squad moving. Shifting formation every few meters. I brought up the rear, on high alert.

No dogs.

Dogs are the first to sense danger. There were none; not even scavenging.

At base, platoon leader Lt. Black updated each position—working the grid. In remote command, as I called it back.

Every step, he knew about it. I made sure.

We moved between buildings. Mainly rigged.

They filled them with gasoline. Tanks of propane. Wired them to remote triggers, while they watched us. Some of the buildings our guys already cleared. They'd marked them, at the doors and windows. But last place to enter any building was the ground floor.

I was looking at one—it had chalk marks by the door; the sign we were using.

Nate spotted something. From the edge of my vision, I saw him put up a signal.

Reconn squad stopped. Nate was looking toward a rooftop—elevated firing position. Stairwell most likely bricked.

I saw him hand-signal his three fire teams. They spread defensive.

Then his lead scout got dropped.

I saw the round—it caught the edge of the scout's kevlar helmet. It hit him in the face. He was dead before he hit the ground.

The shooter was front, right-flank, less than fifty.

The forward fire team pulled the immediate-action counter-ambush drill—running right; to the enemy. To a concrete wall.

The moment they reached it, a burst of automatic rifle fire ripped from the left. A derelict house. Two more hit.

A prepared field of fire.

Cover. The marked warehouse.

Something stopped me.

I put my three teams on Nate's retreat, the squad SAW suppressing.

The same split second, the brick warehouse exploded. A ball of flame rolled across the street.

Bricks and debris flying. Everybody down. Firing, front-left, front-right.

Somebody pulled an M203. Put a high explosive round at the house.

We had to break contact—break, not engage.

I grabbed the radio. Waved for Nate to peel right.

A machine gun opened up behind us. Third floor window of a bombed out office building.

Behind us.

We couldn't pull back.

⋏

Paisano Pass, TX.

Five years later.

I pulled Michael from his vehicle—for the second time in my life.

I rolled him on his back, saw the blood in the sand. It was leaching through the sweat top, the black cotton soaked around his right arm.

There was more blood on his left leg.

Tennille covered the pair of us with her shotgun.

I knelt by Michael, grabbed the sweat top, dragged it up over his stomach.

Tennille backed away, to Michael's truck. She stood by the rear tire, eyes searching the pick-up bed.

I worked the sweat top over Michael's head. Saw the bandage on his arm.

He'd got something over the wound, but blood was still oozing out of it. His head rolled in the dirt; eyes flickering open.

"Hey," I says.

He gave a bare nod.

Tennille searched inside the truck cab. The barrel of the shotgun resting on the seat.

I called out, "What the hell are you doing?"

"Shut up," she says.

The blood on Michael's jeans was dark. I put my hand to the leg wound.

"How bad is this?"

"A nick…" His voice was ragged.

I pulled the sweat top back onto him. Tennille was still searching, ripping through a hold-all inside the cab. She tossed it aside.

From the ground, Michael turned his head in her direction.

Then he lookcd at me. "There's no fuckin' money…"

I watched her reach underneath the seat. She pulled out Michael's P250 Sig.

She put the pistol in the pocket of her hunter's jacket. Took the shotgun in both hands.

She stepped from the pick-up cab. "You owe me…"

"You half kill me? You hit me with the butt end of your shotgun." I shook my head. "I say we're even."

Michael pushed himself up on his elbows. He stared

down the pass—down the line of the dirt track.

"The hell is that?"

In the distance, a vehicle was approaching, a bank of dust trailing behind it. No way to make it out.

He pushed himself straighter, the weight off his bad arm. Whispering under his breath, "Get the fuck out of here…"

I looked at him. His eyes never wavered.

Tennille raised the shotgun to her shoulder. "Get up," she said, "both of you."

I steadied myself, grabbed at Michael. Put his good arm over my shoulder, pulled him up.

Michael breathed, "I can rush her…"

Tennille raised the barrel straight. "Shut up. Whatever you're saying."

I stared down the pass.

Whatever it was, it was headed straight for us; less than a half a mile off. Some kind of big four by four.

Tennille swung the shotgun. "Get him in the truck…"

I shifted my weight. Took a half-step to Michael's pick-up.

"Not his," she snaps, "mine…"

I checked step.

"*Move*," she shouts. "Get him in the back seat." She jabbed the shotgun at me.

"*Your* truck?"

"Get the hell moving."

I gripped Michael, we turned, ran, stumbling—Tennille tracking us, with her gun.

"Get him in," she shouts.

I pushed him forward. "What about me?"

"Get in the front," she says. "You're driving."

⋏

The Nine Hill.

A trail in the mountains, headed north.

Michael was slumped against the window, behind me on the back seat.

Tennille beside him. The 250 SIG in her hand.

I checked the rear-view. The shotgun was propped in the door frame in back.

"Can you see anybody behind us?" she said.

I didn't answer.

The four by four had followed us out as far as the edge of the pass. Then it'd turned back, toward Michael's pick-up.

"It must have been somebody off the ranch," she says.

"Yeah. They would've seen you pointing a gun at us. They must've called the police."

In the driver mirror of the truck I saw Michael push himself off the window. He tried to straighten up.

"Gil?" His voice a rasp. "Why didn't you come…"

I thought of Terlingua, the power outage. The miner's house.

I turned in my seat to stare at Tennille.

"Just keep driving."

"You know these tracks?"

"I grew up here. Why wouldn't I?"

"Where the hell are we going?"

She didn't answer.

⟡

Alpine.

A lowering sky stretches out across the empty horizon. Whicher steers the Silverado along the two-lane into Alpine.

Spiny grass, the color of sand, shifts in the wake of his truck.

He stares at a ridge of dark hills rising in the south.

His cell phone rings. He picks up the call.

"This is Benjamin Zemetti."

An educated voice. Late middle-aged.

"Alpine police department gave me this number."

"Mr. Zemetti?"

"Doctor, actually. I'm calling from Brooke Army Medical Center."

Whicher thinks of the USMC file.

"You wanted to make an inquiry. About a patient in my care?"

"Yes, sir. Heywood Black. US Marine Corps. It's in connection with a serious crime."

The doctor clears his throat. "Yes," he says. "I'm afraid I don't quite follow."

Whicher looks out through the windshield, at the unyielding land.

"Captain Black was invalided out more than six months ago," says the doctor.

"He was in charge of a rifle platoon," Whicher says, "in Iraq. A lieutenant, five years ago."

"Five years?"

"I'd like to discuss an incident that occurred while he was in command of that platoon."

The doctor's silent on the end of the line.

"I'd just like to ask him some questions," says Whicher.

"I can't guarantee he'll be able to help you. Captain Black was invalided out suffering a severe intra-cranial injury…"

"*Intra-cranial*, that's a head injury?"

"Correct."

"Is he still, uh…"

"He can function," the doctor cuts in. "But he's pretty severely impaired."

"Can I speak with him? Under your supervision?"

"You'd have to come in…"

"To Brooke—to San Antonio?"

"There's no question of him going anywhere else."

Whicher stares at the snaking line in the center of the highway. "No, no. Of course." He pauses. "Doc, I don't mean to be blunt about this. Thing of it is, if I come on out there. What I mean is…"

"He can talk."

Whicher nods.

"That's all I can tell you. Do you still want to see him?"

CHAPTER 13

Popeyes Chicken & Biscuits. I-10. TX.

A parking lot. The back of a fast food restaurant, close to the interstate.

I stood by the red and black 350. The lot deserted. Tennille pointing Michael's SIG at me through the pocket of her hunter's jacket.

"I need to get him inside. Get him something to eat."

"You go," Tennille says. "He stays here. Bring him something out."

Michael leaned against the door post. His black sweat top oozing at the arm.

I says, "You trust me not to pull something?"

She gave me her dark-eyed stare. "I don't think you'd do anything to put your friend at risk."

"Of what?"

"You don't come out of that restaurant, I'll drive him to the nearest police station. They can take care of his bullet wounds for him."

I looked at her.

"But you're not about to do that," she says. "I'll give you that."

From the truck, Michael held his bad arm.

"I'm going in and get you something," I says. "You got to eat."

"I'm alright." He tried a smile. It died before it was half formed on his face.

"Get back in the truck," she said to Michael.

His eyes moved from her to me. "Go ahead," I said. "Sit tight."

He gave the slightest nod. Got in the rear of the crew cab. Let his head fall back against the rest.

Tennille stood in the parking lot, hand still in her jacket pocket, holding the pistol.

I went inside. Bought chicken. A bunch of sodas.

I watched her through the window, pacing up and down in the lot. She stared at Michael, in the truck. Then broke off, to check the entrance to the restaurant lot for any cars, anything coming. Turning the silver bracelets at her wrist. Thrusting her hand back in her pocket, to the bulge of the gun.

I paid the guy at the counter. Carried everything in a cardboard tray. Back out in the glare of sun, hot wind raking the asphalt, straight off the desert.

Michael was passed out, sitting in the back of her truck.

Tennille had climbed in the truck bed. She was closing up the tool-chest, wind pushing hair into her face.

I knelt by Michael, took his shoulder. Shook it, not too hard.

His eyes opened, a familiar blue.

My man Michael—with the life draining out of him. In a chicken joint car park.

"Hey," I says.

"Hey."

"You okay?"

He gave me a grin. "Fuck, no."

I took a cup of soda out from the tray. Opened it for him. He took it in his good left hand. Chugged down the ice cold, sweet liquid.

Sweat was running off him, slick on his skin. Dark and matted in his blond hair. Like a shipwrecked Swede. In an ocean of desert. Waves of heat blowing off the battered lot.

"We in a spot, huh?"

He lowered the cup from his mouth.

I says, "I got your back."

His eyes seemed to brighten.

"Eat something." I put the cardboard tray of chicken on his lap. Put his hand on a piece, raised it up, toward his mouth.

Tennille jumped down from the back of the F350.

"I put the shotgun in the toolchest," she said. "Locked in. So don't be getting any ideas."

She had a cigarette in one hand. She kept the other hand on Michael's pistol, in her pocket.

"Half a mile from here," she says, "there's another interstate. It connects with I-10."

"So?"

"I-20," she said. A strange cast of light at her face. "Runs all the way to Dallas."

I stood up. Left Michael eating chicken. Walked to the middle of the lot, to stop him hearing.

Tennille followed.

"You need money," she said. She slipped the brushed steel Zippo from her pocket. Flicked it open. Sparked a flame.

"What the hell are you talking about?"

"There's a gas station at the intersection. Where the interstates meet. You need money. So do I…"

I just stared at her.

"There's something else." She lit the cigarette. Flicked the long dark hair from her face. "The two of you need a car."

I crossed my arms over my chest.

"I'll drive," she says. "You go on inside. Rob the place. Steal somebody's car." She took a hit on the cigarette. "Then get out. Meet me. Give me half the money. That's it."

I glanced at Michael, in the truck.

She says, "He stays with me."

He was watching us, now. He called out. "What's going on?"

"You've got no money," she said. "And no car."

"Are you for real?"

She says, "Are you?"

"That's what you've been thinking on?"

Her chin juts. "You have a better idea?"

I shook my head. But she was right.

We needed a car. And money. Fast.

"It's a gas station," she says. "It services two interstates. It's big enough."

"You need money—that bad?"

She didn't answer.

"I can't do it," I told her. "Not alone. It'd take at least two."

She looked across the lot, to Michael.

I says, "Forget that. No way he can do it."

She stabbed the cigarette to her mouth. A wild look behind her eyes. She span on her heel. "Mierda…"

She crossed to the far edge of the parking lot. Turned, blew out a thick stream of smoke.

I walked to the truck, to Michael.

He put down his piece of fried chicken. "The fuck's going on, man?"

"Just keep eating." I picked a soda off of the tray.

I crossed the baking lot, to Tennille. Cars and trucks on the interstate, an endless stream of them. Who could say where they were all headed? It's like a drone in the background; a drone that doesn't ever go away. I thought of the night Steven and Michael and me first talked about carrying out a robbery. All the way back in Lafayette. The same sound playing—like some hex.

"You," I says, to Tennille.

"Me, what?"

"You can do it. With me."

I sipped on my cup of soda. Ice butting up against my teeth.

"You've got to be kidding."

I took another pull on the drink.

She started to pace back and forth.

I glanced at Michael. "Look at him. He can barely sit upright." I thought of robbing a gas station. Stealing a car.

She was talking to herself. Mouthing words under her breath; "Mierda, mierda…"

"You could do it," I says.

She stopped.

"All you got to do is wave your shotgun. Look mean."

She cocks her head at me. "Are you trying to be funny?"

I just watched her. Watched the flush at her face, in her dark skin.

"I get to leave with nothing." She looks at me. "Or I get to rob a gas station…"

She clamps the cigarette to her mouth again.

"That husband of yours? Does he really want you dead?"

She threw the cigarette on the asphalt. Ground it out under her heel. "He wants our daughter."

She stepped to the edge of the parking lot. Staring out across the scrub.

Neither one of us spoke. A long moment passed.

Her world. Mine. Cold choices.

"You'll have to give me the SIG. That pistol in your pocket."

She glared at me.

"You do what I tell you," I said, "if we're going in. You

freak out, I might kill you myself."

Nothing.

"You do what I tell you. Understand?"

Nothing but her look.

"What you firing with that shotgun? Buckshot? Not a slug round?"

"No."

"What is it, 870?"

"Remington. Yeah."

"Regular four load. You got a choke in there?"

"What?"

"In the barrel. To keep the spread tight."

She nodded.

"What's the set? Mid-range? Longer?"

"Mid. I guess."

"You guess?"

I saw her jaw tighten. "It'll take the head off a fence post at fifty yards."

"How about flesh and blood. You draw a line on that, too?"

She only stared back at me. Eyes hot and narrow.

I already knew the answer.

Alpine.

Whicher pulls into 5th Street—two blocks back from the main drag through town. He spots Lieutenant Rodgers' Crown Vic, parks up next to it, climbs down from the Silverado.

There's a group of uniform men, two patrol officers, plus the lieutenant. They're standing beside a light truck—a ten-year old Nissan Frontier.

Whicher tips the Resistol hat back on his head.

"What do you have here?"

"This thing," says Rodgers, "is the truck belonging to Steven Childress. We've been through it. There was close on two hundred thousand dollars inside."

"We're talking about the money from Lafayette?" says Whicher.

"Yes, sir."

"The money stolen at the airport?"

"It sure looks that way."

Whicher stares at the dull white paint on the battered sides of the truck.

"How come nobody spotted this till now?"

"Everybody's out on the roads, marshal. There's hardly a soul left in town. We're trying to cover a big area…"

"Yeah," says Whicher, "the Trans-Pecos, I know. I got the low down from Sheriff Emory, out at the roadblock."

He kicks a boot toe against the tire of the Nissan.

"Alright. So, the boys that pulled that robbery up in Lafayette is the same bunch tried to pull this. What do we know about it?"

"Not much. Lafayette police are sending down everything they have."

"Know something? I just got off of the phone to some doctor. In San Antonio."

Lieutenant Rodgers leans against the truck.

"Brooke Army Medical Center. They got a captain up there. Former unit CO, for Gilman James."

From the other side of the Nissan, a patrol officer calls over; "Lieutenant. There's a radio message coming in here for you, sir."

The lieutenant steps to the Crown Vic. Squats by the car's open door.

Whicher scans a strip mall. A Dollar General. The dome of a church in the distance.

He watches the lieutenant sitting on his haunches at the curbside. Then reach in his car and replace the radio receiver.

"What's going on?"

"Some rancher just reported a vehicle abandoned. Paisano Pass. A pick-up. Blood stains on the seat."

Whicher looks at the lieutenant.

"Louisiana license plate. A girl and two men. A young woman—pointing a shotgun at them. They took off in some truck."

"Where you say this was at?"

"Paisano Pass. About ten miles west of here."

"This rancher feller? He get a number for the truck they took off in?"

The lieutenant shakes his head. "He said they were too far off for him to see it."

"We better get somebody the hell up there."

"You want to put out a general alert?"

"Two guys and some gal riding in a truck?" says Whicher. "We'd have to pull half of West Texas off of the road."

"You don't want any action on it?"

"Put out the alert. And check for a description of the truck from the rancher."

The lieutenant reaches for the radio.

✦

I-10 intersection Tx.

At the turn for I-20, I made a right. Tennille smoking in silence. We swung around a bend in the road.

Now, we could see it. I pulled over. We sat there, staring.

"What?" she says.

"Nothing. Let me get a look, okay? Just give it a minute."

There were people coming in and out of that gas station, a lot of people. Two interstates feeding it, state roads, farm roads. I didn't like the way it sat there.

I took out Michael's SIG, slipped the magazine; Smith & Wesson .40 caliber. Fourteen rounds.

I ran a finger up the length of the magazine, felt the sheen, flexed my hand on the pistol grip. I turned to Michael, in the back of the cab.

There was a point more life in him. His face still pale, blue eyes sunk.

"Me and her'll get out behind the gas station."

He nodded.

"You drive the truck—back to Popeyes. You good for it?"

He pushed himself straighter in his seat. "Half a mile?" he croaks.

"All you got to do."

Tennille took a hit on the cigarette. The set of her face hard as stone.

She rolled the window, flicked her ash.

I stuck the truck into drive.

"We'll park up in back," I says, "sit a minute. See if we can get it clear. Probably won't happen, though."

I pushed at the big throttle pedal.

"When I say go, you follow me inside."

She flashed me a look.

"Stand in the door with your shotgun. Don't let anybody in. They see you, they probably won't try. I'll already have a pistol in the cashier's face. You know I never done this before?"

"I know…"

"I don't know what's going to happen. We'll take whatever we can get—but we got to be quick. Then we take a car. Any car. You drive us out."

"Why me?"

"I'm on covering fire."

She took the shotgun out from under her seat. Fed two slugs into the tube mag, fast—bending forward, the gun below the line of the window.

"Put it on your lap," I says. Heart pumping.

We turned in to the gas station. Looking everywhere; at every car. Through the glass-front of the store, a guy and a woman were moving around inside. It looked like two cashiers behind the desk.

I drove the truck around back, where we could just see

the forecourt. Motor running, blood banging in my ears.

Another car pulled in. Sweat was running cold on me.

Tennille staring straight ahead.

A green station wagon swung in from the road.

I put my hand on the door lever. Jumped from the truck.

Michael slid out from the back of the cab. He could barely stand, I had to hold him.

He climbed in the driver's seat, pulling himself up, hanging on the wheel.

Tennille was out of the cab, gripping her shotgun.

Michael gave me a last look. He pulled out in the truck.

I ran, with Tennille—straight inside.

A woman in a blue dress. A guy in a brown Stetson.

First cashier—a black mustache, thick glasses, skinny.

He was making change for the guy in the Stetson. I headed straight in for the desk.

Second cashier was younger. Red hair. He clocked it first.

I had the SIG by my side, pointed at the floor.

The guy in the brown Stetson was taking his change, head down, stuffing dollar bills in his wallet.

I raised the gun in the air. "*Everybody on the floor…*"

There was this split second of silence. Always happens, even with soldiers.

The guy in the Stetson looked up; frozen.

"*This is a robbery.*"

I showed them the gun.

"You guys on the desk. I want all the money. Right now."

The Stetson guy dropped to the floor. The woman in the blue dress was still standing, eyes fixed on a spot behind me.

I checked it—Tennille in the doorway, facing out on the forecourt, shotgun up to her shoulder.

People outside were starting to stare. Some running away. Tennille shouting, *"Get the hell out of here…"*

The Stetson guy was down on the floor already, the woman starting to get down.

I felt the red-head kid do something, don't ask me how— I spun to face him, his eyes locked with mine. He was trying to reach down to something below the counter.

I put a single shot two feet to his right. Clean through the plate-glass behind him.

He reeled back. The second cashier was staring at me through quarter-inch thick glasses. Eyes giant, magnified; unreal.

"Get a bag. All the cash money. Put it in."

He grabbed a paper grocery bag. Opened it; holding it by the badge on his shirt. It read; 'Howdy. I'm Jonah ~ always Happy to Help!'

His mustache twitched—like he had to think about it.

I flicked the nose of the SIG at him. "Get it in there…"

There was something about the guy—all skin and bone, big veins on his hands; a baseball hat high up on his head. Like he wasn't the full ticket.

I shouted out; *"Nobody pulls any shit."*

A radio was playing, off in one of the back rooms. Christian Country.

Outside, people were trying to edge back into their cars and trucks, heads down, closing doors like they were dynamite. Nobody looking to come in.

Tennille was blocking the doorway. I could only see the back of her.

At the corner of the forecourt, there was an old man by an air-line. He was watching it all go down.

I turned back to the counter, the cash-register was about empty. "Take out the tray, too."

"How's that?" Staring through them glasses, like a dumb beast.

"The divider…"

The red-head was about to freak; "The *tray*, Jonah, come on, the *tray*."

I reached over. Grabbed the tray out of the cash-drawer. There was a bunch of fifty-dollar bills underneath. "Everything in the bag," I says. "Come on, *move*…"

The red-head tips it in.

"Get that other register open."

Jonah's black mustache twitched again. Then he reached into his pants pocket.

"What the fuck're you doing?"

"*No*," the red-head shouted, "the keys. He's just getting the keys. It's locked."

"You get 'em. Get 'em out of his pocket. Eyes on me…"

He reached into Jonah's pocket—picked out the key. Opened up.

"Empty it all in the bag."

He tipped everything in.

"What else?"

"Nothing, man," the red-head said, "that's everything…"

"Bullshit." I waved the SIG closer to him.

"Most of the pumps, you got to use a *card*. That's all they'll take. We don't carry cash…"

I grabbed the bag. It felt light, even to me.

"What else?" I says, "come on."

"That's it."

"It's the truth, mister," Jonah said. "Company come take the money every two hours. All the cash money…"

There was a noise behind me.

I turned, fired two shots into the doorway of the back room—where the radio's playing. Chest-high and abdomen.

Tennille swung around with her shotgun.

Somebody was calling out.

The red-head saying, "Oh my God."

I shouted at Tennille, "*Get a car—now.*"

She looked; then went.

Outside, the old man dropped the air-line.

He started walking toward us.

I was moving into the doorway—taking Tennille's spot.

She ran toward a car pulling in at the nearest pump. Big sedan. Woman driver in a business suit.

The old man was still marching, straight toward me.

I checked behind, two customers both still on the floor. Jonah and the red-head just standing, dead-still. A bullet hole and broken glass behind them.

Nothing from out of the back room, where I fired.

Tennille had her shotgun leveled at the woman in the business suit. She was out of her car, a Dodge Intrepid, stumbling away.

I leveled my pistol at the old man. Looked in his eyes.

He stopped. He didn't back off, he just stopped.

A telephone rang, inside.

I turned, to see Jonah, making to pick it up.

"Leave it. *God damn it.*" I locked the SIG on him. He froze.

A wave of anger started to flood in me, finger curling around the trigger. Feeling its pressure, almost squeezing; semi-automatics can be light.

Jonah's staring. "Please, mister—I got four kids…"

The telephone stopped.

There was silence, except for the tinny little radio. I stepped out on the forecourt—Tennille already in the driver seat of the sedan.

I jumped in, she floored it, swung out onto the road.

My mind was racing, full of this rage; confusion, checking every movement. Looking everywhere, remembering; lines of sight, arcs of fire.

On I-20, driving like crazy, there was a police cruiser. It turned down an off-ramp, skidded across the road. Then it was gone from sight, behind an earth bank.

The sign for Popeyes was sticking up over the bank, less than a quarter mile off. "We got to ditch this and run."

"We're not ditching it…"

"It's too late," I said, "he's already seen us."

There was some kind of feature running the direction we had to go, a dirt slope; drain gully, down to cast concrete.

"Get off the road, down that cut there."

Tennille swerved. Braked hard. And we were skidding down a shallow incline, no way to stop.

We hit the bottom, the engine died.

"Get the bag, the money, I'll get the shotgun. Take the bag…"

She grabbed the money. Pushed open her door.

"On me. Follow me. Do what I do."

We ran along the bottom of the gully. Out of sight from the road, but blind, too.

The gully passed beneath the interstate, through a concrete tunnel, a steel mesh bolted over it, no time to get it off. I crawled up the earth bank on my hands and knees. If we could cross the road, nobody seeing, we could jump back in the gully, and follow it right back to Popeyes.

A brace of trucks blasted by.

"Alright, get up here…"

We ran out behind the pair of trucks. Threw ourselves down the other side. Michael's SIG stuffed in my pocket, Tennille's shotgun in both hands.

We slid to the bottom of the gully. Then ran fast, at a crouch toward a wood-panel fence around the lot in back of the restaurant.

I opened up a lead on Tennille. Ten yards in back of the fence, I was about to run around the side, when I stopped.

I threw myself straight to the ground.

Voices.

There were voices in the lot.

Chapter 14

Popeyes Chicken & Biscuits. I-10.

"**Get a look** at that light show…"

Tennille crawled up beside me. The smell of cigarette smoke curling into the air.

I held a hand over my mouth, showed her two fingers on my left hand. She nodded.

"*Slow down, boy.*"

"He's going for the gas station," the first guy again.

There was the sound of a police siren; closer now.

I drew the SIG from my pocket. *Where was Michael?*

"Yeah, well," the second guy talking again. "You 'bout through? Let's go on in. I got to take a piss. I'm drinking too much coffee."

"Break don't hardly last a single smoke. Winston's get shorter, I swear…"

We stayed dead-still, listening, just breathing. Among the weeds and highway trash.

I kept my voice a whisper. "Let me go around first."

I put the shotgun down, stuck the pistol in back of my pants. And walked around the side of the fence, making out I was doing up my fly.

There were two cars in the lot. Plus Tennille's truck.

Michael was still in there, the windows down. He was slumped forward in the driver's seat. I called over my shoulder; "Come on round, quick…"

Tennille walked onto the lot, the paper grocery bag clutched in her hand.

"Go on and get in the truck."

I checked the restaurant door—then edged around the side of the fence and grabbed the shotgun. No way we were leaving it.

I ran back, ripped open the rear door of the truck cab and threw it in.

Tennille was in the passenger seat looking out through the rear-view mirror. Michael was passed out in the driver's seat. Tennille's eyes locked on a spot—somewhere behind me. Something behind me; someone.

Somebody coming out the restaurant.

The pistol. Fuck. It was sticking out the back of my pants.

I spun around. It was a couple, in their sixties. I looked beyond them, at the restaurant door, like I was fixing to go in.

The guy was thinking; something wrong there, I could tell. He turned toward a cream Oldsmobile, car keys in his hand. But the woman stopped.

She glanced at Michael, slumped at the wheel. She called

over; "You folks all right?"

"Yes ma'am. We're fine. Thanks." *Go. Get the fuck out of here.*

Tennille was smiling out the window.

The SIG felt like it was about to fall out the back of my pants and blow somebody's foot off.

The woman nodded, but there was some kind of look in her face. She hurried across to the Oldsmobile.

I watched it back out, fast, and pull out on the road. I could see her glance back.

I wrenched open the driver's door. Michael half fell out on the lot.

I caught him, "Buddy, we got to go…"

I could hear the siren on the cruiser. Angry sounding. I wiped the sweat off my forehead. It was running off of me like water.

Tennille had the bag of money.

I says, "You want to count it?"

"We've got to get the hell out of here."

I laid Michael out in the back seat, straightening his legs, blood oozing from the gunshot wound in his arm. His mouth was open. He was breathing fast, burning up.

Tennille pulled a fistful of cash from the grocery bag. She stared inside it.

I watched the back door out of Popeyes. "Keep it," I says, "you keep it—take it all. Just get us out."

She fixed her eyes on me.

"Let us out some place," I says. "Me and him. You keep the money."

She stared, hair loose, a wild look in her face.

"I got to take care of him."

"Get in the back," she says. "Lay down. Out of sight."

I looked her in the eye. "Yes or no?"

She snapped her head around, got behind the wheel, fired the engine.

Whatever she was thinking, she didn't look back.

Highway 118 out of Alpine.

Whicher stares at the desert where it stretches out south beyond the empty highway. Mile after mile, unrelenting. He thinks of the pick-up truck with the Louisiana plate. Some girl waving a shotgun. Two men.

Whoever it was, they'd be long gone by now. The lieutenant could cover it, no point him going out there as well.

He thinks of the mileage down to Terlingua, right down on the border. The store owner. The message from Alpine, at HQ. A store owner that thinks he's seen Gilman James—back on Monday, the day of the raid.

It's the first lead that actually places James in the area, the day of the bank getting robbed. But what was he doing there, that far south? It didn't make a whole lot of sense.

The radio flashes up inside the big Silverado.

"Marshal, it's Lieutenant Rodgers."

"Go ahead…"

"We've just picked up an all-units from Reeves County.

A gas station robbery. Man and a woman."

"Jesus Christ."

"It's right up on the interstate…" The lieutenant waits at the end of the line.

"You think it's them?"

"I don't know. I'm still up here at Paisano Pass. Up with the abandoned vehicle."

Whicher stares at a bank of cloud filling the sky out of Mexico. He thinks of the interstate—the towns of Odessa and Midland just east of Reeves, El Paso only a couple hours west. It could be anybody. From any of those places.

"What do you want to do, marshal?"

He can stop the truck. Turn north.

"Listen. Maybe it's them, maybe not. I'm half way to the border here. I want to speak to this store owner in Terlingua. It's a solid lead."

"Okay. Copy that."

Whicher shakes the thought of a gas station robbery from his mind.

"There's a lot of blood in the cab of this pick-up, marshal."

"That patrol sergeant of yours?" says Whicher. "He reckoned the guy escaping the bank was hit, right?"

"Definitely."

Had to be, then. Had to be one of their pick-ups.

"What about the witness—that rancher. What'd he say?"

"He said it looked like it was some kind of a fight going on."

"A fight?"

"He gave us a description of the three of them, but it's

not real good. One guy kind of dark—a possible for Gilman James. He was holding onto the second guy…"

"The shot guy?"

"Most likely."

"How about the girl?"

"Youngish. Dark hair."

"You run the plate on the pick-up?"

"Yes, sir. Toyota pick-up registered in Lafayette. To a Michael Tyler."

"Twenty bucks says he's a Marine…"

The lieutenant hesitates.

"I spoke with Lafayette police. They say Tyler's a bum. Some loser, lives out on the skids. They've had him DUI twice this year."

Whicher scowls at his reflection in the window. "Alright. Head on up to that interstate, you get done. Call me on it. You got that?"

"I got it."

The marshal snaps off the radio. Pushes down harder on the gas.

☀

Davis Mountains.

I pulled the 350 off the dirt route, high in the hills. Parked in the shadow of a cottonwood.

I jumped out. Wrenched open the rear door of the crew cab. Michael was burning up. The black top clinging to his body, skin shining with sweat.

"I need to get him help."

Tennille stepped from the truck.

"You can't take him anywhere. Not with a gunshot wound."

I worked Michael's top over his torso, the cloth sticking to his back. "Think I don't know that?"

Tennille pulled a cigarette from a hard pack, one hand gripping Michael's pistol.

"You're not through," she said.

I didn't answer.

The bandage around Michael's arm was soaked with blood. He was in and out of consciousness. Mostly out.

"I got to stop the bleeding."

She nodded.

"You got something?"

"No."

I grabbed the sweat top, tore a rip in it with my teeth.

"I can get him help," she says.

I tore at the rip, pulled it—loosened the blood-soaked bandage.

"I know somebody," she said. "A woman that could treat him…"

Underneath the bandage the wound was a mess of blood and skin. I glanced at Tennille through the open door of the truck.

"She used to be a doctor."

"She get drugs?"

Tennille nodded. I laid the ripped strip of cloth on Michael's arm.

"It's an hour since that cruiser saw us," she says.

"So?"

"They'll never find us—in these hills."

I wrapped the strip around the wound, pulled it tight. "What do you want?"

She didn't answer. She stared at a ridge covered in desert olive and goatbush. Held the silver bracelets at her wrist.

I tore a second strip out of the sweat top.

"I can get him help."

"You in this, now?"

She took a pull at the cigarette. Blew smoke out the side of her mouth.

I tied the second strip around Michael's arm. "You get him help. Then what?"

"You're not done. I heard you say so. Neither am I."

I eased Michael on his side, tried to prop him against the seat back.

"We get him somewhere safe." She walked to the hood of the truck, eyed the pistol.

I looked at her. "And?"

"How are they going to find us?"

CHAPTER 15

Terlingua.

Marshal Whicher stares out the window of the gas station diner. Past the pumps. To a big rock, that rises on the road north; rust red, against an iron gray sky. Every place else, the land is wide open.

He sips on a cup of coffee. Twists his watch. Waiting for the owner of the place—name of Stinson.

He scans the other diners. He's the only man in the place wearing a suit.

It's day two. Wednesday.

A kid named Steven Childress is in the Alpine morgue. His Nissan Frontier plus two hundred thousand in stolen money—in police custody.

There's a Toyota pick-up. A Michael Tyler. And a Gilman James.

All the main roads south are covered. Check-points, Brewster County cruisers on rotation. The marshal stares out of the diner window. West Texas goes on forever.

Paisano Pass a witness saw something. Still no word yet from Lieutenant Rodgers—on the robbery up at the interstate.

A big man approaches the table. There's sweat on him, his shirt sleeves are rolled to the elbow.

"Sir? You're the sheriff? Out of Pecos?"

"Deputy US Marshal. John Whicher."

"Excuse my workin' an all."

"Not a problem, Mr. Stinson."

"Everybody just calls me Lem."

The two men shake hands. The owner sits. Hutches his chair.

"Alpine Police Department says you called them this afternoon. That right?"

"Yes, sir."

"You think you seen a man we're after finding?"

"Yes, sir, Mr Whicher." Lem pushes up his sleeves. Leans in to the table. "Monday, he was in here. Right here. In the diner."

"And how do you know that?"

"I seen the picture. One they're circulating." He leans back in his seat.

"Police have been in here?"

"Yes, sir. And distributed them papers."

Whicher pulls out a photocopied picture of Gilman James. He puts it flat on the table. "This the boy?"

"Hell, yeah. It was the morning of the power outage. Start of the week."

"Power outage?" says Whicher.

"He was staying at the motel. Over yonder."

"Staying how long?"

"Reckon just one night. Sunday."

Whicher pulls out his notepad. Writes down the detail.

"He had that truck," says Lem. "The one y'all are looking for."

"The F150?"

"Yes, sir. Red, Ford F150. Just like the *de*scription."

"That's him, then," says Whicher. "How'd he seem?"

Lem reaches up. Scratches on the back of his neck. "Shoot. Kind of hard to say."

"Notice anything about him?"

"Well, sir. I'll say he was wanting to get back on the road a ways."

"I don't follow?"

"Wasn't nobody going no place, no how. We all were powered out."

Whicher throws him a baffled look.

"The man needed gas for his truck. We couldn't pump any."

The marshal leans forward, in his seat. "*What did you say?*"

"Don't know what all happened to him," says Lem. "We closed up the store the middle of the afternoon, account of the outage. Went on home."

"Was he still here then?"

"I can't say."

"But he was out of gas?"

"He was gone next morning. Is all I know."

ⵣ

The Solitario.

Across the miles of scrub and rock to the south, a telephone repeater mast cut the long horizon. Thunderhead moving behind it.

I steered the truck across the primitive ground. Tennille by me, up front in the passenger seat. SIG in her hand.

"I left my truck someplace like that."

I pointed at the land ahead, through the windshield.

"There was a long canyon. North of a big repeater mast."

"The Solitario," she says.

"You know all of this? Your way around it all?"

"This is my country."

"I dumped the truck," I says.

She looked at me.

"I got in a canyon running east. Couldn't get out. I followed it to that old miner's house of yours."

"Why do you even need it?"

"You really want in this?"

She didn't answer.

"We got to move that truck," I says. "Hide it. Make everybody think we're gone."

From the back seat, I could hear Michael.

"Where are you, man…"

I twisted to see him. "Right here."

Blood showed red, through the bandage at his arm.

I'd get gas from her truck. Wait for night.

"Take it easy," I told him. "Rest up. We're going to stop soon."

Nightfall, we'd break—cross the border, for Mexico. Get the hell out. Forget her.

Tennille rolled the window.

"Why'd you fire those shots? In the doorway of that gas station. Those two shots," she said. "You think you hit anybody?"

I felt a chill at my skin, despite the heat. I thought of Jesse. We had something between us now; a connection, more than blood.

She reached down to the floor. Picked up the paper grocery bag.

"My life," she says. A kind of hot-looking flush in her face now.

I glanced at her.

She cocks her head over. "My life. In a bag."

"In a bag, huh?"

"It's too small. You see that?"

"I see it."

"What's inside isn't enough."

"We're talking about the bag. Right?"

She opened it. Reached in. Pulled out a handful of crumpled bills.

She started to count, trapping money under her leg. "A ride. For fifty thousand dollars…"

I looked at her.

She put a loose strand of hair behind her ear.

"I just pulled a robbery."

She was silent. She thrust all the money back inside the bag.

"Nobody needs to know. You could go home," I said. "Forget this."

She gave an empty laugh.

"What about your daughter?"

She turned the silver bracelets at her wrist.

"What's her name?"

She picked up the brushed steel Zippo from the dash. Flicked it open. Flicked it closed.

I held the truck steady on the worsening ground, the chassis bucking and shaking. Trying to keep from throwing Michael around in back.

"Maria…" she finally says.

I couldn't picture her with any kid. Some child, to take care of.

There was something about her, something hard.

All I needed was two hours, three, till it was dark. I'd cross the border, take Michael. What was she going to do?

Across the border, I'd find a doctor; it couldn't wait. Michael was passed out on the back seat.

I owed him a life.

⋏

At the bottom of a scree slope, there was an overhang of rock. I stared through the windshield at a clump of evergreen sumac.

Blind, we'd come in. What I'm used to; you do that and

get it wrong, somebody'll put you in the meat-locker.

Every trail and track, Tennille seemed to know. I'd let her pick the route, trusting her. She couldn't risk being seen, no more than us.

The red tailgate of the F150 was poking out from beneath the mess of sumac. I scanned the empty land around us. The truck seemed undisturbed.

We pulled up. I cut the engine, climbed out—listening to the silence.

I opened up the cab of the F150. Felt the broiling heat inside.

"You know it needs gas."

"Siphon some out of mine."

"I got a length of hose," I says. "In the tool-chest."

I climbed up in back. I took the keys from my pants to open up the lock on the tool-chest—and stopped dead in my tracks.

Somebody'd bust the lock off of there.

Somebody knew I was there.

Terlingua.

Whicher writes fast in his notepad.

Across the diner table, Lem Stinson sits and watches with his arms crossed.

"There anything else?"

"Well, sir, maybe yes. Maybe no."

The marshal puts down his pen.

"I never told them boys up to Alpine. Only heard an hour back my own self. Seeing how you were headed down here…"

"That's alright. What d'you hear?"

"Well. I'm raisin' Cain the hot side of the kitchen, we were talking about how you were coming down. Coming down this way. The *in*vestigator—on the case, ain't that right, sir?"

"Criminal investigator. That's correct."

"Damn me, if Shorty don't pipe up…"

"Shorty?"

"Alvis. Alvis Town. Delivery driver. Little feller. Everybody calls him, 'Shorty'."

"Okay."

"I start in about how I seen the man y'all are hunting. And Shorty starts in about his truck."

Whicher leans on his arms. "Nobody's seen that truck in two days."

Lem rubs at his chin.

"This guy, Shorty?"

"Well, here's the thing. But maybe it's just talk. I don't know…"

"What'd he say?"

"Word is the truck been seen. Up in the hills. The backcountry."

Whicher's eyes narrow.

"Maybe it's just a dumb rumor. But word is somebody found it. Out in the desert. Hid away."

"Where?"

"You'd have to find the guy that reckoned to see it. You'd have to look hard on that, though."

"This guy that found it?"

"Comanche feller."

"You know where he's at?"

"Man likes to move around a piece."

The door of the diner opens. A Mexican guy walks in. Gray coverall, carpenter belt, T-shirt at the neck, covered in paint.

Lem calls over; "Hey, Esteban…"

The man looks back, wary.

"I thought y'all was fixin' to come by this mornin'?"

The man shrugs. "We needed two-by-fours. At the lumber yard."

"Get over here, can't you?"

The marshal feels the man's reluctance. Not marking it against him. The suit, busted nose, big hat. Lot of guys wary around Whicher.

"This Comanche guy," the marshal says, "what's he called?"

"Goes by the name of Joe Tree."

Whicher writes in the notepad.

The Mexican walks across to their table.

"If you were looking to get a hold of Joe Tree? Where you want to look?"

Esteban's face gives them nothing.

Lem turns to Whicher. "The two of 'em work together, time to time."

"That right?" says Whicher.

"It's alright," says Lem. "Mr. Whicher here's a US marshal. It ain't about Joe…"

"Like to talk to the feller is all."

"I told the marshal, Joe likes to move around a piece. Ain't it?" Lem grins. "Anybody knows where to look, reckon you'd be it."

Esteban shrugs.

"How 'bout that land of his?" says Lem. "Out in the hills. And them trailers. Up by the Labrea place…"

"Labrea?" says Whicher.

"It's just an old house, out in the desert. That stretch, folk know it by that name. Joe Tree bought a parcel of land by it."

Whicher stares out of the window at the light beginning to fade. "Labrea. Maybe I'll go take a look…"

⅄

Black Mesa, Terlingua.

I drove my F150 behind Tennille, in her wheel tracks. She kept Michael with her—he was barely conscious on the back seat of her truck.

I lied we could hide the truck in the barn at her place. As long as she seemed to think we were in it together.

Whatever she had going on, I couldn't figure it. But it was still too light to head for the border.

We had to wait it out, her place was safer.

I'd get Michael, when it was dark. Take our chances, we'd taken worse.

Somebody'd bust the lock off the tool-chest on my truck. Nothing taken. But somebody knew. Sooner we got out, the better. It could only be a matter of time.

I didn't plan on hurting Tennille. It wouldn't come to that.

She might be crazy, I didn't have her down as stupid. She'd have to let us go, no way stopping us. She couldn't turn us in, not after what we'd done.

I followed her up a dirt trail towards a ridge of bedrock. The land starting to come in shade as the sun got low.

To the south, black cloud was building over the high mountain—in the west the sky clear, the light in streaks across the ground.

I could see the adobe house. I closed in behind her.

A dog ran among the scrub. Barking. Turning circles. Then it was gone.

At the house, I drove past her, down the sloping field to the barn.

I put my truck right inside it, out of sight, the keys left in.

I ran back up the field, toward the house.

Tennille's standing on the porch steps. Eyes on the hills. "Somebody's been here…"

She moved to the window, it was open, marked up on the frame.

We stood, listening.

From across the flat, the dog set to barking.

Tennille stepped to the front door. Pushed at it with a finger. It was open.

I kept my voice low. "Where's the SIG?"

She pointed toward her truck.

I moved silent, eased open the truck door. Picked up the pistol, glanced at Michael, breathing shallow, eyes shut.

I left the truck door open. Climbed the porch steps. Put my boot against the door.

I pushed it all the way back. Raised the SIG, stepped inside. From the dim corridor, I checked each room, finger on the trigger, no quick moves.

It was clear.

Maria's room, the window had been forced. The front door unlocked from the inside.

"That bastard, Leon," she said.

She walked from the house. I followed after her.

She headed across the flats. To the dog, still barking. It watched her. Feet rigid in the dirt.

I could see it was her dog. She reached it, knelt, then stiffened. Her hands moving to something at its back.

"That son of a bitch…"

I walked towards them. The dog jumped, tried to bolt, but she held it.

I walked slow. Saw the fear in its eyes.

There was blood in its coat.

"Don't come any nearer."

I was close enough to see the long, jagged cut all the way down its back.

She shook her head. "Leon did this." It struggled to break free. She held it. "It's alright, it's alright…"

I backed away. "I need to take care of Michael."

"Get him inside…"

"You think he's out there?"

She held the dog tight. Scanned the hills looking for the slightest sign. In the dust blown gloom.

CHAPTER 16

Lights out. A bare room. Michael on a blanket, on a guest bed. I watched him. Night creeping in. Willing the darkness around us.

If her husband was trying to break in the house, cut up the dog, what next? I had to get Michael out in time.

"How is he?" Tennille, in the doorway.

"Weak. Leg's not too bad. The arm's still bleeding."

"You have any idea what you're doing?"

"Just some basics."

She looked at me.

"Ten years a Marine…"

"Oh?" she says.

"That was then."

"I called my friend. Connie."

"She the doc?"

"Ex doctor."

"You really trust her?"

Tennille nodded.

"When's she coming?"

"Tonight. If she can. Connie doesn't work regular hours exactly…"

Michael looked sick. Sweat was drying on his skin. We couldn't stay all night. If her doctor friend didn't show, we'd be better just to go.

Tennille stepped from the doorway into the room.

She watched Michael flat out on the bed a moment.

She passed behind me, I heard her lift the blind and look from the window. Then she walked from the room, down the hall.

Michael. All my life I'd known him. Him and Nate. From second grade.

The three of us were like brothers. He never would've joined the Corps but for Nate and me. Six months after us, he signed up.

The day of the patrol his company was maybe four miles up the Euphrates, from where we were. Neither Nate or me would've lived, if not for Michael.

Let him rest.

I left his bedside, crossed to the back of the room, to the small table I'd left the pistol on.

The SIG was gone. She'd taken it.

I walked from the room, sat out on the front porch. Tried to think.

If I challenged her, how would it go?

I watched the track leading from her property. Listening to the wind, stomach screwed tight.

I took a walk. Light fading minute by minute.

I crossed the sloping field in front of the house, reached

the barn, stared inside—into the dark interior. My truck. The busted lock. I put it out of my mind.

I went back up the field again, to the house. Sat on the front porch. Thought of Leon, the gun.

It was close on eight. Wind lifting dirt off the ground. Juice in the air. I could smell it, feel it.

In the sky over the mountains, flat bursts of dull light. Dry lightning.

I thought of the robbery. Two shots I fired in the doorway of the back room. Trying to make myself see it— what was there.

I heard the door creak behind me.

Tennille came out. She was wearing a red sleeveless-shirt; the skin of her bare arms velvet-dark. Her hair loose; a black swathe. Silver bracelets at her wrists.

No SIG. She stood watching me.

"Where's the dog?"

"Out there," she says, "somewhere. He won't come in."

"You think he'll be alright?"

She didn't answer.

"You count the money yet?"

"Five thousand, three hundred and eight dollars." Running a hand through her black hair.

"This daughter?" I says.

"What about her?"

"Where is she?"

Tennille sat. "Somewhere safe," she says.

"Some place her father doesn't know?"

She let her gaze run out to the distance. Staring into near

darkness. "I crossed a line today."

I put my hand up to the bruise on my skull. "Last night. You really thought…"

"I knew you weren't any hiker. After I hit you, I searched you."

I thought of the M9 Beretta. Nate's gun. It'd been in my jacket, somewhere at the back of the house. She hadn't found it.

She shivered softly. "I think a storm's headed in."

This feeling came over me, from way back. Something I used to think on; wonder on. First time I remember it was my first morning F.L.O.T. The forward line of troops. Our unit came under attack. And I learned what it felt like to have another human being try to kill you. I mean *kill* you, do everything in their power. How strange it was. Different from anything you'd imagine. The speed. Guile. The absolute intent.

Afterward, this feeling, this strange mix. Wondering what the hell we just did. Empty sky overhead, smoke hanging. The smell of burning. Hunkered in the rubble of a stone wall. Watching dust falling out of the air. Everything changed. Everything still the same. Wondering what was the difference?

She was looking at me. I could feel her staring at the side of my face.

"What is it?"

I shook my head.

"Those shots?" she said. "Those two shots you fired?"

I thought of the moment I span around, firing. The blank

doorway in the gas station. The speed. *Absolute intent.*

I thought of the big-veined hands on that cashier. His dumb face. Giant eyes, hardly blinking.

She said, "You couldn't see what you were shooting at? You don't know what happened?"

"Sometimes it's like that."

Wondering what the hell we just did.

"What are you supposed to do with that?"

I didn't have an answer.

We sat. Darkness coming in all around us. Breeze blowing up a gust, dropping again.

I could smell rain.

"Being out here takes me back," I said. "Overseas. The desert."

"You think a lot about the past?"

"I guess," I said. "It just won't quit."

I watched a fork of lightning spit white in the distance. Felt the pressure fall, set my shoulders against the dark. The first sound of thunder came. It was far off, rolling, barking around the mountains.

Down by my boot, yellow-head flowers of a rocknettle set trembling. I dragged a line in the dirt with my heel. "You think he could come back?"

She nodded. Lit a cigarette with a kitchen match. Her face in the flame glow. Like the first time I saw her.

"Tonight?"

"Maybe."

"I ask you something? About him?"

She threw the match out into darkness. I watched it trace

this arc of orange light. It guttered on the ground. For a second it caught again, then it was gone.

"If you want."

"You live here together?"

"Most of my life, I've lived here. We had horses." She pointed across the dark flats at the side of the house. "The Labrea Ranch. We had about thirty."

"Why'd you stop?"

"Poppa left. They left with him. It's not the same, now they're gone."

I watched her smoke.

Rain came. At first it fell sparse, in heavy drops. In the dark, I watched it spread out on the parched wood of the porch floor. The wind came up, an edge in it.

She eased herself up off the steps. Shoved her hands in her jeans. "I'm going inside."

Rain started to hiss on the ground. I wanted to be in it. I could feel the wetness on my clothes, as the wind blew sideways under the porch. I didn't care. I waited. Still looking out.

It got later.

It was a storm now, regular storm. I moved out of the light from the window of the house.

As the rain fell, and bounced up again, a mist rose up, like smoke. I thought of her 870 Remington. I could get it, keep watch. Tell her. In case of Leon.

I could put a line-of-fire to the perimeter, all the way out to the edge of the property. With that choke she had.

A burst of lightning split on the nearest hill; not a quarter mile distant. Something moved, at the edge of my sight.

I snapped my head around, strained to see through the dark—past the straight-edge of a fence broken up by ocotillo. The desert came right up to the house, but there was a mess of brush and scrub for cover. It wasn't any animal. I thought I'd seen the outline of a head.

I jumped off the porch, kept low, ran towards it.

I was unarmed, but if I broke off I'd lose it. Keep the contact.

I slipped down the line of the fence. Tried to listen above the hammering rain.

I picked a stone up from the wet dirt; the size of my palm, slippery in my hand. Sharp on one side, like a blade.

A black shape stepped out from a clump of brush.

I was looking into a snub-nose. With rain dripping off.

𝗔

I stood staring as the black figure stepped in closer—gun-arm motioning at me. I could see his eyes, a sort of grin in them, like a wolf. He wasn't smiling, though.

"Man, put your hands on your head."

I did it.

"Where is she?"

For a second, we stood squinting at each other in the pouring rain, the snub-nose-38 the judge of both of us.

I jerked my head in the direction of the house.

He stabbed the gun arm toward me. "Let's see her. Move."

I thought of going for the gun—I'd have to pick the moment.

We started to walk back, through the rain, feet sticking in the wet ground.

Every step, he kept a pace out of reach. We came to the porch.

"Get her," he said. His voice harsh, grating.

"You want to see her?"

He grunted.

"She ain't expecting nobody…"

"Call her."

I climbed the porch steps. Opened up the door. Shouted inside; "*Tennille.*"

I heard her answer; "Hold on…"

I stepped away from the door—tried to edge up closer to him.

"Stand against the wall," he barks.

Tennille came out. She stopped, mouth open; staring at the two of us.

Light from the window spilled out on the porch. I could finally see him. He had a big, flat face. Mean eyes—hard to read. Long black hair, all tied back. He was rough looking; like a bar brawler. I guessed around forty.

I'd seen him, somewhere—I felt like I'd seen him before.

He was Native American. Indian. From his size I'd have said he was an outdoor man, a physical guy. A rain soaked cape draped his chest and shoulders. The pistol too small in his big hands.

Then I remembered. The motel pool. *It was the guy I'd seen back in the pool.*

"Joe?" she says.

"You alright?"

"What're you doing here? What's going on?"

"I came for my horse. Esteban told me you had her…"

There was just the sound of rain on the porch roof, drumming down. Nobody moving.

"I called up Esteban," Tennille said. "Since you don't have any phone…"

He stared at her.

"You want to put the gun away? Joe?"

He shook his head. "You got yourself a mess of trouble."

He scowled in my direction, eyes like black stone—the .38 locked onto me.

"Yesterday," he says, "I was up to the Gatlin spring. There's been deer. They're coming up for water."

She was just watching him.

"A couple miles from there, I found something. Something shouldn't never have been there. I found me a *truck*."

His eyes searched mine for a reaction.

"Joe…"

He held up a hand to hush her—like he didn't want to hear her try and lie. "This morning, I was down to Terlingua. There's talk. About a raid, Monday, at Alpine."

Tennille's face was blank in the light from the house.

"I heard the cops is looking for that truck…"

"Joseph," said Tennille, "did you tell anyone?"

"I was coming to get my horse," he said. "I came by the barn there…" He raised the barrel of the .38 an inch towards my chest. Eyes on mine.

I held his look.

"I saw it in there," he says.

Nobody said nothing. There's just the rain, siling in on the roof.

I had to get Michael. Get him out fast.

The man straightens his gun arm a fraction at me. "Hey. Don't be making no move."

"This is my neighbor," Tennille says. "Joe Tree."

"Hey, Joe."

All he gave me was a fuck-you stare.

"Joe lives out the other side of the hill," she said. "There's no need for that. For the gun…"

"Hell there ain't."

"Can we at least go inside?"

He shifted his weight. The rain-soaked cape dripping water at his feet.

"At least come out of the storm," she said.

He waved the .38 at me. "Move."

He made me walk in front of him, into the house.

Inside, in the kitchen we edged to opposite walls, under the bare light. Tennille set a bottle of Jack on the table. Like it all was a regular evening.

He was staring at me across the room.

"I seen you," he says. "The motel. The day of the power outage."

I nodded.

"You were in the pool." He looked uncertain. Then, to Tennille; "I went to fix the roof, for Molly Kane."

"At the RV park?"

"The power went. Couldn't cut no lumber." He made a face like he bit on a sour apple. "What I heard; the guy they searching for was one of them done Alpine. I seen him Monday, my own two eyes…"

"Look, Joe," she said.

He stared at me.

"Can we talk?"

He gripped the revolver in his big hand. Didn't answer, looked from me back to her.

"You and me?" she says. "Just a minute, on our own…"

His eyes shifted a fraction. But the gun held level.

She reached for the bottle of Jack. Filled three glasses to the brim. "Gil; you want to leave us alone?"

I picked a blanket off the chair back in front of me. Pulled it on my wet shoulders.

His eyes met mine, then cut to Tennille.

She put a shot glass of bourbon in my hand. "Get some air…"

I stepped out slowly from the room. Walked to the porch. Set the glass of Jack on the floorboards.

Then jumped, and ran to her truck.

I wrenched open the door—no keys.

I ran back to the house, got up on the porch, stood listening to the sound of their voices.

We never should've come—what were the chances anybody else knew? What would they do, send a car up—a lone car. Wait; put a team together? They probably wouldn't wait.

I heard a chair scrape across the floor.

Tennille came out.

She stood in the doorway, in front of me. "We can't stay here tonight."

She turned, stepped to the side.

Joe Tree walked out behind her. Instead of a gun, he held a set of keys in one hand. The bottle of Jack in the other.

He stomped off the porch, toward her truck.

Tennille's dog ran out from somewhere in the dark as he opened up the cab. He climbed inside, the dog leaping in beside him.

I turned to Tennille. She's just watching him.

He started up the truck. Snapped on the lights. Rain shining silver in the beams.

I looked at her; "What the fuck is going on?"

Chapter 17

"Get Michael," she says. "We're leaving."

I says, "You want to go *with* him?"

She stepped to me. Grabbed my arm. "You want your friend to get help?"

"We ain't going nowhere."

"Joe's got a piece of land—he says it's not safe here."

"The hell is it to him?"

She let go my arm. Took a step back. "I already called Connie. She's coming out. Coming to Joe's."

"Jesus Christ."

"His place makes here look like 6th Street, Austin." She stared at me. "You want to just sit and wait all night?"

"He's offering to *help*?"

"Not you," she said. "Me."

I watched him sitting in her 350 truck. His big frame, black outline at the wheel.

"Does he know?"

She nodded.

"About the gas station? You told him?"

"I told him I'm in trouble."

I stared in her eyes—shining in the light spill from the kitchen.

"The way he lives," she said, "is different. The edge of things. Not like us."

"Yeah? That it?"

"You want to wait till somebody shows up, your buddy in a God damn coma, bleeding to death…"

I watched the rain falling in the headlight beams. "What is he, ex-jail bird?"

"What do you care?"

"Forget it. You really trust that son of a bitch?"

"Their law's not his."

The door opens on the 350. Joe gets out. He stares at the two of us on the porch. "*Get the hell moving…*"

She ran a hand through her hair. "I stepped across a line."

I watched Joe Tree standing in the dark.

He bunched his big shoulders, shook the rain off his cape.

"You're not through," she said. "Neither am I."

"You keep saying that."

"There's patrols everywhere. Joe told me. We've got to get out, right now."

Joe turned, climbed in the truck. The dog shifting in the seat beside him.

"Connie's going out there. Get Michael," she said, "if you want her to see him."

I ran in the house.

Michael had to get help.

I'd stay ready, the hell ready.

In the spare room, he lay sunken on the bed, a blanket half on him, half off. In the dim light from the hall I could see him breathing, labored now. "Michael," I says.

His head moved on the pillow.

"Michael, it's Gil."

He didn't answer.

"I've got to move you, man."

"He's not hearing you," Tennille, behind me.

I put a hand on his shoulder. Felt the coldness of his skin. "Shit…" I took his good arm, put it around my shoulder. "He's losing too much blood. Come on, help me get him up."

Tennille took the weight of his right side, we lifted him, she pushed his legs off the bed.

"Get the blanket," I says. "Put it on him."

His legs gave out as I pulled him against me. We dragged him out, down the hall, got him on the porch.

We staggered to the truck.

Joe Tree twisted all the way around in the driver's seat, his black eyes unblinking.

I pulled Michael in the rear of the crew cab.

"I've got to close up the house," Tennille says. She ran back.

Joe raised the bottle of Jack, took a swig, snatched it away. "She didn't shoot you," he says. "I will."

I didn't answer.

"I'll shoot you if you fuck her over."

I shook my head. I would've laughed.

"Her old man Leon cut the pair of you up." His big face leering. "See what he did to the dog?" He looked at Michael. "Carve him up, too…"

"That ain't happening."

Joe Tree wasn't smiling no more. "Maybe he won't live that long."

᛭

Packsaddle Mountain.

From the door of the trailer, a set of headlights snaked its way up the mountainside. Joe's place was in the hills; rough land, barely a track in. Three trailers on it. Nothing else showing in the pitch black and rain. I watched the headlights coming closer.

I heard Tennille, moving behind me in the trailer. She came and stood by me in the open door.

I felt the closeness of her, inches away. She wore a jacket of Joe's, draped around her, like a rug. She pulled out a pack of cigarettes.

I says, "That better be her."

She took the brushed-steel Zippo from her jeans. Sparked a flame.

"Anybody else likely to be coming up this hill?"

Tennille lit her cigarette. "Not very."

Joe was in the second trailer. With the bottle of Jack. Messing with a lever-action Marlin.

I told Tennille, "Keep watching."

I went back by Michael, laying on a canvas cot. I knelt to him, he was cold, his blond hair in clumps. He was breathing shallow. I put his hand in mine. He didn't grip it.

When I lifted his arm, it was like a dead-weight. I laid it back by his side.

"This friend?"

Tennille took a pull on her cigarette. "She lost her license."

"She was really a doctor?"

"Fifteen years."

"What happened to her?"

"Too many drugs."

I stood up. Crossed to Tennille, at the trailer door.

She shrugged. "A lot of folk around here need a Connie."

I could see the vehicle now— big SUV, a beat up Chevy Tahoe.

"That's her."

She rolled in slow between the trailers. Cut the lights.

The driver's door swung open, a woman got out. She was carrying a satchel bag. Mid-forties, hair in tight brown curls.

"Over here," Tennille called out.

The woman ran through the rain to the trailer. She glanced at me, then at Tennille.

Up close, her eyes were quick; pained. A worn face, older than her years.

I stepped aside.

She turned to Tennille, "What's going on?"

Tennille backed into the trailer, to Michael on the cot. "Connie, this is the guy."

She put down her bag. Knelt by him. "Gunshot," she says, "yes?"

Tennille nodded.

I said, "There's two wounds. Right arm—where you can see. And left leg."

"How long?"

"Two days. Monday."

"Jesus." She pulled the bandage from his arm. Lifted the blanket, to look at his leg.

I said, "The leg's not too bad…"

She glanced at me over her shoulder. "He's in stage four hypovolemic shock."

I just stared at her.

Tennille said, "Can you do something?"

"He needs oxygen, a drip…"

"Do you have that?"

"You've got to be kidding, honey."

I watched her kneeling by Michael.

"He's been shot two days," she says. "Bleeding out. Joe doesn't even have running water…"

Tennille said, "There must be something…"

Connie stood. Crossed her arms tight on her skinny chest. "Not for this."

ᛉ

Terlingua.

Whicher sits on the bed at The Old Mission, watching the storm outside the window. It's late. Now there's nowhere left to go.

He glances at the night-stand, his Ruger revolver laying flat on it; Glock still at the gun belt around his waist.

Nothing's moving on the road outside. The room silent, except for the creak and moan of the wind. The lights are dim. There's a stillness in the motel air as he leans his weight back against the headboard, and swings up his legs. He stares at his boots, splayed on the bed. At the lines etched deep in the leather.

His hand rests on a report. A file printed earlier in the day, back in Lieutenant Rodgers' office, up at Alpine.

USMC Dated xx xx 20xx
RECONNAISSANCE PATROL
Platoon Commander: Second Lieutenant H Black
Patrol Leader: Staff Sgt G F James

Security Team: Staff Sgt G F James
Reconnaissance Team: Sgt N Childress

Patrol Objective: xxxxxxxxxxxxxxx
Movement to Depart Point: 12:24—13:00
Depart Friendly Lines/Area: 13:00

He thinks of two Marine sergeants. One a suicide. The other an outlaw.

He watches the rain on the black window. Wind pushing it upwards, in crazed patterns against the glass.

It's two hundred miles home, to Pecos. Too late, the storm the way it is. She'll be asleep. Lori. Eight years old.

Or maybe still awake. With the sound of thunder.

Her mother would leave the door ajar. Maybe he should call. How come Leanne didn't get back anyhow, she must've picked up the message—letting her know he'd be staying out.

Three hours up there. Four, maybe, in the rain. He thinks of two souls, as he sits alone in the motel. Two souls that never leave him.

He could've gone up. But first thing in the morning, he'd have to have been all the way back down again. He wouldn't have seen Lori, even if he went. Leanne wouldn't thank him any. Showing up, turning everything upside down. Disappearing again next morning.

Forty years old, to have a first kid. Life already half done. Everything set, the routine of days, too much to do, no time ever.

But still. One was enough. More than the sum, what folks said. A light, in all of it.

He thinks of the doctor, at Brooke Army Medical. Dr. Zemetti.

A combat Vet puts a gun against his head. Little brother holds up an airport, three weeks later. With the same gun. Then heads out to rob the bank that used to pay his wage check.

Michael Tyler. Some bum. Gilman James. And some gas station, up in Reeves, on the interstate.

He pulls out his cell phone. Dials the number for the Alpine police department, the number the lieutenant gave him.

It's diverting. The guy must've left.

He'd be home with his family. His right place. Whicher thinks of hanging up the call as he rubs a hand against his jaw.

Give it another second.

It's answering.

"Lieutenant?"

"Marshal."

"You don't mind me calling?"

"Not a problem."

"I'll make it fast," he says. "That gas station? What's the word on it?"

"We've been looking at VT. I was going to call you."

"You think it's them?"

"It could be James. It's inconclusive, but pretty close."

Whicher sits up straighter on the bed. "We get his face?"

"They had a camera behind the counter. But it's blurry."

Whicher stands, takes a pace around the room.

"Send a copy of the VT to Arlington. US Marshal's headquarters. In my name. They got a bunch of IT guys out there might be able to get a confirm."

"Okay."

"They're using bio-markers, facial algorithms—whole bag of tricks."

"I'll do that, marshal."

"Tell me what happened?"

"According to witness statements, a man and a woman showed up. Robbed the place. Stole a car. Then took off."

"That's it?"

"Pretty much."

"Anybody hurt?"

"Three shots fired, but no injuries. They didn't get much, either…"

"How about this woman?"

"VT only got the back of her. She had a shotgun pointed at the forecourt. Young woman, possibly Hispanic. Long hair."

"What about vehicles?"

"Zip on that. One old-timer said he thought some truck showed up, just before. Some big truck, double cab."

"You check back with that rancher feller? At Paisano Pass. He reckoned to see a truck…"

"I've been trying to get a hold of him, asking him to call back."

"Chase that."

Whicher thinks of a woman and a shotgun. It's not a fit. Not with the other robberies.

Childress, Tyler and James were all from Lafayette. Linked to the airport robbery, by locale at least.

The bank at Alpine, they had Childress. But where was a gas station in that—what was the link?

"You think it's just a drive by?"

"I don't know," says Rodgers.

"Listen, I'm down in Terlingua. Noon tomorrow I'm flying out of a strip airfield in Lajitas; to Brooke AMC."

"Brooke?"

"In San Antonio. The military medical center. CO of James' former unit is going to talk to me. I can't afford the drive-time. Say you know this strip? Is it okay?"

"I never heard it wasn't. You think you'll find anything in San Antonio?"

"My job, ain't it? Alpine and Lafayette are linked, ATF have got that right. But not this gas station. Either there's a link I can find, or it's random. Which case, we'll be picking up the pieces till we're scraping 'em off the floor."

"How badly injured is the CO?"

"I'm guessing pretty bad."

Neither man speaks for a moment.

"Before I go on out there, first thing tomorrow morning, I'm heading out to check on a report James' F150 has been found. Got a local guy coming to show me around. Sergeant, name of Baker. You know him?"

"Yeah, he knows that area real well, the local informants, too. There are a lot on the border."

"That's what I heard. The guy that owns the diner here reckons Gilman James was stuck Monday. With no gas."

"Really?"

"I know. None of it stacks up. I want that F150 truck, lieutenant. If it's out there. Everything else, we're chasing shadows."

🛩

Packsaddle Mountain.

Joe Tree sat on a wheel rim in a trailer full of auto junk. Flush of whiskey at his face. Marlin rifle in his hand.

"Connie's here," I says.

He grunted. Worked a screw at the receiver on the Marlin.

"She wants to know, do you have any clean water?"

He picked up the bottle of Jack. Sat hunched on the wheel. The rifle like a toy against his big frame. "No," he says.

Tennille's dog lay in a corner. Blood dark on its back. A single light-bulb hung from the roof. Wired to a battery from a wrecker.

"We're not staying."

Joe took a pull at the bottle. He gave me a sour grin. Set the gun across his lap, tilted in my direction.

"Her old man really want to kill her?"

"Man wants a bullet," Joe said. "Between the eyes."

He worked the lever on the rifle. Peered in the side-ejector.

"We're leaving," I said.

"Your buddy ain't going nowhere, but. He ain't making it…"

I turned my back on him. Stepped out of the trailer.

I crossed the rain-slick ground toward the first trailer, to Michael. Staring at the Chevy Tahoe. And then at Tennille's 350. Michael had to go down the hill in one of them. Either that, or he was going to die.

I'd seen it, in the field, fatalities from shock. From loss of blood.

I'd checked the rounds weren't in him, he seemed okay. The leg pretty much a deep graze; a lateral hit. But the arm had an exit wound, two ways to bleed.

I stared into the black night. Rain swirling in the ragged air.

I'd take him down the hill, find somewhere—some place they could treat him. At least he'd live.

We were hours from the nearest town. Connie ought to know the nearest place that could take him. They'd call the cops. It was too late to do any different.

I thought of Nate. Dead. His brother, Steven.

Michael had to live.

I stepped in the trailer.

Tennille was standing with Connie, by Michael, flat out on the canvas cot. There was an edge in their voices. They stopped talking as I stepped inside.

Tennille shoved her hands in her jeans pocket. "There must be something else."

Connie dipped her head. "There's a house…"

"What house?"

"It's a place I use. But I can't take him there…"

Tennille looked at her.

"It's a safe house," Connie said. "A place if somebody needs more treatment…"

"Then why not?"

Connie held her arms in tight across her chest. "Sugar, I'm talking about girls with no health insurance. That need a termination, or something. Right?"

I stepped in closer. "What's the difference?"

"Between that and treating a gunshot?"

"Nobody's going to know," said Tennille.

"Five to ten years, honey. Jail time."

"You won't treat him?"

"It's too much of a risk."

Tennille stared at her.

Connie shook her head. "No." She picked up her satchel bag from the trailer floor.

Tennille stepped in her path.

"Darlin', this ain't no hunting accident. Alright? Let's not pretend with each other."

I said, "Where's the nearest hospital?"

"The nearest place that could treat him?"

I nodded.

"You know they'll call it in?"

"Where is it?"

"There's a clinic in Presidio. It's not a hospital, but it's the closest thing. Hour and a half, you could be there."

"Five thousand," says Tennille.

Connie took a step back. "Honey…"

I looked at Tennille. "I'm taking him. I'm taking him in to Presidio."

Connie twisted the satchel bag in her hand.

Tennille reached in her hunter's jacket. "Cash," she said.

I grabbed her arm. "Forget that…"

She shook off my hand. "You keep him at this safe house, till he's stable."

Connie squinted through the deep lines around her eyes.

Tennille started to count off the money she was holding—the money from the gas station.

"Maybe just a couple days. IV. Oxygen. Antibiotic for any infection…"

"Take it," says Tennille, eyes on the money, not looking up.

Connie put out a bony hand. Dry lips drawn back, her teeth cracked and worn.

I just stared at Michael in the dim light.

"Take him," said Tennille. "Keep him alive."

Chapter 18

ANBAR PROVINCE, WESTERN IRAQ.

A **pipe barely** *big enough to crouch in. Pitch black. Reeking.*

Platoon commander back at base found it, on his map. A sewer network running beneath the streets. New orders. Clear the ambush. Get out; down it.

Four of us. Down that stinking pipe. Nothing more than pistols in our hands. Nate Childress. My car man. A private from my second fire team.

Thirty meters in. We heard their voices. Opened up. A noise like hell inside that tiny space.

I still dream about those seconds. Live them.

After. Praying they were dead. Pushing on, right over them, walking on top of their bodies. A shaft of sunlight from a drain grill. Nate first out, into a deserted street.

Two parked cars. To left and right, either side. No intel. My car man shaking his head.

Nate. Grinning under his helmet, running out, down that street.

The right hand car went off. It blew, threw him through the air, he landed on his back. He didn't move.

I ran. Rounds flying, ripping through the air. I reached him, saw the blood running out of both ears. I grabbed his vest. Light-caliber smacking into the ground.

Dragging him, unconscious, back to the sewer. Then back the length of it, through—back to the patrol.

I radioed in. Told Lieutenant Black; no.

We moved the wounded to a walled garden, a derelict house. Six wounded, three dead. Nate unconscious. But breathing.

Base ran a check—units close enough to get to us.

Michael volunteered.

Five up-armored Humvees.

Fifty cal M2s. Michael leading it.

By the time the column made it, we were on last rounds. My M9 pistol in my hand.

They came in like the end of the world. Cleared the street.

Before the RPG hit Michael.

And I watched him burn.

"whoso sheddeth man's blood,
by man shall his blood be shed"
Genesis IX : 6

Chapter 19

Salt Grass Road, Terlingua Creek, TX.

A Chevy Silverado bucks its way down a desert track. Behind it, a column of dust rises, in the still air. It hangs against a sky the color of stone.

Marshal John Whicher steers the big pick-up; V8 humming under the hood. Sergeant Troy Baker of the Brewster County sheriff's department sits beside him. Ice air, all the way cranked.

"According to Lem Stinson," says Whicher, "this Joe Tree feller lives someplace out near the Labrea land."

"Labrea Ranch."

"You been out there?"

"I know it some."

Whicher peers through the windshield. "These here back trails, there a lot of 'em?"

Baker nods.

"They go where? Old ranches, farms?"

"Yes, sir. And mine workings. Such like."

"Any houses?"

"A few, yes sir."

"And parcels of land like Joe Tree's."

"Not so many of them. A lot of this land folks tried working. Horses. Livestock. But ain't near enough water. Or feed."

"Yeah, I noticed."

"Worse now. In summer," Baker says. "Goats can stand it."

"Lot of money—in goats?"

A shadow flicks along the ground from a buzzard, wheeling high. The only living sign upon the land.

The marshal shakes his head. "If a man was after getting around, using the tracks to navigate? Miss out on the roads?"

"It's possible. You'd have to know 'em pretty good."

You'd have to know them. Or else, be with somebody that did.

If some type like Joe Tree found Gilman James' truck, how could he be at an interstate a hundred eighty miles north? In Reeves County. And rob a gas station with some girl.

Whicher had called Lieutenant Rodgers. First thing that morning, before setting out. Got him to run a check—stolen cars; anything, a hundred mile radius of Alpine.

It took fifteen minutes for Rodgers to call him back at the motel. There were no reports of any. In the last three days.

If he didn't steal one, somebody had to be in helping this guy.

Sergeant Baker raises an arm, pointing out the window.

"That's the turn. Up there."

Whicher takes his foot off the gas. He lets the Silverado slow against the slope. His eyes follow a pitted track kicking off in the hills. It disappears in the low scrub.

"You're telling me there's actually something the other end of that?"

He pulls the truck over and stops. He opens the door, climbs out, sets the tan Resistol forward, against the glare of sun.

Sergeant Baker leans over in the cab. "Everything alright, marshal?"

"Just fine. That pump-action shotgun behind your head? You see it? In the rack there?"

Baker turns his head. "Uh-huh."

"Time to break it out, sergeant."

"You want me to take it out, sir?"

"I sure do."

Baker unclips the straps. He slides the shotgun clear of the rack.

"Alright." Whicher takes another look at the stony track. Barren hills. Heat blistering on them. "Keep it where you can get it."

He climbs back in, sticks the truck in low. Pulls away.

"This guy, Joe Tree? He got a sheet?"

"Couple of larcenies on his file."

"Like?"

"Car theft. Horses."

"Old school," says Whicher.

"He keeps out of the way, mostly."

"He an incomer?"

"Local. About as local as a man can get."

"Kind of guy'd know his way around? The tracks and trails, an' all?"

Baker nods, "Definitely."

"You think he could've found a truck abandoned? Bank robber's truck?"

"Joe gets around. He sort of roams the hills. Some folks here are like that, sir."

"Living in their own world," says Whicher.

He steers ahead to where the track drops away between hills of withered brush and Texas agave. A mountain of bare rock behind it.

"That's it, marshal."

"The Forgotten Valley…"

The Silverado rolls forward, slow. Rocks crumbling from the dust at the edges of the track.

There's three trailers, a bunch of junk, stacks of firewood. Whicher pulls up in front of a pile of rusted oil drums.

Both men climb from the cab, sun lighting them up. Into air like an open oven.

Baker carries the pump-action at the waist. Barrel to the ground.

They both listen; the silence like a tangible force.

Whicher moves forward, stepping between the litter of debris on the ground. All three trailers are shut up. There's a camp fire. Whicher kneels to it. It's cold—the ash wet. Last night's rain. Or doused. No way to tell.

He walks to the nearest trailer—tries the door. It's locked.

"Check 'em all."

He reaches to his shoulder-holster. Takes out the .357 Magnum Ruger.

Baker looks at him. "What kind of trouble you expecting, marshal?"

Whicher walks towards the second trailer. "Hard to say…"

He tries the door. It's locked. There's a small window at the side, blacked out, no seeing inside.

Sergeant Baker tries the third trailer. He raps on the door. "Anybody home?"

He tries the handle, it's locked.

Whicher picks his way through the dusty camp. An empty lean-to, rusted water tanks, spools of fence wire. There's something, though. It feels like there's something. Maybe it's just the wind. The hills. The empty space.

Sergeant Baker searches at the back of the trailers.

Whicher walks to the Silverado, eying the surrounding land. *What else?*

Baker swings the shotgun up to his shoulder. "I guess he could be anywhere."

"He keep a vehicle?" Whicher points the tip of his boot at the ground. "Tire marks there. Bunch of 'em."

Baker scratches at his arm.

"What else is out here? What about the Labrea place?"

"It's just an old place, marshal. Other side of Packsaddle

Mountain. Ol' ranch. Max Labrea's place."

"Labrea? What's he like?"

"He's not living there any more, sir. He left. His daughter lives out there now."

"Daughter?"

"Yes, sir."

"Kind of age?"

"Young. Twenties. Late twenties."

Whicher tips his hat forward a notch. Holsters his pistol.

"Get in," he says, "let's go take a look."

Casa Piedra.

Tennille drove the big 350 up a gravel ridge. Ahead of us, Joe Tree drove an old Dodge Dakota.

"You learn your way around," I says, "off of him?"

She glanced at me from behind the wheel.

"I know what I know."

We were topping out on a steep-sided pass. Below us, a disused rail line. A dry creek, a group of buildings, part stone built, part adobe—flat roofs of fiber cement.

Some kind of old homestead, it looked like.

No sign of people. An old van parked in the shade of a barn wall.

Joe started his truck to roll down a drift of grit and sand.

"This Connie's? The place she uses?"

Tennille didn't answer. She shifted gear, followed after Joe.

I'd slept maybe an hour, since Michael had gone. Connie took him. I helped her get him into her Tahoe—told myself it was the only way.

Joe reached the foot of the drift. He drove the Dakota across the old rail track.

I scanned the run-down homestead, trying to get a fix. Where the rail line ran out there was a sheet-iron sign on a post. Letters faded on it; *Texas Pacifico Transportation.*

Joe crossed a dirt ford through the empty creek. He was slowing up, approaching the buildings. He turned toward them in his pick-up, then circled back.

"What's he wary of?"

Tennille's eyes were everywhere.

Joe parked. He didn't get out.

"Where the hell are we? This where Michael's at?"

She braked the 350 to a standstill. Shook her head.

"After, I'll take you." She eyed me from behind the wheel. "First," she says, "you're going to tell me."

"Tell you what?"

There's a thin line of sweat at her forehead.

"What else. What else you were planning on robbing?"

An hour's sleep on a floor in Joe's trailer. A girl that said she stepped across a line. Michael with a crank-head doctor. I thought of going for the SIG in my pocket.

The door opened a crack on Joe's Dakota.

I says, "It's three hundred miles from here."

"How are you going to get there?"

I could see Joe, holding his rifle.

He pushed a boot at the door of his truck.

"You're going to need help."

I didn't answer. I thought of Jackson Fork; the place next on the list.

Maybe.

Maybe she could get me there.

I thought of Nate—he'd been living there. Five miles out of Jackson Fork. He'd been living on a farm, trying to make an honest-to-God go of things. I thought of his widow, Orla.

"Tomorrow," I says.

She looked at me.

"Ten miles shy of San Angelo."

"Why? Why there?"

"Couple hundred thousand dollars. In cash. Maybe more."

Joe stepped out of his truck. He stood, scanned the hills.

"What's he looking for?"

"To see if anybody followed."

A door opened in a wall of the main building. A man stepped out. Hispanic, wearing a gray coverall and carpenter belt.

"Who the hell's that?"

"A friend."

I turned to her. "What's going on?"

She says; "Why tomorrow? Why all the way up there?"

"We planned this shit, right? All of it. Michael and me. It ain't random."

"I can take his place."

I didn't answer.

Joe Tree approached the man in the coverall.

"Come on," she says. "We're getting out."

I climbed from her truck. Kept my jacket on. SIG in the pocket.

Joe Tree turned back to scanning the hills. Light cover on them. Sotol and tanglehead.

The man in the coverall approached Tennille.

"Hola," she called. She stepped away from me, toward the house.

The man turned, but stared over his shoulder at me. Then he walked with Tennille to a wooden slat door.

They stepped inside.

Joe Tree stood in front of me. "Not you."

⅄

Black Mesa.

Whicher loosens his neck-tie. He leans forward in the seat of his truck—pushes his shirtfront into the cold air streaming from the vents.

He steers across the broken up ground.

"Sometimes I wonder how they could stand it."

"What's that, sir?"

"Folks out here. Before, you know…"

"AC? Cold beer?"

"It's like the surface of Mars."

"Take that track," says the sergeant. "Other side of that emory oak…"

"That's a *track*?"

Baker grins.

"I'm sure glad I brought you along."

"I guess you ride horses, you learn your way about."

"That it? You a horse ridin' feller?"

"Mainly."

Whicher nods. "Come out here a piece?"

"Time to time. Labrea's used to run a few. Joe Tree's got a couple of head." Baker turns a fraction to Whicher. "Marshal? I ask you something?"

"Go ahead."

"Why the shotgun. Just now. And that .357. What's Joe Tree about to do?"

"Not him," says Whicher. "Gilman James. You mind telling me which way I'm supposed to be heading?"

"See that rock? Up ahead?"

"We taking a bearing?"

"Just head toward it, sir. There's no reason to think Joe's caught up in any of this, is there?"

"You prefer him not to be?"

"I mean, he's a local guy…"

"Yeah. But if he found that truck we're looking for, how come he never reported it?"

"Maybe he didn't know—that all of this has been going on."

"Maybe."

"No sign of anything at Joe Tree's place…"

"Tire tracks, though," says Whicher. "Alpine police department are putting Gilman James in a robbery up in Reeves County, yesterday."

Baker gives a low whistle. "That's a long damn way from here."

"Right. It's impossible, too. Unless someone's helping him."

"Head over to the right, sir. Around the side of that bluff."

Whicher steers on. Thinking on Gilman James. No way he got that truck out of West Texas. Not on any road. They would've caught him. Between the Brewster County sheriff and Alpine police department, they had the road network taped. Either James was still out there. Or he took to the backcountry—somebody showing him how.

Ahead, through the windshield, Whicher sees an adobe house. Raised porch around it. A few scattered trees. Outbuildings. A line of fence.

"That's the place," says Baker.

"Alright, same routine, sergeant. Take the shotgun."

The marshal steers the truck up to the gate at the front of the property. He switches off the motor. Reaches for the revolver.

He steps out, finger on the trigger guard.

Baker holds the shotgun at his midriff.

The two men walk forward, toward the house. Their feet crunch on gravel. A path winds out in front of them, bunch of cacti, set out like a garden.

"That robbery," Whicher says, "up in Reeves County. If it *was* him, he had an accomplice. A young woman."

Baker climbs the porch steps. He stops in front of the door to the house. Looks at Whicher, a question in his face, now.

Whicher shoots him an eyebrow.

The sergeant moves to a window, tries to peer inside.

He steps back, staring at the frame.

"Bunch of marks around this, marshal. Somebody's forced it." He lowers his shotgun, hand against the glass. "It's closed now. But somebody broke in…"

"You're sure?"

"Yes, sir, marshal."

Whicher climbs the stairs and knocks on the front door.

"Hello? *Hello in there*?" He takes off the Resistol. Wipes at the sweat on his brow.

"Police officer. Anybody home?"

He tries the door. It's locked.

"This girl live alone?"

"She's got a young daughter."

"Any husband?"

"She's separated from the father, far as I know."

Whicher lowers the Ruger. "Let's take a look around back."

He puts on his hat. Climbs down the porch steps. Baker behind him, with the shotgun.

No sign of anyone. But maybe James had been up there—looking to steal something, get a vehicle? He could've broke in.

At the back of the house, Whicher stops. The wall is burned, right up to the roof. "The hell's that?"

Baker moves forward. He kicks at the mess of charred wood on the ground. "Looks like they had a pretty good fire back here."

Whicher takes a long look at the house. A break-in, a fire.

"What else you know about these folk?"

"Max Labrea built the place. I think Leon Varela owns it now."

"Who?"

"Father of the little girl. Reckon Leon bought him out after he married the daughter."

"But he doesn't live here any more?"

"He lives in Lajitas. She stayed on, with the girl."

"He left, they stayed?"

"That's all I heard."

"No sign anybody's here."

"No, sir."

Whicher steps from the house toward a ridge at the front of the property. He sees a rooftop on a barn down a sloping field.

"How about there. On down in that field?"

Sergeant Baker follows his gaze.

"Take a look, sergeant. I'll check the house again. Make sure nobody's home."

Baker holds the shotgun at his waist. He walks into the sloping dirt field, scanning the ridge of mountains rising in Mexico.

Whicher holds the Ruger loose in his hand. He walks to the front porch, climbs the steps, bangs on the door.

"Anyone home?"

On the porch floor, in a shot glass, is a measure of bourbon. Untouched. Against an upright stud.

He stands and listens. Silence. Nothing from the house.

From the porch, he can just see the sergeant, at the side of the barn. Coming around the front, to where its doors are open.

Baker steps back sharp. "*Sir!*" he shouts.

He swings the shotgun out before him. "*Over here, sir!*"

But Whicher's already running.

Chapter 20

Casa Piedra.

I stared at the bleak land surrounding the homestead. The disused rail track running north-south, between the hills. The track bed was on a bank of crushed stone above the dry creek. A line of switchgrass growing from the hard-baked dirt.

Nothing moving, no sound. Just the sand blowing down the draw. Tennille's black and red 350, ticking heat.

Joe Tree stood by the Dodge Dakota. A harsh look on his face.

"You think there's somebody out there?"

He leaned against the truck. Marlin on the roof of the cab. "Leon, maybe."

"Leon?"

"Or one of his."

I looked at him.

He says, "They want to know where she is."

I put a hand in my jacket, on the 250 SIG. Closing my

fingers around it. "They want to know where Tennille is?"

He shook his head. "Maria."

"She's got her daughter out here?"

"Been here a week."

I turned to look at the group of buildings. Mud brown walls. An outpost, all it was. End of the line. One brick had a date stamp; 1932. It wasn't hard to picture, it couldn't have changed. Mules. Sheep, maybe. Desolate, my reckoning. The day they built it, and every day since.

"She has to hide her daughter," I says. "A place like this?"

Joe leaned into the truck roof. Raised the rifle. "You think she wants this?"

"What's that mean?"

He looked along the barrel. Eyes squinting into the sights. "This. You."

I broke off looking at him. Stared at the waves of heat above the hard pan.

Behind us, there was a noise from the house. The rough wood door was opening. The guy in the coverall was coming out. He had his hands in his pockets.

Beside him, a woman, Mexican-looking, her hair tied back from her wind-burned face. Rebozo over a worn cotton dress.

Joe turned from the Dakota. Rested the butt of the rifle on the ground. "Esteban," he said. "Elaina…"

The man nodded. There was no smile on the woman's face. She scanned the outlying hills. Barely glancing in my direction.

Behind them, Tennille stepped out through the door. With a girl, maybe seven years old. She had a mane of hair, eyes too big for her face. Tennille took the girl's hand, knelt in the dirt. She put both arms around her, kissed her face.

"Tomorrow night, baby," she says. "Just till then."

The little girl looked at her. She stole a look at me. And Joe in turn.

"Tomorrow, I'll come. And we'll go find him. Tu abuelito. Yes? Your Grandaddy. In Mexico…"

But her daughter only held her. And leant in closer. And didn't answer.

⋏

Lajitas.

At the border, the Rio Grande sits low in the flood plain. The settlement of Lajitas deserted in the mid-day heat.

Whicher parks the Silverado by a freight yard down near the river. Through the mesh wire fence, a truck mechanic in a baseball cap works the axle on a stepdeck.

According to Sergeant Baker, Varela owned a freight business as well as the ranch in the hills. Whicher had left him back at a trading post on the highway; the sergeant after making a couple of calls to see if he could raise a friend, some school teacher, on account of the kid.

At one edge of the freight yard, there's a flat-roofed site office. A red Camaro parked alongside it. The marshal makes a note of it. Leon Varela's car.

He steps from his truck and crosses into the yard. The mechanic working on, no word, no kind of greeting— watching, from the corner of an eye.

At the site office, a big Hispanic stands in the door-frame. Six two. A hundred ninety pounds. In jeans. A tight black vest. Silver cross and chain on his chest.

"Mr. Varela?"

The young man rocks back on his boot heels. Around thirty. Good-looking, matinee type. King in his own yard.

"My name's Whicher. Deputy US Marshal. You know where your wife is at?"

Varela flexes his neck, the silver cross drawn tighter. "No."

"How about your kid?"

The veins on the man's neck stand a little higher. "She better be alright."

"Y'all still married?"

"Separated."

"You own a ranch property up in the hills, correct?"

"So what?"

"We found a vehicle. Belonging to a suspect on a bank robbery."

Varela gives a flat, disbelieving laugh.

"Know anything about that?"

"Are you for real?"

"Just answer the questions…"

Varela bugs his eyes.

"You don't know where your wife was at yesterday? How about your daughter?"

Whicher sees the reaction, at the second mention of his child.

"I haven't seen either one of them. In weeks."

The marshal turns sideways in the young man's stare. Watching the mechanic, working the axle on the stepdeck.

"You don't have much to do with 'em? This point in time? That about it?"

Varela doesn't answer.

"But you do own that ranch?"

"I hate the place."

"That right?"

"I've been on the road. If you're asking. Yesterday, I was driving a flatbed load down from Clovis, New Mexico. If you want to check it, man, I'll give you the number for the yard."

"Somebody broke in the house up there, Mr. Varela. That property of yours. You know anything about that?"

The young man's eyes narrow.

"How about that house fire they had?"

Varela runs a hand through his slicked back hair. Face blank now, eyes guarded.

"Bad luck," says Whicher, "fire out there. No help. The middle of no place."

"Hey, man. What the hell's that mean?"

"I'm asking the questions, son."

Varela's hands twitch by his sides.

The marshal stares at the younger man's muscled torso. Let him twist. Son of a bitch.

"So you ain't seen 'em. Don't know nothing."

"I got work to do."

"That it?"

"Why don't you get the hell out of my yard?"

"Guess I know where I can find you." Whicher tips the brim of his hat. "You have a fine day, you hear?"

Varela turns back into the site office. Head side-on he spits into the dirt. And pulls the office door closed behind him.

Whicher crosses the dusty yard back toward his truck.

The mechanic looks up from his set of wrenches. Underneath the cap, his skin is weathered dark.

"She's afraid," he says, Spanish-sounding, more than Texan.

The marshal looks at him.

But the man pulls down his cap. Picks up a wheel nut. Turns back to working on the trailer.

Whicher strides from the yard and climbs in the Silverado. He fires it up—heads along the grit road back to Lajitas.

He hits the radio frequency for Alpine police department. Waits while they find Lieutenant Rodgers for him.

"Lieutenant?"

"Yeah."

"News on that gas station robbery. I think we got your perps. You send that VT to Arlington?"

"I did, marshal, but it didn't come back yet."

"No matter. Looks like we got a confirm for Gilman James. And the girl's Tennille Labrea—age twenty-six."

"I'm writing that down…"

"We found his truck. In a barn. A ranch property, middle of no place. "

"Anybody there now?"

"No. But the ranch is occupied by her. Description fits the girl at the gas station. And seen at Paisano Pass."

"That description was pretty loose…"

"She has a bank robber's truck parked in her barn."

There's a pause at the end of the line. "Alright, sir. Does she have a vehicle?"

"Ford F350. I'll have Sergeant Baker radio up the details, I'm about to go pick him up. There's a daughter, second-grader. Some kind of trouble, with the father. Guy runs a haulage business, on the border. Lajitas. I'm down there now."

"Any record on either of them?"

"On her, no. Varela's got a juvie file, according to Sergeant Baker. He runs more than drill parts south of the border…"

"That make her a gas station robber?"

"Where is she? Where's the kid? That's what I want to know."

"Copy that," says Rodgers.

Whicher switches out the call.

He swings the truck onto a two-lane highway. Runs along the road. Scattered buildings at either side—ocotillo and desert candle. Ahead is the low shape of the trading post. He slows up, steering toward the lot in front. Sergeant Baker waiting beneath a shaded gallery.

Whicher parks and jumps out. "Any news on the kid?"

"Child Protection Service have been up there, marshal."

"How come?"

"She's been cutting school. They've had anonymous reports the mother ain't fit. And ought not to be living up there."

"You find this school teacher feller?"

"Inside, sir."

The marshal thinks of the fire again, up at the ranch. The break-in.

"Why's she stay living out there, you think? With her kid?"

Baker shrugs. "Her father built that place. Him and Joe Tree, what I heard on it. Guess she ain't looking to quit the family plot."

⅄

A ceiling fan turns inside the darkened interior of the trading post. Whicher surveys the double room; a combination bar and general store. In one corner is a stuffed goat. Long-neck bottle of Lone Star in its upturned mouth. A painted sign above it reads: Henry Clay—Mayor of Lajitas. *'Vote for the Goat'.*

Standing alone is a man in his late thirties. Rimless glasses. Sleeves rolled on a checkered shirt.

"I'm Jed Reynolds."

Whicher steps forward. "Sergeant Baker here tell you what this is about?"

The man pushes the rimless glasses up his nose.

"Tennille Labrea. Mother of one of my students, Maria."

"The kid's been cutting school?"

Reynolds nods. "She's missed some, yes. Like I told Troy."

"Enough for Child Protection to hear about it," says Whicher.

"The school's obliged to make a report, if it goes beyond a certain number of days."

"She was a regular wildcat when they started in about her daughter," says Baker.

"Troy," says Reynolds, "that's not real helpful."

"What I heard, is all."

"There's no denying the family have had problems," says Reynolds.

"But?" says Whicher.

"That intervention was heavy-handed and totally unnecessary."

"You here to defend her?"

Reynolds reddens.

"She is a hell of a looker, Jed," says Baker.

A bar-keep in a cut-off T-shirt comes out from in back. He eyes the sergeant in his uniform. Whicher. The suit, big hat.

"Gentlemen. I get you something?"

"Just business," says Whicher. "Another time."

The cooling air from the ceiling fan washes over him. Reynolds shifts his weight from one foot to another.

"Considering the harassment from the father it's not surprising there have been problems."

"What harassment?"

"He wants his daughter. He's made all manner of threats."

Whicher turns to Sergeant Baker. "Any of that make its way to police?"

Reynolds cuts in; "There's a perception around here it wouldn't make any difference."

"Hey, Jed," says Baker, "she didn't file any report."

"She knows nothing'll happen."

Whicher folds his arms across his chest. "Don't start in, that kind of crap."

"A lot of families around here are different," says Reynolds. "Not exactly conventional."

Whicher glances at the stuffed animal in the corner. "No shit."

"Is Tennille in trouble?"

"Could be."

"Am I allowed to ask in what way?"

"Armed robbery."

The school teacher's face blanches. "Good Lord. I didn't realize, Troy."

"Heavy-handed or not," Whicher says, "the law is the law."

Reynolds stares at the bare floorboards through his glasses. "There's no mother more committed to her daughter in my school. I hope you're wrong about Tennille, marshal."

"Yeah. Keep hoping."

"If Maria ends up losing her mother, whatever chance

she had in life gets snuffed out pretty early."

Whicher chews on the side of his lip. Thinks of Lori, his little girl, back home.

"Everybody I ever busted is a nice guy. Or girl. I'm the son-of-a-bitch gets the job cleaning up after 'em."

The teacher looks past the marshal, to the far corner of the room. "I do a little cleaning up the mess myself. Not everybody voted for the goat…"

Antelope Mesa.

We followed Joe Tree's Dakota over a wide desert plain. Tennille driving the 350—Joe's truck kicking up a rooster cloud of dust ahead.

I watched the waves of heat bending the horizon. Thought of Michael. He should've never joined the Corps.

Nineteen years old, blond haired, blue-eyed, what he was then. Girls fighting over him. Living the life.

Connie had him now. A doc with no license—no license and a taste for crank. Whatever happened, I'd get him out.

The Corps was Nate's thing. Nate Childress, best Marine you ever saw. He was always going in, from day one, ever since I knew him.

Me, I had nothing better, that's all it was. My mother dead, no father. Only family Nate and Michael. And maybe Orla—Nate's girl, from second grade. We grew up a part of each other's lives. Closer than blood.

Michael joined six months behind us. He was kicked

back, then some—a typical southern guy. But he put himself to catching up, he told me. First time in his life he ever really tried.

I scanned the flat-topped hills in the distance.

Tennille watched the rear-view. She checked behind every few seconds.

She was something. Hiding her daughter in the desert, an outpost like that. I thought of Orla Childress. Two kids to feed. Some ways they weren't so different, one from the other. Her and Tennille.

I glanced at her, silent, steering the truck.

Up ahead, Joe started making a turn, moving out, away on the right flank. Tennille drove on towards him.

The Dakota was stopping, dust swirling around it.

Tennille hit the brakes. She stopped the truck.

It was the middle of nowhere. Miles from any road.

She's looking at me.

I pulled the SIG from my jacket.

"You don't need that."

"What the hell are you doing?"

She says, "Getting out."

"You're taking me to see Michael."

"No, Gil."

I held the pistol level. "You told me we were going to see him…"

Out the window of the truck, Joe Tree's standing with his rifle.

"I told you that," she said. "But we're not doing it."

"The fuck we ain't."

She says, "Can we get out?"

Joe swung the rifle to his hip. He pointed it in the cab of the 350, right at me.

I sat a foot apart from her in the truck cab. Hardly breathing.

"What do you want?"

"I want to get out of this truck." She put a hand on the door lever. "Are you going to let me?"

Her twelve gauge was propped between us, between the two front seats. She didn't try to reach it.

She pushed open her door.

I tracked her with my pistol.

Joe held the rifle at his hip, pointed straight at my chest.

I slid out, held the SIG on Joe.

Tennille looked at me. "Nobody's shooting anybody."

I didn't answer.

Joe Tree only grunted.

"I'll take you to Michael," she says. "But not today."

She stepped away slow, eyes on mine. Till her back was against the battered sides of Joe's Dakota.

"Michael's supposed to be pulling a robbery with you tomorrow." She shaded her eyes against the sun. "Now he can't."

I looked from her to Joe. "This your idea?"

"My idea would be shoot your ass."

"Yesterday," Tennille says, "I turned my life upside down."

I kept the SIG on Joe.

He watched me with shining eyes. Long hair loose, black as a crow's wing.

"I robbed a gas station," she said. "I've got to get the hell out—to Mexico, with my daughter."

"I want to see Michael."

She held her hand to the glare of light. "I crossed a line. No going back."

"Let me see him."

She just looked at me. "You'd rob the next place alone," she said. "If you had any choice. We're taking Joe's truck."

I turned to him. "Yeah?"

He gave me a sick-looking smile.

"Joe's switching with us."

He grunts, "She might as well hang for more than gas money."

"Then what?"

She says, "I want half."

I laughed. No sound came out, though.

"After, Joe can meet us. I'll take you to Michael. That's it."

In her eyes I saw the streak of sadness. For the first time, behind the lick of flame.

"How about you, Joe," I says. "Ready to pull the house in on yourself?"

He stood by his truck, some thought working inside. He held the Marlin rifle flat. Pointed it at the horizon, sweeping a line along it. "Take a good look around…"

"At what?"

He cracked his mean smile. "That's just it."

I turned to Tennille. "You getting any of him?"

She took a pace from the Dakota. "What he means," she says, "is nobody's coming."

"What?"

"Nobody's coming to help."

Joe set the rifle at his hip. The muzzle gaping towards me. "My kind no more than hers."

I stood facing the pair of them. Gripped the SIG, desert sun at my back.

All she said was; "Yes or no?"

CHAPTER 21

Brooke Army Medical Center, San Antonio.

A plastic chair. A waiting room. The office of Dr. Benjamin Zemetti. Neat magazines, a coffee table, pot plants.

Whicher takes off the tan Resistol. Reads the posters on the cream colored walls. Group healthcare, family counseling. Support numbers. There's a giant pin board, with upcoming events. Wheelchair basketball. A surfing clinic for amputees.

The door of Zemetti's office opens. A silver-haired man in his sixties emerges.

"Marshal? If you'd like to follow me?"

Whicher grabs the Resistol.

"Captain Black is down at the neuro care facility."

The doctor steps into a well-lit corridor.

"I could use a walk."

The corridor stretches out, silent, under squares of light. Whicher tries not to think of the melancholy pull waiting, somewhere just out of reach.

Twenty years gone, his own time, 3rd Armored Cavalry. All different. The Persian Gulf War. Six months, start to finish.

No multiple tours, no bombs, no civilians, no kids with C4 taped to their bodies.

He thinks of the report again. A reconnaissance patrol.

"Don't suppose y'all get a lot of visits from law enforcement."

"You'd be surprised, marshal."

The two men reach a set of stairs descending to an open plan area. Floor to ceiling windows, flooded with afternoon light. There are men in wheelchairs, on crutches. Reading the sports pages, drinking coffee. A terrible asymmetry. Bodies missing arms, missing legs.

"Some of the people we deal with have a highly diverse mix of problems," says Zemetti.

The room runs on, section after section. Stretching scale to the distance.

Whicher looks at the doctor, a question in his face.

"They can be hard to predict."

Ahead is a reception desk, manned by two Army nurses.

Zemetti leads Whicher past it to a circular ante-room, a smaller unit, leading off into private suites. He stands before a wood-veneered door. Knocks sharply.

"This is Captain Black's room. And marshal, I have to ask you not to show any outward sign of distress at the captain's physical appearance. Also, you may need to adapt any questions to fit the situation here."

Whicher nods. "Is everything alright with this?"

"Yes." The doctor meets his look. "Well, no. But you'll see…"

Inside the private suite at a picture window, a man, silhouetted, watches the leaves moving on the trees in the wind.

From the threshold of the room Whicher sees the motorized wheelchair. The back of the man's head. No left arm. No legs.

The doctor leads Whicher to the center of the room.

"Good afternoon," he calls out. "How's it going, Cap?"

The man still stares out of the window. He wears an olive T-shirt, one sleeve flat against his side. "There's two birds in the tree over there. Yesterday there were no birds."

"We have a visitor. The marshal—wanting to speak with you?"

The man moves his fingers on the armrest of the wheelchair. It swivels to face the room.

Whicher sees the burns that have consumed the man's face. Erasing the features once there. The hair line, at the front is raised, grafted. A reconstructed nose and lips. Too small for the dimensions of the skull.

Whicher shows no reaction.

"Can we sit?" Zemetti asks.

"What?"

"Do you mind if we take a seat?"

The man in the wheelchair looks at them blankly.

Zemetti gestures Whicher to a suite of soft chairs by a couch at the back of the room.

"Captain Black," says Whicher, "I appreciate your seeing

me. I'll try to make this brief. It's about two men from your former command."

The man's eyes move behind his still face.

"Staff Sergeant Gilman James. And Sergeant Nathaniel Childress."

"Childress? Childress was a medical discharge. James is still in."

"No," says Whicher. "James left, also. A few months back."

The man in the wheelchair looks at the doctor.

Zemetti shrugs, lightly. "It must have been after you left."

The captain looks from one man to the other. He pulls at the T-shirt, fingers and thumb pinching the letters in capital across the chest—U.S.M.C.

"Sir," says Whicher, "I'm investigating an armed robbery the last couple days—and it seems like there could be some connection with these two men."

"My men?"

"There's evidence to support that."

"You'd have to talk to the CO."

"Excuse me?" Whicher looks at Zemetti.

"If you're thinking of putting them on a charge."

"It's alright," Zemetti says. "Marshal Whicher only wants to ask some things about them."

"Oh." Captain Black stares into the middle distance.

"Sergeant Childress left the Corps a while back?"

"Yes."

"Can you tell me anything about that? He was injured in

the fighting. Is that right?" Whicher sits forward in the soft seat.

The captain sits with his mouth partly open, head completely still—sucked back inside himself.

Outside, through the picture window, trees move soundlessly, indifferent.

"They had it in writing," he says.

Whicher inclines his head.

"Under '*Logistic Support*'…"

"Sir, what was in writing?"

"The patrol warning order."

Whicher looks at Zemetti.

"I think it's a sort of notice," the doctor says. "Before they set out on a patrol."

"Yeah. I know what it is."

"No medical evacuation by helicopter," says the captain. "No fire support, no air support. It was in writing."

His eyes move quickly behind the mask-like face.

"Don't tell me they didn't know…"

Jackson Fork, TX.

A block-shed. Sitting with Tennille at the Jackson Fork cattle auction—looking down from a bank of raked seats. Another steer moves through the run, behind galvanized bars.

"How much longer?"

"They're almost through," I says.

There's maybe twenty people in the shed. Most of 'em in

Stetsons and John Deere caps. Rocking chairs, flicking on sheets of paper—tappin' a hat rim; making bids.

The last animals are coming in now. A sale by the head, not a batch.

A TV screen hangs from the ceiling, prices on it, running by like ticker-tape. Feeder steers, slaughter cows. Breakers, boners. Ain't sure what. There's an auctioneer at a microphone—singing, a language I can't get.

Fans rotate the smell of beast and dirt in the air.

"These are all ones and twos," I said. "The little guys."

It's fast. A gate opens, an animal runs in. It takes just a few seconds.

It looks around, feet trampling the dirt. Bids. A sale. End gate opens, and they run it out. Another one comes in.

"Doesn't look like anybody's getting rich."

"Not today," I says. "Tomorrow's the big sale. Come on, let's head out. We don't have long."

We climbed down the bare concrete steps. Headed outside, toward the holding pens. Through the dark sheds. A wall of smell. Churned up mud.

There's rigs and trailers everywhere. Hoses feeding water tanks, sluicing out the pens.

"There's an office," I says. "A trailer they use. Green trailer. Me and Michael clocked it; out back."

The site's a sprawl. The middle of a bunch of flat fields. Like a fair, or a rodeo came in. Cars and light trucks one end. Rigs and trailers at another. The pens, the shed. Out on a flank, a couple of hundred yards off, past the last pens, there's a group of trailers.

In front of the green office trailer, there's an old Ford van. E-Series. Faded yellow.

"That's it."

"That's what they move the money in?"

Across the hard ground, there's nobody—the sale's still running, everybody busy. Alongside the E-Series, there's a Chevy Blazer.

"Anybody asks," I says, "we're looking for the john."

The trailer's got a window running the length of one side. It's dark behind, no light. Piece of plastic from a grain sack taped across one corner. No faces looking out.

"Let me check the van. We couldn't get this close last time."

"Watch it," she says.

I glanced in through the van windshield.

"What're you looking for?"

"Extra security."

Inside, the cab seemed normal. A couple of worn-looking seats. Regular steel bulkhead dividing off the rear. No armor. I tapped on the short hood.

Tennille says, "Let's not hang around."

We turned away. Headed back to where the rest of the cars and trucks were parked.

We found the Dodge Dakota. Climbed in. Rolled the windows.

"We're about ten miles shy of San Angelo," I says. "We need to hit the van the first three or four miles in."

"You work this all out?"

"Me and Michael. We got to hit before they reach the

highway. Only thing is this terrain—it's real open."

"We can't go any closer in to town?"

I shook my head.

"You're sure of their route?"

"I want to check it's the same today."

I took a look at where the gate led out onto a farm road across the fields.

"We used to hate these kind of roads. Flat out hate 'em."

"We?"

"In the Corps. Out in Iraq."

I pushed the door of the Dakota all the way open—to let out some heat. A couple of flies banged around the inside of the windshield. Over and over, tangling, flying on back against the glass.

"They'd blow the shit out of you, places like this. Mine the road."

She swung her door wide, the breeze catching it. "This remind you?"

"Maybe it's just the feeling."

I stared at the cars and trucks parked all around us. The safety of steel, solid metal, what most folks think. An IED would rip any one of 'em in two.

She says, "Did you see it a lot?"

I let my eyes rest on the flat line at the horizon. Big sky, brown scrub. Dry fields; an indefinable haze rising up. The light seemed to flicker on the hot wind.

"Worst thing is multiple severe injuries…"

I felt my shirt clinging to my skin.

"I don't know how you get used to that."

"Secure the ground," I says. "Black Hawks lift 'em out. Forward surgical teams get 'em."

I watched the rear-view in silence as the dirt lot began to empty. Surrounded by animals. Dumb beasts, for slaughter. Baying. Not understanding. Feeling something, maybe. Penned-in, constrained. In the lowering sun

People were going home. Cars and trucks peeling away. Going back to something—a thing I couldn't come to imagine any more.

Jesse was a farmer. Most folk don't get it. There's no way back.

In the rear-view mirror I could see two men.

I started the engine in the Dakota.

"That's them…"

⅄

Brooke AMC.

From the suite of chairs in Captain Black's private room, Marshal Whicher takes out a notepad and pen. "This patrol. You tell me anything about it? It was under your command directly?"

The marshal glances at Dr. Zemetti.

"I had them on radio," the captain says. "They came under attack."

"They were ambushed. They couldn't get out?"

"We got them out…"

"Yes, sir," says Whicher. "But there was a high casualty rate. According to the report that I've seen."

Zemetti clears his throat. "Marshal? Why do you want to go over all this?"

Whicher taps his pen against the notepad.

The doctor leans back. Hands clasped against one knee.

"Those two sergeants? The one of 'em ends up half-dead; on a medical discharge. The other gets a nomination for the Navy Cross."

The room is silent.

The captain staring at a wall. He picks at the letters on his T-shirt.

Whicher continues. "Sergeant Childress took his own life three weeks back."

The doctor sits forward, stiffly.

"And we can put their Marine-issue service pistols at two crime scenes."

Whicher pauses. Looks to Captain Black. No response.

"Sergeant James' gun is in possession of the Alpine police department, as evidence. One more thing…"

Zemetti watches the marshal from the seat opposite.

"We got Childress' kid brother, Steven. Dead at one of the scenes."

The captain's truncated body twists in the motorized wheelchair.

Whicher leafs through his written notes.

He reads aloud. "Two rifle squads. Three fire teams per squad. Twenty six men." He looks up. "Is that right? All in, on the patrol?"

The captain doesn't answer.

"Out of twenty six men, there were fifteen casualties that

day. Including seven dead."

Inside the room nothing moves but the shadow of the leaves on the trees, blowing, dancing in the wind outside.

"No," says Captain Black.

"No?"

"Casualties were high. But it was three groups. It wasn't fifteen from twenty six…" He turns to the doctor.

"It's alright," Zemetti says.

"I ordered them out. James refused…"

The marshal glances at him.

"There was an evacuation route."

"Sergeant James refused an order from you?"

"He delayed the evacuation. There'd have been no need for a mounted section…"

"Mounted."

The captain nods. "No air. No artillery. There was no separation from civilian lines."

"The vehicles got attacked, too?"

"It wasn't fifteen from twenty six…" The captain clenches his hand on the armrest of the wheelchair.

"Why did they delay evacuating?"

In the silence, a switch clicks. Cold air spills from the A/C vents in the wall.

"All of this was looked into," says Captain Black.

"Why was that, sir?"

The man in the wheelchair nods. As if confirming something to himself.

Whicher makes another entry in his notepad.

Doctor Zemetti cuts in; "I imagine the casualty rate…"

The captain's head snaps upright. "This is about Tyler, isn't it?"

Whicher's pen stops.

"Tyler took it in…"

"*Tyler.*"

"Michael Tyler. From B Company."

"You had a Marine named Michael Tyler?"

"He volunteered, he led the rescue effort. But he's gone, invalided out. He was one of the casualties."

Whicher writes fast in the notepad.

The wheelchair turns.

The captain moves back to the window. He stares at the trees, speaks his words to the bright glass.

"James never answered. For that delay…"

⋏

Jackson Fork.

It was the same men coming out to the yellow E-series. The same two I'd seen with Michael. Late-thirties. Jeans, Western hats, all guts and arms. One of them carrying a brace of metal-alloy flight-cases. The other sporting a shotgun; blue-black finish. Mossberg 500. Extended tube mag; eight shot, at a guess.

They opened up the van and climbed in. I saw the tail-pipe shake as they sparked up the motor. They backed out. Turned. Bumped by us.

Tennille says, "They're going to see."

They rumbled across the lot in the E-series. Turned. And

went out through the gate.

I gave it thirty seconds and pulled out from the line. Swung the Dakota through the gate, onto the road.

"We'll keep back. They better take the same route."

We followed the van about a half a mile down the farm road.

"He's got his blinker on," she says. "He's making a left."

The van turned down a single track road. No markings, no signage. Flat fields stretching out at either side.

"So far, so good."

It was open, every direction. There was nothing, all the way out, as far as the eye could see. Just the road, the worked earth. Irrigation booms, five, six span, maybe more; a thousand yards.

Tennille scans to left and right, out the windows of the truck.

"How's this going to work? There's nowhere to hide."

The van's three hundred yards ahead. Like a colored brick. Kid's block, out on the mud.

There's power lines running down one side of the roadway. Wooden poles and cross spars. A busted single-wire fence.

"We picked a spot," I says.

Up ahead, coming in at the right-hand side of the road, there's a line, dark green, against the flat field. The road's arrow straight—running north-south, but there's a barn, to the right, no sides just a tin roof. The dark green line stretching out is a row of Arizona cypress—a planted row. Maybe a quarter-mile long.

"That's the place."

In front of the line of trees, is an old freight car; stock container, painted red. Right by the side of the road. No wheels on it. A store, most like, an improvised store. But it's solid cover. And it makes two points, with the line of trees.

"Alright, I'm pulling over."

"You'll lose the van."

I pointed out the windshield where the road stretched out ahead.

"You see anything else out there? Anything else at all?"

She shook her head.

"It's here or nothing. We already checked."

I pulled the Dakota off the road, by the freight car. It was beat up, weathered old, red paint and rust against the brown field. *Santa Fe Railroad*, marked in faded white.

Thirty yards further up, behind the line of trees, a grit track ran the length, hidden in behind. The track made a right-angle where it met the road. At its eastern end, it led to an abandoned farmhouse, among the fields.

I got out of the Dakota.

Tennille watched me.

I started to count off the distance, in strides.

"What are you doing?"

"Getting the range," I says. "From the tree line."

She calls from the truck. "What for?"

"Figure you're going to be in behind that freight car. I'm going to be in behind the trees, with the Dakota. I want to know you can hit 'em from back there."

"I'm not shooting anybody."

"Got to know the range."

"Gil…"

"I know. I heard you."

It was thirty two. Thirty two strides. Maybe thirty five meters, at the outside. I think in meters, when it comes to range.

Good enough. My reckoning. 870 Remington on a full choke.

I walked back to the freight car.

"You're in behind this," I called to her, "on the shoulder of the car." I showed her. Stood where I meant for her to be. "They don't see you, as they're coming up the road."

Tennille got out of the truck. She stood there, looking at me.

"You got the rear of the van," I says, "as soon as it passes by the freight car."

She put her hands on her hips.

I ran back over to the line of trees. "I got the Dakota in behind here, they're not going to see me, any more than you."

"Then what?"

I put my hands out in front of me, like I had them on a steering wheel. "I pull out from behind the trees," walking forward, "and park it across the road."

"That's going to work?"

"Time it right, yeah."

"How come?"

"They got no time to make a play."

She says, "So, what happens?"

"I get it right, they got just enough time to stop. Before they hit me."

I ran back to the freight car, Tennille's position.

"Soon as they come past, you move." I ran out, still showing her. "You get up behind the van. Shoot out both the rear tires. Boom. Move. Boom."

"Just like that?"

"Like that. They can't see you, can't hit you. You're safe."

"That's going to get their attention."

"I already did that parking a truck across 'em. Plus I shot out the windshield and put a couple on the engine."

"They're taking fire both ends…"

"And then, we offer them a way out."

"Which is?"

"They offload the money."

"You can get them to do that?"

"I'll be doing my best to be persuasive."

She looks at me. Takes a hand off one hip. Rubs at the side of her neck. "Then what?"

I bent down—picked up the imaginary flight-cases from where they threw 'em out of the van. "I get these."

"What do I do?"

"Point your 870 the hell at 'em."

"No shit."

"Then I drive us out of here."

"You?"

"Yes, ma'am."

"How come you?"

"I'll make it fast. At 10 miles-per-hour we put 14 feet

between us and them every second."

She looks at me.

"At 30mph, that goes up to 44 feet. Per second. Speed, speed, speed."

"What am I doing, covering them off?"

"After the first ten seconds, it don't matter. We're already gone."

"You sound pretty sure."

"It ain't like, my first. It's an ambush, right?"

She stared at the line of trees. Past the old freight car.

"I ain't no criminal. But I got this."

She runs a hand through her dark hair. "I think maybe you do…"

CHAPTER 22

Terrell County, TX.

From the single-engined Cessna, Whicher sees the great sweep of land stretching beyond the Edwards Plateau—Texas, the Rio Grande and Mexico. To the west, the evening sky is filled with broken cloud. In the south, a bank of solid gray approaches; a moving wall, a mile high.

The pilot works to trim the aircraft; fifth time in as many minutes.

Whicher points through the cockpit windshield.

"We got some weather headed in?"

The pilot, name of Logan, cracks a gap-toothed grin. "Mexican monsoon," he says. The sound of his voice metalized in the headsets. "It's kicking up a lot of turbulence. This plane about flies itself if you trim her right. Not tonight."

The sheer face of the storm cell is solid. Dark as a bruise. "Everything okay?"

"Just fine," says Logan. "Except we may have to divert."

"Really?"

"We're on visual flight rules," the pilot says. "Not instruments."

Whicher looks at him.

"Can't fly if we can't see. Can't land, either."

"I came up out of Lajitas, earlier." The marshal stares out with a brooding eye. "Clear as hell, then."

"Lajitas? Who you fly with?"

"Big guy. Not much hair. Wearing a leather jacket."

"Sounds like Dusty."

"You know him?"

"Ex-crop duster, I used to work with him. Now I know why you're gripping on the sides of that seat there."

"If we can't go to Alpine, where can we go?"

"Let me run a check on the weather. See how fast that thing's moving."

Whicher turns to looking out under the high wing. He thinks of Brooke AMC. The patrol.

Whichever way you cut it, it'd been a disaster. The report, the one he'd seen, was just the half of it. Rescue attempt was a separate action, classified—detail withheld.

Michael Tyler was a DUI to Lafayette police. But he was a Vet. A brave one, after all.

Whicher searches the empty desert beneath him. Tries to shut out the drone of the engine.

Brooke had left him depressed. Before leaving, he asked Zemetti what'd happened to Captain Black. Car bomb, the doctor told him. Six months back. In Iraq.

Whicher'd handed his security tag to an army nurse—

while an orderly worked a motorized cart across the floor.

"Apart from the loss of limbs and the burns," Zemetti'd said, "there's severe head trauma. Memory loss, behavioral change. He doesn't even really know he's had a brain injury."

"Why not?"

"He lacks the cognitive function to perceive it."

Brooke was an incredible place, but no-one walked away unscathed.

Whicher stares down from the plane. He thinks of three robberies. Lafayette. Alpine. An interstate gas station.

From the pilot's seat, Logan taps him on the arm.

"Word on that Mexican monsoon…"

"How's it looking?"

"Moving north-east a little fast. Could be marginal."

"Will we have to divert?"

Logan nods his head. The sun at the horizon blazes off his gold-rimmed Aviators.

"We'll have to run north a little. We're good for fuel." He taps into a GPS screen, brings up a flight chart. The position of their aircraft shown in the center. "Where do you want to go?"

"North from Alpine?"

Logan zooms the scale on the chart. Scrolls north and west. "We can do Fort Stockton," he says. "Or Pecos?"

"Pecos."

Logan types the identifier, PEQ, into the GPS.

"Runway 14. Elevation, two six." He points to the top corner of the GPS screen. "That's your ETA…"

Whicher thinks of the girl; Tennille Labrea. No links. No direct evidence.

But where was she? Where was the daughter?

He thinks of the teacher back in the trading post. Jed Reynolds. His little speech. Standing up, defending the folks you lived among.

Something got the whole thing started. Nate Childress; it had to be on him.

Three weeks back, he'd taken his own life. His kid brother and two ex-Marines up and get on some kind of a rampage.

Whicher gazes at the hills to the west, deep ravines of shadow stretching out as the sun begins to slant past the horizon.

What happened to Nate Childress, after Iraq?

From a mile above, the ground begins to shift shape, the wall of rain already threatening, about to blank out everything.

Smother every point of reference.

⚔

Christoval, South of San Angelo.

Rain. Rain full of fine dust. Of desert, the way I remembered—from night patrols, thousands of miles from there.

The wipers beat time in the Dakota. I had my window rolled, wiping my wet arm on the side of my leg.

Tennille was by me. Her shotgun against the door of the truck.

A stitch of light. Cars moving on the highway, in the distance. Our tires hit standing water, running off the fields at the side of the county road.

Shining out of the dark ahead, is a mess of lights.

Tennille opens her mouth to say something. I can't hear, the rain's so hard, railing on the roof.

I slowed up to where the light spilled across the wet roadway. Pulled over, to an empty gravel lot. A diner. Lit up in neon. Red, white and blue, like the flag.

"You think it's open?" she shouts.

"That's a hell of a light bill, if it ain't."

I snapped off the engine. Stared at the bright panes of glass lit up in the black night.

Tennille pulled the hunter's jacket around her.

"Let's get something," I says. "We've got to eat."

I grabbed my jacket. Felt for the weight of the SIG. Jumped from the truck.

I ran across the gravel lot, into the diner. Nobody in there. No other customers, but it was open. I dumped my jacket on a seat. Slid into a booth

I checked the menu card. Tennille walks in. She stands by the booth.

I looked up at her, at the rain running down the skin of her flawless face. Hair black and wet against her shoulders.

"Get something," I says.

She sits down opposite. Turns her face to the window.

From a door in back, a guy comes out behind a long counter.

Tennille's just staring into the darkness, outside.

The counter guy comes over with a notepad open in his hand. He's late-fifties, a glass-cloth on one shoulder, worn-looking, but friendly.

"Evenin' to you."

"Evening." I picked up the menu card. "Can I get a steak?"

"What kind of size?"

"Sixteen ounce, medium."

"Any side?"

"Little okra. Corn. Cup of chilli."

"Got it," he says. "Ma'am?"

She shakes her head. "Just coffee."

He puts his pen behind his ear. Walks on back to the counter.

Outside, on the road, nothing's moving in the pitch black. I stared out the window. Thought of Jesse. Out there, riding through the dark land. Or was it all in my mind?

I stared at my reflection. Distorted. Like somebody I didn't even recognize. I caught her watching me, in the glass.

"Why don't you eat something?"

She didn't answer.

I thought of Michael, of dragging him the night before— getting him into Connie's Tahoe. Face drained, how it was. The weight of his body. Out of it. Unconscious. In stage four shock, from loss of blood.

I looked at Tennille. "You don't have to do this."

Her hands were resting on the table between us. She picked at the silver bracelets.

I thought of Connie. The crawl of skin across her cheekbones. Pained eyes. Ten years burned out of her face.

You took up a gun, your world could turn upside down in a heartbeat. A bank. A gas station. A patrol, the other side of the world.

Or a robbery, the fields of Texas.

You stepped off, the fall could be an inch, a mile— unending. Nobody to save you, nobody there. Except for people like Connie. With ravaged faces, in forgotten rooms.

"You can change your mind," I said.

She didn't answer.

"I could take that van without you."

She messed with her bracelets.

The counter guy brings two cups of coffee to our table.

Tennille picks up the menu card. "Can I get a slice of that sheet cake?"

"Yes, ma'am. Right away."

The guy walks back to his counter.

I looked at her.

She says, "I want my share."

Along the walls of the diner were row after row of old-time photographs. They were lining the place; guys in Model Ts from the thirties, box-front trucks from after the war. Walls of memorabilia. A country on the move. Everybody going some place, in farm trucks and Fords. Horses and wagons.

"Go home," I told her.

I heard the door swing open from the kitchen in back.

"You got Michael hid away in them hills. What am I going to do? I'd give you the money anyhow…"

She didn't answer.

The guy comes out from the counter with our order.

Tennille sat in silence staring down at the table. It was covered in knocks and scars. Everything in there clean, not new, but made the best of.

The counter guy sets our food on the table. I told him, "Thanks."

"You got it."

He went on in the back.

Tennille says, "The people you're planning on taking care of?" She cuts a corner off the sheet cake. "The ones you're stealing for…"

I looked at her.

"You said you're not a regular bank robber."

"I said that."

"They know what you're doing? In their name?"

I watched the parking lot. The road beyond it. "I'm doing it. They don't have to know."

"It's for people you fought with?"

"Them. Their families."

"What kind of injured are they?" She set her pressed-steel fork in the crook of her hand; balancing it on her finger like a weigh-scale.

"TBI, worst of 'em," I says. "Traumatic brain injury."

She's just watching me now.

"Bomb goes off by the side of the road, you're either

dead or cut in half. Or the shock-wave hits your head so fast, so hard, your skull's moving like a rocket's strapped on it, but your brain, inside there, can't keep up. Like being in a car wreck. Times fifty."

I felt the distance between us.

She turned the fork in her hand. Cut another edge off the sheet cake. She put a piece up to her mouth."You think that gives you the right?"

I held her look. "You think taking care of your daughter does?"

I turned back to the steak on my plate. Cutting hungry, through the fat and meat.

"Why here?" she says. "Why this place? Why a cattle auction?"

"Why Mexico," I says, "with your daughter?"

She sat back from the table. Shook her head. Looked at me.

"A guy I grew up with, went to war with. He came back. Severe TBI."

I stared along the photographs on the near wall. In one polished frame, a young soldier with a canvas kit-bag. A Forties uniform. Grinning, by a roadside garage.

"After," I said, "he lived on a farm. Near here."

I stared at the grin on the young soldier's face. Square set of his shoulders. Behind him, a workshop. Tractor wheels. Metal rack of tires.

"We grew up in Lafayette," I says. "Nate, his name was. After he got hurt, he came here. His wife had family, grandparents that owned a farm. They retired, Nate and Orla moved out. Took it on."

"They say that's a hard life."

From the corner of my eye I could see the counter guy. He'd seen me staring at the photograph.

He walked towards our table—wiping a beer glass with his cloth.

"That there's my old man," he says. "Just back. After World War Two."

"Fine picture," I says.

"They came home, the world was a better place."

Alongside the black and white photograph was a color photo, newly taken. Another soldier. In a desert uniform. I recognized the blue and white square on the sleeve.

"3rd Infantry."

"My son," he says.

"They were out in Iraq…"

"Three times," he says. He looks at me; "You?"

"Marine Corps," I said. "Four tours, I'm done now. When's he coming back?"

The guy put a hand on my arm. I felt its slight pressure. And he took it away.

He stood in front of his rows of photographs. Hard wind rattling against the windows. He reached up, straightened the frame of the color picture. Glass cloth trailing from his hand.

"I buy you one?"

"How's that?"

"Cup of coffee," I says.

He stepped away from the picture. Nodded. "Sure."

He turned. Walked on back to the counter.

Tennille looks at me. A frown of question in her face.

I says, "You want to ask him?"

She shook her head.

He brought over another cup of coffee. Tennille made a space on the diner seat.

"Wild ol' night," I says.

"Yes, sir."

"Ain't great for business. Don't suppose."

He shakes his head. "Wind and rain ain't the problem. I seen worse."

"We were out riding," Tennille says. "Couldn't hardly see."

"It'll do that. This time of year."

I tried to think of something guys from around there might talk about. "Guess the farmers get a bunch of water. If nothin' else."

"Farmers all gone," he shrugs. "Leastways, the ones I knew."

I nodded.

"Got all them super-farms now," he says. "Don't know who owns 'em even. No idea. Folk back east."

He straightens the menu card. Wipes at a loose grain of salt on the table.

"People worked themselves to the bone. Them parcels of land…"

I says, "You had the place a while?"

"Grandaddy started it. The Great Depression. Just a roadside garage, it was then."

238

"Long time. I guess a lot changed."

"Everybody's broke. Same as then."

I rubbed at my chin.

"Grandaddy's time, so many folk were on the road, looking for work, oftentimes, he'd fix their cars, charge 'em nothing."

"That right?"

"Gramma'd cook by the side of the road. Before the diner got built. She fed 'em, waved them away again. Couldn't take a cent."

The guy stares unfocused, out the window. He drains his cup of coffee, leans forward on the table-top.

"I don't reckon there'll be a fourth generation."

"Maybe things can come good again," says Tennille.

"I ain't no different from anybody, ma'am. Nowadays, it's all chains, ain't it? Big ol' chains. Restaurants, hotels. Even the damn farms." He slid out of the booth. "Elsewise, a man might stand a hope."

He turned back to his counter.

We broke off looking at each other. Set to finishing our food.

A score of weathered faces stared down from the photographs, eyes like glass, caught in a moment. Who could step out of the stream, slip the frame.

I thought of the border. High hills in the wind.

"What about Joe Tree?" I said.

"Joe?"

"Where's he fit?"

"He's his own man," she says. "He's got his horses. His

land. People say he talks with the dead."

"Oh, they say that?"

"You think he cares a damn?"

I reached inside my jacket to a bundle of scrunched up bills. And thought of that gun. In my pocket. And all the things inside me, that pulled at my gut.

I took out a fifty spot, trapped it under my cup.

"Come on," I says, "let's get the hell out of here."

I looked back to the counter, but the guy was already gone. I pushed the big glass door open against a blast of wind and rain.

We ran—back to the Dakota. Got in.

I fired her up. Cranked the wipers full.

Tennille grabbed a cigarette. Pulled the lighter from her hunter's jacket.

I stuck the Dakota in drive. Headed her back out on the highway—bagged it down the soaking road.

"What's burning you?" she says.

I glanced at her in the glow of the dash.

She sparked the flame. Lit the cigarette.

"I came back."

She snapped the Zippo shut.

"Expecting what?"

I stared out at the dark land. With no answer.

She takes a hit. "It's not out there," she says.

In the rear-view, I could see the last specks of light that still showed, in all of that blackness. Shining, from the diner. Its brave neon lights. About to disappear, consumed by night.

"War's not out there," she says.

I watched it going, to nothing.

To nothing.

The red, white and blue.

Chapter 23

A **third floor** window. Friday morning, coming in hard. Across an asphalt lot, thin trees throw scant shade in the bright heat. Whicher's gaze drifts across the empty parking spaces. A water tower on the skyline. Past the donut shack, cars are starting to pull in from the strip. To America's Pizza. Welcome to lunch.

Whicher sits on a corner of his desk. Under flat light, in the hum of office machinery. A faint headache, from last night, still working on him.

Leanne had come out—met him, picked him up, when the Cessna got in. His wife but not his daughter. No Lori.

Her best friend had invited her over; Leanne already told her yes. No knowing if he'd be home, or not, or when. Same as it ever was. And so he'd seen her ten minutes, before bed. Stole another minute while she brushed her teeth. Leanne trying to get her down, tired, wrung out. While he chased his ass around the country.

Somewhere, they were out there.

Brooke. Brooke'd got him down.

Not the hospital, not the injured. A sense of something that lingered, unformed. His war was short; the Persian Gulf. Now everything was unending.

When Lori had called down, awake, he'd gone up grateful. To sit in the dark, on the floor, his back against her bed. And listen to her breathing. Close his eyes.

There's a knock, at the open office door. "Yeah," he calls out, "'mon in."

US Marshal Reuben Scruggs enters the room.

At sixty-one, the skin of Reuben Scruggs' face is like waxed leather. Tan saddle leather. Eyes that seem to dance with mischief. He wears a suit, a crisp collar with a shoestring neck-tie. In one hand he swings a high-top black Stetson, the hatband marking a deep line in the cropped white hair about his scalp.

"Mornin' to you, John."

"Good morning, sir." Whicher pulls out a chair by the desk.

"You looking to keep me here a piece?"

"Be just as quick as I can." He picks up the sheaf of notes on the desk. Squares them.

Marshal Scruggs sits. His back straight. A little stiff. "I'm up to fixin' a pit-roast this weekend. Mrs Scruggs got her sister comin' by."

Whicher nods, "I heard that."

"Am I going to see you in Church, Sunday?"

"If I get the time."

Scruggs places his hat on top of one knee. "You ride up from Alpine?"

"I flew into Pecos last night. Out of San Angelo. Account of that damn monsoon."

Scruggs gives a grunt. "I heard Alpine police department released all the cruisers to regular duty?"

"Border Patrol are keeping watch."

"Okay, John. So, where're we at?"

Whicher scratches at his temple. "Last solid lead was twenty-four hours back. Thursday. Outside Terlingua."

"Y'all found this boy's truck."

"Ford F150, yes, sir. In a girl's barn."

"We got her for an accomplice?"

"Sure looking that way."

Marshal Scruggs nods. "You think this situation is ongoing. Like ATF say?"

Whicher pinches the bridge of his busted nose. "I get the feeling I'm about to get burned."

"I'm division marshal, right? My ass, then. You're the investigator, do your job."

Whicher nods. Reaches for the top sheet of paper on his desk. "First up, we're confirming Gilman James on that gas station robbery at the interstate. Wednesday."

"You got evidence?"

"Strictly speaking; circumstantial."

"What about that CCTV?"

Whicher leans his head on one side. "Not good enough to take to court."

"This girl ride him out there?"

"Tennille Labrea."

"She help pull the robbery?"

"Matches the witness statements, yes, sir."

"Any direct evidence?"

Whicher shakes his head. "It's them, but…"

"Yeah, I get it, John."

"We found a car belonging to a Michael Tyler. Abandoned outside Alpine. Blood all over it. Tyler's former Marine Corps; I found out at Brooke. He served with Gilman James. We think Tyler's the guy that escaped from the bank. Alpine police confirmed the blood type with USMC."

Scruggs' eyes dance in the creases of his face. "Tell me something? Anybody catches these birds, there any reason not to take 'em down? With both barrels."

"They're armed and dangerous. No reason to cut 'em any slack."

"Alright." Marshal Scruggs looks around the room. "I like to know, is all."

"I found out at Brooke that Michael Tyler was invalided out along with the brother of Steven Childress. Direct result of some patrol. James was still in the service till six months back. But prior to discharge, they were seeing him— disaffected. He had a lot of friends got hurt. I guess it's just bad luck. But a lot of free time, he ends up spending on hospital visits."

Scruggs flicks the brim of his black Stetson. "Not sure I follow."

"I don't know," says Whicher. "Maybe I been thinking on it too much."

"I want you thinking. What about this Labrea girl?"

"She's got trouble with her ex. There's a kid involved. Threats, the husband wants the kid. I can't find a connection to any Marines…"

"Her place empty now?"

"No sign of her. No sign of the kid."

"Anyone watching the place?"

"There's not enough manpower. She has a 350 truck—police are looking for it."

Marshal Scruggs lifts the Stetson off his knee. He flips it over, holds it upside down peering into the high crown. "Feller that sold me this hat told me the weave is tight enough to catch rain in. This here felt."

Whicher rubs the back of his neck.

Scruggs flips the hat back over again. "Take a drink out of it, you've a mind to."

"Fine hat, sir."

"Only damn thing in here holds water." Scruggs raises an eyebrow. "What else?"

"There's a neighbor. Native American. Name of Joe Tree. I tried to pick him up. Owner of the gas station in Terlingua told me it was this guy found that F150."

"You got him in this somewhere?"

"I don't know. Record shows he owns a Dodge Dakota pick-up. No sign of it, when I searched his property. I put out an alert for it…"

"That don't get us anywhere."

"James could've stolen it?" says Whicher. "Maybe he got out that way, with Tyler."

Marshal Scruggs blows the air from his cheeks.

"Brewster County sheriff's office has a sergeant, name of Baker, bringing up my truck, from Alpine."

Scruggs looks at him.

"Then I'll get back out there. For what it's worth, I think they're on the move, after pulling something else."

"Why's that?"

"Kind of fire and maneuver."

"It's what?"

The phone rings in Whicher's office.

"Go ahead and take it," says Marshal Scruggs.

"Whicher. Hello."

He pushes his chair back from the desk. Stands. Walks to the window.

Scruggs' sharp eyes search Whicher's face.

"Y'all are *where* now?"

He grabs a pen.

"When was this?" He scrawls something on a sheet of paper on the desk. "How come I'm only hearing it now?"

He listens a moment longer. And snaps off the call.

"Two hours ago, a Tom Green County patrol car spotted a blue Dodge Dakota. Partial read on the plate. But fitting the description. They left a message for me back in Alpine. Thinking I was there. You believe that?"

"How come nobody called?"

"Desk clerk at Alpine was waiting on Sergeant Baker coming in."

"But you had him up and drive your truck here," says Scruggs. "John, the Lord sent his own son to walk the earth. But you got to ride in that Silverado?"

"Three hours closer to San Angelo, ain't I?"

"See, them smarts of yours is what I like…"

⋀

Jackson Fork.

An abandoned farmhouse at the end of a tree-lined track. Rotting Santa Fe freight car across the field.

Through a broken window of the empty house, I could see the Dodge Dakota, parked in back. Hidden from view.

Two hours. Two hours waiting on the money van from Jackson Fork.

The weatherboarding on the farmhouse was shot. Paint peeled. Flaking. Dirty streaks running off the nailheads. Pieces of the shingle roof hung down, to swing in the wind. The porch was still good enough to take a man's weight. But the steps were gone—burned at a corner of the yard.

I tried to visualize the yellow E-series. Picture it, coming up the road. They had at least one shotgun with them. Both times, I'd seen it. First with Michael. Then with Tennille. Mossberg 500. Lethal at close quarters. Maybe they had other weapons, concealed.

I pushed open the door of the farmhouse. Walked inside.

A front hall. An old staircase. Marked up walls. It's like the bones, somebody's life. It ain't them, but what's left. Everything they was. And tried for.

A mirror, blown, misted. Outlines where pictures used to hang.

I stepped on through to a parlor room.

Out the window, the line of trees stretched all the way down the drive, to the road, across the fields. The old drapes still hanging. Shredded, stained by rain. But the room was stripped. Stripped to dust and rubble. A trash fire blackening the grate.

Through a broken door I walked into the kitchen. Only things left were screwed onto the walls. Cupboards, all open, doors gone on some of 'em. Space where a stove used to be.

Through the back window I could see Tennille. Sitting in the Dakota. Smoking on a cigarette. Tight-looking, with not long left.

I crossed the peeled-up flooring. Staring at the feathers of a dead bird in the middle of the room. I thought of Orla Childress.

First time I seen her, she was eight years old. A school yard in Lafayette. Hair the color of chestnuts. Green eyes, too big for her face. Like Tennille's girl, Maria. Or like her own daughter; Bonnie.

Orla moved from Texas at seven. Her old man left Jackson Fork, he never wanted the family farm. He got a job in Lafayette; Southwestern, the engineering department. From then on she was part of all our lives.

But Michael and me were just a sideshow. Nate was the one. Right from the start. Head of curls on him like a gun dog shaking in a bar ditch. The same as his son, now, little Josh.

Last time I'd seen them all was three weeks back. Together. At the side of an open grave.

⋏

Christoval.

A loop off the highway, a town less than five hundred strong. Whicher sits in his truck, staring down the main drag. A handful of one room stores and empty grass lots. Houses scattered among the Mexican blue oak.

Twenty miles south of San Angelo. The message from Tom Green County; *Possible sighting. Christoval.*

Vehicle last seen exiting off a side road. Officer unable to re-establish visual contact.

Maybe. Maybe them. Maybe nothing.

The Dakota was a long shot—Joe Tree's truck. But his place, so close to the Labrea ranch—somebody broke in the house there; James'd been in the area. They found his F150 in a horse barn.

If Michael Tyler was with him, he was injured, no doubt on that. Blood all over the cab of the pick-up outside Alpine.

Tyler hurt that bad—would they even be looking at something?

Christoval. Nothing about the place was right.

Twenty miles to the north, the city of San Angelo. Any number of places to rob. He could call Lieutenant Rodgers. Have him put in a request to USMC. Get everything the Corps had, on all three of them. Maybe San Angelo was in there, somewhere. The way Alpine had been.

He lifts the radio receiver. Puts in a call to the local dispatcher.

"Tom Green County sheriff's department. Go ahead."

"Deputy Marshal John Whicher here. I'm off of Highway 277, in Christoval. Following up a sighting on a Dodge Dakota?"

A moment's silence while the officer locates the log. "Yes, sir."

"Suspects in an armed robbery…"

"Logged this morning, got it, sir."

"I'm out here checking on possible targets. Anything they might be interested hitting. I called in a couple of places; the garage, the store, the post office. But I'm not seeing it. Too small, way small."

"I couldn't say, sir."

"I advised the locals to remain vigilant. Especially the post master. I'm thinking, maybe San Angelo."

"We can put out a general alert to San Angelo police department?"

"Do that," says Whicher. "There's something else you boys could do…"

"Go ahead, marshal."

"Have somebody pull out a phone book, search on-line—look for anything else this vicinity. Businesses registered close by."

"Alright, sir."

"It can't hurt. I'm going to take a ride around."

"I'll get right back. Stay on this channel…"

✦

Jackson Fork.

I slipped the 250 SIG out from inside my jacket. Dropped the box magazine from the pistol. Staring at the ceiling in the farmhouse; cracked, a brown stain of water in its center.

My boots crunched across broken plaster on the floor. The sound of it sharp, the air dry and still, too long unchanged.

Everything was different. Harder. Maybe the hardness was in me.

I ran a thumb over the first round in the magazine. Fed it back in again, felt the weight on the trigger—standard reach, double-action only. I stepped over a broken floorboard, walked back to the landing. Down the stairs, to the hallway, to the front door.

Along the tree-lined drive the wind was stirring. I tried to imagine what it used to be like. All of us leaving, or we already left.

I came down the porch boards, jumped off, turned the corner by a border of dead shrubs. Tennille waiting in the cab of the Dakota.

She swung the door open, stepped out. "We ought to get moving…"

"Let me have the shotgun."

She flicked her cigarette butt on the floor. Twisted it out under her heel. "What for?"

"Last checks," I says. "Habit I ain't broke."

She reached in the cab of the Dakota. Slid the 870 Remington out off the seat.

I took it from her, took out the cartridges. Two and three quarter inch, double-ought buckshell. Nine to ten pellets, per cartridge. Like a bunch of .38 special slugs coming right at you. In the barrel end the choke's a point-zero-three. Maybe zero-three-five. Full-ass, anyhow.

I loaded the cartridges back in. Chambered one up.

"Are we moving?" she says.

"We're moving."

We got in the Dakota. I fired her up.

We ran out slow, down the grit track.

Stones snapping under the tires.

Highway 277, South of San Angelo.

There's a burst of static on the radio receiver hanging from the roof of the Silverado.

"Whicher. Yeah."

"Tom Green County sheriff's department, marshal."

The Chevy barrels down a gun straight highway, headed north. "Go ahead."

"Can you confirm your locale?"

Whicher looks out of the window, at the low trees spinning by. Blur of grass at the side of the road.

"Eight to ten north of Christoval. On 277. Coming by a ranch. Something. There's a turn up ahead a ways. Road left."

"To the airport? To Mathis Field?"

"Son, I don't know."

"It sounds like you're near Jackson Fork."

"The hell's that?"

"We've just been taking a look. It's one of three businesses registered that area."

Another static burst. The signal drops, then comes back in.

"Sir?"

"I hear you."

"You could take a look at this place, you want to."

"What is this thing?"

"Jackson Fork. Auction sale business."

"What kind?"

"Livestock."

"Really?"

"Yes, sir. You're around three to four miles off of there. We called, they had a sale day today. Big sale, moved a lot of stock."

"They tell you that?"

The yellow-paint on the road doubles into a central reserve. Whicher sees the turn off for the road approaching ahead. "I'm at the turn, son. Left. Do I take it?"

"There should be a right turn, also. Small road—a farm road, headed right?"

"Yeah, I see it."

"Make the right, sir."

Whicher slows. Steers the Silverado off the highway. Up a road heading out into fields. "Y'all have a number for this place?"

"Yes, sir."

"Hold, up—I'm going to pull over and write it down."

"Copy that, marshal."

Whicher pulls over by a wild hedge of feverbush. He hoists his hip, pulls out a note pad from his pants pocket. Grabs a pen off the seat. "Go ahead."

"485—8291."

"Got it. Right."

"It's straight ahead, sir. Down that farm road you're on."

"I'll get back to you." Whicher clicks it off. Reaches for his cell.

He punches in the numbers, pulls the Silverado back onto the road. No sense not taking a look.

He steers with one hand—the cell clamped against his ear. It picks up.

"Jackson Fork—livestock auctioneers."

"Afternoon. This is Deputy Marshal John Whicher…"

A silence. "I just had the sheriff's department on here."

"Yes, sir, that was my doing."

There's a pause at the end of the line. "They all call up asking about some ol' truck. Ol' Dodge Dakota."

"Yes, sir. Series one, blue pick-up. We're interested finding it." Whicher's eyes drift across a field of dull white cotton. "I don't imagine you'll have seen it?"

"I ain't, but I got a stock-hand done seen it, right enough…"

Whicher's eyes snap back, straight ahead on the road. "Say what?"

"We just got through talkin' on it."

"Sir, somebody there's *seen it*?"

"Yeah."

"Today?"

"No. Yesterday. I weren't here. I got off of the phone just now, the sheriff's department. I tell my stock-hand, and he starts in how he's seen the durn thing…"

A truck is coming toward Whicher on the farm road. He has to put two wheels on the grass and swerve to give him room.

"Sir? What'd he say?"

"Some feller was looking over one of the vans we got. Raff—that's the hand, Rafferty—he don't like the look on him. Seeing him do it. Like he's up to checkin' on it some. He seen him go on back to his truck, after. Blue Dodge Dakota. Him 'n some gal."

"A girl?"

"Yes, sir."

"What'd she look like?"

"The heck should I know…"

"What's this van? What is it?"

"It's just an old Ford we up to runnin' the money out to the bank in."

Whicher feels his pulse against his collar.

"I take a look at it? This van? I'm on my way up to y'all."

"Ain't here. They done left, five minutes gone…"

A spark snaps in Whicher's belly, like a flare. "They headed out? To the bank?"

A moment's silence at the other end of the line.

"They sure did." Another silence. "Is everything alright? Marshal?"

CHAPTER 24

Jackson Fork.

I'm in behind the tree-line, engine running, hid from the road. Tennille's standing out on the shoulder of the freight car, the blind corner—forty yards out.

She's wearing the hunter's jacket, like the first time I saw her. Jeans, boots, long hair pulled back from her face.

I checked the clock in the dash of the Dakota.

Through the trees, through the low branches, the road's empty. It's got to be fast. Clean and done. And gone.

There's just the fields. The long horizon.

In the blink of an eye, the van. A grille—a yellow hood.

It's coming on, straight toward us.

Tennille puts the shotgun to her shoulder.

"Don't go early…"

I watched the van, trying to gauge the speed, right foot hovering.

Another second. Another. *And go.*

I slammed down on the gas, tires biting, the Dakota

shooting forward—bursting out from the tree line.

I blocked the road, hit the brakes.

The van nose-dived on its front end—wheels locking, skidding past the freight car.

Tennille ran out behind it.

I could see the driver in a denim shirt—beside him, the guard, in a leather waistcoat.

I leveled the SIG at the windshield, high and center— and fired.

The windshield exploded, a shower of glass spilling down the hood, tires locking solid. I fired twice more, on the engine bay. The van at a dead stop.

I jumped from the Dakota, SIG on the guard—there's a deafening shot, Tennille, against the van side, at the rear tire.

I ran for the passenger door, the guard reaching for the Mossberg—a second crash; Tennille at the next tire.

They're stunned, a split second, in the noise. I'm feet away, pistol locked on the guard.

He swings sideways, points the barrel of the Moss straight at me.

I squinted at him down the iron-sights of the SIG. "Drop it…"

He hesitates, face drained, full of shock.

But I'm in deep, too slow, it's too slow.

Tennille's at the side of the van, the driver's window.

She points her shotgun inside. "I pull on this—the both of you are gone."

"M'on Fletch," the driver shouts, "throw the damn thing on out."

His eyes are fixed on the barrel of my pistol.

"Fuck it, man, Fletch. Give 'em the gun."

He tilts the barrel down, one hand on the stock, pushing it out of the shattered windshield. It tips down the hood, hits the ground like a dud. A shell in a fox hole.

I snatched it up—put the stock to my shoulder. "Throw the money out."

I aimed the Moss at the near wheel, shot out the front tire. Racked a second slug.

"*Throw it out.*" Glancing at Tennille; "Move back out of there."

I aimed at the last good tire. Squeezed the trigger, the shotgun kicking and booming, barrel heat spreading into my fingers.

Tennille took a step further from the van. She was staring down the road south—mouth open; about to say something.

I moved to where I could see.

A Chevrolet pick-up was screaming up the road. Silverado. Headed straight for us.

I yelled; "*Get the money.*"

I racked the Moss, ran forward, knelt on one knee.

The truck braked, it turned three-quarter profile.

I aimed high, over the cab, a warning shot. It caught the top corner of the windshield. I pumped another slug.

The driver window was coming down—inside, a guy in a suit and Western hat. Leveling a gun on me.

I fired again, wide of the cab, saw his hand whip up, holding a big revolver.

I rolled flat, saw the muzzle flash, came up at the van

side. There was a clunk on the road, behind me.

Tennille shouted out; "*I've got it.*"

The driver of the Silverado fired again. The round smacked the door-pillar, behind me.

"*I've got the cases,*" she shouts, "*let's go…*"

I aimed straight at the Silverado, the guy threw himself down. I fired, not to kill, but to drive him off; the hell out. Pumping a fifth—firing, running now, in close.

His engine stalls out.

"*Come on,*" Tennille shouts, "let's get out of here…"

I'm at the truck window, the driver's laying across the seat. Arms up over his head, big revolver in his hand.

"Drop it."

He squints at me, a dust of splintered glass on him. He nods, drops the gun on the cab floor, by his hat. He's tough-looking, a square face, busted nose. The look of a pro.

"The hell you think you are?"

"United States Deputy Marshal. John Whicher." A grimace. "I been wanting to speak with y'all."

My heart's pumping, but I'm calm, cold inside, on a set of known rules.

"Get the hell out here." I wrenched open the door.

He sat. Slid out. Stood, his hands out in front of him.

"Lose the jacket."

He put a hand to his lapel—slipped off the jacket, let it fall on the road. He's wearing a white shirt, dark tic, black shoulder-holster; empty. Around his waist is another gun belt. Glock 22.

"Get that off…"

He put his hands to the buckle of the belt, eased it loose.

"Drop it. And get over there. Up by the Dakota…"

He walked ahead, hands in the air.

Tennille was standing at the front wing of Joe's truck. Twelve-gauge at her shoulder.

Through the open door, I could see inside the truck cab—both flight cases, all the money. I glanced at her face, caught the look in her eye.

I pushed the marshal forward; "Get in the back of the pick-up."

He walked on, past Tennille, past the E-series. Stuck a boot on the truck tire, a Western boot, tooled leather.

He swung a leg up into the truck bed.

The two men in the van sat staring out—wall-eyed, a pool of coolant gathering underneath the fender. The driver with his hands locked around the steering wheel.

I turned to the guard. "This here Moss? What is it, eight shot? You rack a ninth in the chamber?"

He nodded.

I looked at the marshal. "Three in the hole."

Tennille shouted out, "*Plus two*." She raised the barrel of the 870.

The motor in the E-series was starting to seize. I told the guard; "Let's leave it at that." I called to Tennille, "You drive. I'll sit up in back a piece."

Her chin juts a fraction.

"Head straight up the road, there. I'll tell you when to stop."

I wrapped a hand around the forestock of the Moss.

Pulled the SIG from my jacket, pointed at the marshal. "Slide on down the back there."

He moved down the truck bed, hard against the tail-gate.

I jumped in, facing him. "Okay, let's roll…"

Tennille ran the truck across the edge of the field. She straightened out, hit the gas, accelerating hard.

Behind the marshal, the E-series sat stranded, all its tires shot out.

"You wanted to speak with me?"

We were barreling down the road now, wind blowing in about us.

"You find what you was looking for?"

He says, "Not exactly."

There was a haze, forming up around the sun. Streaks of cloud, the air thick, snag of dust in the fields.

The marshal's just watching me, hands holding onto the truck sides as we blast down the road.

"I'm a criminal investigator, Mr. James. Been on y'alls tail a piece."

"Since when?"

"Alpine."

"I wasn't there."

He glanced at the Mossberg. "You're pretty handy with that." Watching me—sitting low in the pick-up bed. Dark red tie flying like a leash.

"Had a mil. spec 590. In the Corps. Couple years back. Not unlike it."

"That where you learned to shoot?"

"Right."

"What you plan on doing now?"

I didn't answer.

"Y'all on a streak?"

I watched the road stretching out behind him, a strip running through the fields of cotton, dirty white.

"Lafayette," he says, "Alpine. That gas station, at the interstate. Now this."

I stared at the flat land, dust rising behind us, power lines strung from pole to pole.

Tennille drove the Dakota hard, tearing along the empty road. The van was gone from sight.

"Steven Childress is dead," he says.

A glint of sun caught an irrigation boom.

"Where's Tyler?"

I felt the weight. The SIG in my hand.

"He's shot. Right?"

Thirty ounces. To knock a world off its axis.

"I seen a lot of this." The marshal holds his head to the side. "This kind of thing."

I looked at him.

He says, "It don't end good."

Far enough. I reckoned it far enough. Mile and a half, maybe two.

I slapped a hand on the cab roof of the Dakota. "Alright, here. Pull it over."

Tennille slowed up. She braked to a stop.

I jumped out onto the road. Flicked the nose of the SIG. "End of the line. You're getting out."

He was watching me, wary now. He leaned forward, got

to his haunches. Sat on the side of the truck. "You going to shoot me?"

I stared right at him. "No."

He swung his legs out. Jumped down. Gave the slightest nod. "'Preciate that."

"Don't come looking for me no more."

He stood by the side of the Dakota.

"You carrying a cell?"

"In the truck." He jabbed a thumb back down the road.

"Let's see."

He put his hands in his pants pockets. Pulled them inside out. A few dollar bills and loose change fell.

"We're going to get going now."

He nodded.

"Tell you what, marshal?"

"What's that?"

"Let's not meet again."

He looked up and down the deserted road.

Tennille shouts out, "*Come on. Let's go…*"

There's just the wind, rising, singing in the power lines.

"She worth it?" he says.

"It ain't on her."

He rubbed a hand over his jaw.

"You're right about one thing," I said.

He took his hand from his face.

"If there's a next time, it won't end good."

"I guess that means you ain't…" He stopped. Searching for the right word. "Listening," he finally says.

"Not to this."

He stood facing me, under the wide sky—fields of cotton stretching out to either side.

He pulled at the dark red slash of tie. Undid the top button of his shirt, loosed the collar.

Something in the way he's standing, staring at the road. He kicked at a balled-up piece of mud. "And what *do* you hear?"

I climbed back in the Dakota, stuck my head out the window.

"Voices," I called to him.

Tennille started to pull away.

"*The voices of the dead...*"

⅄

Concho County, on U.S.83. Tennille driving. Thirty minutes, no sign.

In my mind I could see him still. Tearing in, his Western hat, big-frame revolver snapping at me.

Clean and done, it was going to be. Clean and done.

Last he saw, we were headed north. Last-known-direction. We'd switched a dozen times since, east mainly.

Twenty miles, we'd come to a place called Eden. I hauled up the first of the flight cases. Cracked it open. Saw it full. I lifted it, held off my knee, Tennille just staring at it. A feeling, like electricity, nerves snapping—like static across my skull. Stack after stack of money. Neither one of us speaking.

Past Eden, we found farm roads, tracks through the fields of cotton. Deserted. Running south.

"I reckon this at three hundred fifty miles," I told her.

She didn't answer.

On the seat I had the map open, laying on top of the Moss. I traced every possible route south and west, to the border. "By the back roads, it could be closer on four."

She flexed her arms, gripped the steering wheel. Stared straight ahead at the highway.

"Looking at six hours."

She shook her head.

"You know it," I says, "better than me."

"In another hour," she said, "it's going to start getting dark."

I studied the map. Looking for anything. "Worse if it is."

"Worse how?"

"No one else is going to be moving."

To the south-east was hill country. Hardly a town on the map, nothing worth the name. Plenty of space. Broken country—wild mountain.

"We could hole up."

"We have to get back," she says. "Tonight."

⬧

Sixty miles out of Jackson Fork—west of Kerrville. The money still uncounted, both flight cases on the floor.

"It was definitely him," she says.

"That marshal?"

"From the roadblock in Alpine."

"If he's figured out who you are, they'll be watching. Waiting at your place."

She stared straight out through the windshield. Jaw set,

streaks of color at her throat.

I studied on the map. "We go near Terlingua, odds are we'll run right into them."

I thought of Michael, stuck with Connie. Somewhere out in the desert.

Close on three years he'd been scraping by. His lungs were damaged, his brain injured. He couldn't work; neither him nor Nate. But Michael got off better. What everybody said. Compared to Nate.

Non-penetrating. Focal and diffuse. I still remembered some of the words. *Cerebral edema.* Fifteen days before Nate came out of the coma.

A Navy doctor told me we missed the first hour—it might've been different. The night he told me, I sat in a chair, my quarters, in the pitch black. A bottle of hundred-proof whiskey that didn't touch me. The cold light of morning, bone awake. My M9 Beretta in my hand.

Nate's family got him out, got him to Jackson Fork. One time, I visited, only once. Orla running the farm, Nate in the fields.

I pushed the memory away. Watched the light fading on the highway.

No way I figured we could make it back for Michael—not straight out, not all the way.

Tennille was afraid, it didn't need spelling out. She was afraid for her daughter, her little girl.

I looked up from the map.

Tennille was leaning forward, tense in the driver's seat. Staring at something in the rear-view—eyes fixed.

"What?"

I turned to look.

There was two cars, a hundred yards back of us.

A third vehicle behind them—*some kind of patrol car.*

I snapped around back to the map, finger pressing hard in at the paper. "There's a road junction coming up. Get off this, we can make a left."

"If we turn, he'll see us."

"He'll see for sure if we don't."

There was a dip in the road, the outline of an iron-windmill against the sky—the smaller road just behind it, coming in at the left.

"We don't get off, we're stuck on here another twenty miles…"

She comes off the gas, starts to slow.

"Do I signal?"

"Make the signal."

I watched the road out front, praying nobody's about to come and make us wait to cross the lane.

She slows right down. "Fuck, this better work."

She makes the turn.

The side road climbs across an open plain. Buffalo grass, live oak.

She stomps on the gas.

"Don't turn," under her breath, "don't turn," eyes on the rear-view.

He's turning in behind us.

He holds short, like it makes a damn difference.

I ditched the map.

She cuts me a look. "Maybe he was already headed this way."

"Maybe."

Up front the road's twisting, starting to dip and rise. A stone track at the right.

"There…"

"That's going straight in the mountains."

"He can't follow," I says, "in any cruiser."

She wrenched the truck right, floored it out up the track.

We're powering through a stand of trees, climbing fast.

I turned around in my seat to look behind.

"You seein' this?"

"I'm seeing it."

The cruiser's bumping up the hill below us.

Ahead, the track's nothing but dry mud and deep ruts gouged by rain. We're coming to an overhang of rock, stunt trees growing from it.

The cruiser's dropping back on the slope.

We're climbing level with the outcrop of rock, turning a bend that disappears blind. There's a passing place off the track at the side.

I grabbed the wheel, dragged the truck over.

"Stop the motor—turn it off…"

I threw open the door, grabbed the Moss. Ran back.

We were hidden by the bend, he'd never see.

I strained to listen for his motor.

Tennille stepped from the Dakota—twelve gauge in her hand.

I pulled a bunch of slugs from my jacket, tossed a couple

at Tennille. Fed four in the tube of the Moss.

A white Crown Vic swings around the bend. Kerr County Sheriff's Department, in black across the door.

He's alone, head dipped looking for us along the track—window down.

I stepped out, shotgun hard at him.

He stamped on the brakes.

Tennille moves in behind me.

"Kill the motor…"

He reached to the keys. Switched it off. Placed his hand on the top of the door, where I could see it.

"Get out."

He stepped out. Pale-skinned, no hat, sandy hair, thinning. He raised his hands above his shoulders.

"Take off the gun."

He lowered his arms. Unfastened the buckle. "Sir, take it easy…" Letting the belt and holster fall to the ground.

Tennille reached and grabbed the gun belt—the barrel of her 870 never leaving him.

"What's your name?"

He put his hands back in the air. "Officer McBride."

"Know who I am?"

"Mr. James?"

"How long you been sitting back there, behind us?"

"I guess—fifteen minutes."

"Time enough to call it in."

He gives me a look.

"Not enough time to help your ass."

He swallowed.

"You carry cuffs? In the car?"

He didn't answer.

I pointed to a Hackberry at the side of the track. "I'm either going to shoot you down—or cuff you to that tree."

"Right in the front there, inside the car…"

Tennille drapes the gun belt and holster over her shoulder, like a Mexican bandit. She leans into the cruiser, pulls out a pair of silvered cuffs.

I walked him over to the tree.

"Alright, McBride. Get a hold of that."

He leaned against the trunk, reached his arms around, till his hands met. Tennille snapped the cuffs to his wrists.

"You know these hills?" I says. "Think it's set to rain?"

"I don't rightly know."

I stepped across the track to the Crown Vic, put the Moss up by the open driver window. I drew a line on the radio. Pulled the trigger.

I waited for the noise to clear. "What's up the end of this here trail?"

"I don't know, sir."

"Don't know, or you ain't saying?" I racked the shotgun.

"There's nothing out here. Nothing I know of…"

"There a name to it?"

He squints back over his shoulder at me. "Not that I know."

I ran to the Dakota, jumped in the driver's seat. Tennille already scrambling into the far side.

I started the engine.

"He radioed in," she says.

I didn't answer.

She looks at me. "I say we still head south."

I drove the truck back out on the mud track. Put her to a fast climb beneath a solitary desert ash.

I watched McBride disappear in the rear-view.

The ground worsened as it gained in height. There were boulders rolled on flash floods—the soil thin; bare limestone, clumps of poverty weed.

"We find a way off the hill…" I glanced at her, "maybe we could make it down to Kerrville."

She shakes her head. "We're not going in there…"

If we could get down, get close, we could ditch the truck. On foot, we'd be harder to spot.

I steered the Dakota on past a lechuguilla that screeched down the truck sides, like a banshee.

"This place—Kerrville. What kind of size is it?"

She sparked up a cigarette.

"Like Alpine?"

"Twice that. But we're not going there."

It was due east. We'd ran south, so far, up the hill. If we ran east, we could find it. I reckoned it at fifteen miles.

Nothing between us and it. We'd see light a long ways out, come nightfall.

I steered ahead, Tennille smoking in silence.

Up a mountain track; no name, to nowhere.

East.

Town.

Last thing they'd expect.

CHAPTER 25

Jackson Fork.

Half of Tom Green County sheriff's department is parked up by the auction site pens, a grass field, the middle of no place. Whicher sits in the shot-up Silverado. Watching more cars arriving. Every other vehicle is painted metallic gold; a black and bronze stripe along its side.

The cattle still left on site set to bawling at the disturbance.

Still no word.

Three hours back, Whicher'd stood and watched the blue Dakota disappearing up the road north.

By the time he'd made it back to his truck, the two guys in the E-series had already called for help.

San Angelo police took the call. Dispatched two cruisers. Plus crime-scene techs; the white cars boxed in now by the sheriff's trucks. The Silverado was part of a crime scene—techs had to finish before it got released. The time they got done measuring, picking up empty slug cases, James and Labrea were long gone.

KLST sent a TV crew.

Whicher declined comment.

He sat in his truck while the news crew filmed close-ups of bullet holes in the van for the early evening report.

He'd called Lieutenant Rodgers, back in Alpine. Warned him, in case they could be headed his way.

Rodgers told him he'd spoken to the county sheriff's office—found out Tennille Labrea had applied for a protective order against the husband. But not completed her end of the paperwork. Or if she did, she never returned the application.

The lieutenant said he'd call Border Patrol—put out everything they could find.

Whicher thinks of the girl, at the roadblock; Tuesday, the day he'd first arrived. Was she in it then? She must've been.

He thinks of her standing by the yellow van. Not many in the '15-most-wanted' like her.

The radio on the dash lights up. A call coming in. Whicher grabs at it. Marshal Reuben Scruggs.

He grits his teeth. "That was fast…"

"Hey, John?"

"Evenin', sir."

"I got a state commissioner wants to know how come we got a rural crime wave happening in West Texas. And what the hell Division Marshal's planning on doing about it?"

"It was them—Gilman James and the girl. Tennille Labrea. I walked in on it."

"What I heard. You still in one piece?"

"Last time I looked."

"How about that other feller—Tyler?"

"No Michael Tyler."

"Monday it's a bank. Wednesday it's a gas station. Friday, it's a goddamn cattle auction."

"I'm not seeing any pattern."

"Bunch of folk up in Austin want this squared away."

"Me and them both."

"All available resource…"

"We don't know where they all went."

"Wait there till you hear," says Scruggs. "Then bring 'em the hell in. You need anything?"

"My truck could use a week in a body shop…"

The light starts to fade across the auction site.

More vehicles arriving, more officers—in tan shirts and olive pants.

An entire county, plus the seven adjacent counties, on full alert. Whicher sitting in the Silverado. Picking glass splinters out of the seat.

He sees the door of the trailer office pop open.

A sheriff's deputy, a black guy in his early-fifties, running over.

Whicher pushes wide the door.

"We've got a confirmed sight, marshal. Kerr County police."

"Kerr County—that's a hundred miles south east…" The marshal reaches for his hat.

"Patrol officer radioed in," says the deputy, "Highway

83. But now they've lost him. They're sending all available units…"

ᛚ

Kerrville.

Red lights splintered in the rain on the windshield. Tennille drumming her fingers on the steering wheel of the Dakota.

"Either this is smart," she says, "or the dumbest thing we can do."

"They ain't going to look for us in here."

Traffic lights swayed on an overhead cable. And changed to green.

The car in front came off its brakes.

She says, "You better be right."

We crossed the bridge over the Guadalupe River. Into Kerrville, the heart of it, on Main. Four hours since they last had eyes on us. Four hours, inching through the hills, across the grasslands. Lights of town off east, through the worsening rain.

"We get in here," I says, "ditch the truck, get a room."

We passed two-story brick builts, old-style from the thirties, and fifties. A hospital, car lots. Squinting at the road panels, bouncing on the wind.

"Keep going," I says, "straight up there—Fredericksburg."

The traffic wasn't much, but there were people moving, trucks and cars. Street lights shining on the wet road.

We drove north-east away from the river.

"Hey…" she says.

Up ahead was the Kerrville police department. Flat-roofed block of concrete. Black and white cruiser out front.

"Just roll by," I said. "Nobody's out there." Feeling on the seat for Michael's SIG.

I threw a glance at the station house. On a pole out front, the flag of Texas hung heavy in the rain.

We crossed an intersection. By closed up restaurants. Past a rental lot, a Walgreens. A brown stone church. Auto parts store.

"Last place they're looking for us is here."

Tennille shook her head.

"Keep going," I says, "there'll be someplace. Up near the interstate."

"You're going to get us killed."

Already, half a mile on, the town's starting to thin. We passed a gunsmith. A Dairy Queen. A high school football field.

"Up by the interstate, there's bound to be a couple of motels."

"You don't know that," she said.

"We can get a room."

"There's going to be cops near the interstate…"

We kept on, past the strip malls and furniture stores. Starting to climb again, the road already lifting out of the valley floor. Hardly any vehicles, now, we're maybe a mile from the river, the center of town.

Up ahead, to the left, there's a bunch of lit-up signs, names of motels. Cars parked up in front of the rooms.

"How about there?" There was a yellow sign on a

motel—a light still showing from its front office. "Looks like they're still taking business."

Tennille pulled in.

It was a two-story motel, maybe forty to fifty rooms. Steel balcony, running along the top floor. Not more than a dozen cars in the lot.

"Park where it's dark, away from the lights."

She found a space behind a line of bushes, hidden from the road. "You want me to get the room?"

"I'll do it," I says.

"What if they recognize you?"

"Leave the motor running."

I slipped the SIG into my jacket. Took out a roll of money from the topmost flight case.

"I'm not out that office in five, you go. Get the hell out."

She gave me a look.

I stepped out of the Dakota. Ran across the parking lot, dodging rain. There was a light showing in the office window, it was definitely open. I pushed at the door.

Inside, there's a guy sitting behind a counter, the room dim.

"Evening."

He looks up over a pair of thick glasses. He's in his sixties, long white hair, a beard, check-cloth shirt. Tattooed arms.

"Like a room. For the night?"

He grunts. "One night?"

"Yes, sir."

He reaches on the counter. Spins a printed price card

around, so I can see it.

"Them's the room rates. Cash up front. I'm going to need you to fill out a registration card."

"I'll take a double."

I pulled out some money, laid it on the counter. Scribbled some made up lines on the piece of card.

He took a key from the board behind him on the wall. "Ten o'clock, going to need you out of there. There's breakfast. In the lobby, from six-thirty."

"Obliged to you."

"First floor, down at the end. On the right."

He counts the money. Folds it into the pocket of his shirt. Puts the key on the counter.

I picked it up.

He's staring at me now, from behind his desk. Magnified eyes, searching my face. "You traveling far?"

"Louisiana." I rubbed at the back of my neck. "Just came in off of I-10. Figured I had about enough."

"Lock up good tonight."

"How's that?"

"Got a manhunt." The bare office light bulb shone in the lens of his glasses.

I felt the weight of the SIG against the counter.

"Up in the hills," he says. "Bunch of guns is closing in on 'em. Bank robbers, what I heard."

I nodded. "Well. I'll take that advice."

I pocketed the keys, stepped from the counter. Slow, no hurry. I pushed open the door.

Tennille's out of the Dakota, smoking on a cigarette. I

pointed to where the room was at, at the far end of the row.

I walked fast, beneath the steel balcony, rain dripping from it.

Tennille runs across with the flight cases.

I opened the door, flipped on the room light. Tennille put the cases on the bed.

"I'm going to move the truck. See if I can't find a spot around back."

She leaned over the cases, unfastened the latches. Raised both lids. The second case was full like the first had been.

I headed back outside, jumped in the Dakota. I drove it around the side of the building. There was a ramp down to another lot, three or four cars parked—I stuck the Dakota in behind them. Two shotguns in the cab. Police officer's gun belt and holster. If I tried getting them in the motel room, anybody saw me, they're dialing nine-one-one. I put 'em on the floor, pushed back under the passenger seat. Locked up. Headed back to the room.

Tennille was leaning against a set of drawers just staring down at all the money.

"You going to count it?"

She turned, a blank look on her face.

I says, "You want to count this? Or what?"

"Fuck. I don't know. I don't like being here."

"It's too dangerous out on the road. Nothing's moving."

"You think staying here's all fine?"

I tried the door—made sure I'd locked it. Leaned my back against it. "We're never going to make it out of here. Not like this."

She folded her arms across her chest.

"We get another vehicle."

"Right," she says.

"You think we're going to make it back—in Joe's truck?"

She didn't answer.

"By morning, we got to be gone." I looked at her. "You want to walk?"

"Yeah, Gil."

"We steal something, or maybe we can buy something. All that money. Whyn't you count it? Make a start. It's not like we're going to get any sleep."

"What about you?"

"I want to scope around, check what's happening. Guy on reception says they're running a manhunt in the hills."

"And you want to stay here?"

"You want to tool out on the highway?"

"But what did he say?"

"Yeah, he really thinks we're it. Coming in to catch a few."

"We could still try to get back."

"It's four hundred miles."

She shook her head. Leaned down. Picked out a thick stack of money.

"Ten minutes, I'll be back."

I slipped out of the room and closed the door.

The rain was starting to ease up, a few sets of headlights still coming up from town.

I walked along the main drag, jacket pulled tight. Past a

building supply, a couple of houses. Down a side-street there's a car rental.

I studied the line of vehicles on its lot.

I walked on down to an intersection. Nothing going on. Just a wet night, small town Texas. Friday night, everybody gone wherever they was going. No sign of cops. No cars, nobody patrolling the street.

If any search was going on out there, everybody must be on the hill.

I stood in the shadows a minute. And turned around, started on back.

Two hundred yards from the motel, a cruiser's coming down the strip—white cruiser, light-bar strung across its roof.

He was headed in from the direction of the interstate.

He was too far away to see me. But I got in behind a rig and trailer on a strip of waste ground—just to let him pass.

He was slowing. Most likely finishing a shift.

There were no other cars, no other traffic—but he was stopping.

Right in line with the motel.

His headlights swung through the rain as he turned in.

I couldn't see him no more.

As I broke cover.

Started to run.

Chapter 26

Guadalupe River. Hunt, TX.

"You figure it's set to rain all night, McBride?"

"I don't rightly know, marshal. I'm no expert."

McBride pulls the zipper on the rain jacket, all the way up to his throat.

"I grew up in Beaumont. East Texas. Only been out here six years."

"Thought you all was local boys?"

"No, sir." He huddles his shoulders for warmth. "You know, you're the second person to ask me. About the weather."

"How's that, son?"

"The guy did it. Gilman James."

The marshal stands in the headlight beam of the Silverado. Glancing up the hood, the windshield cracked and crazed .

"Yes, sir," says McBride. "He asked me what I thought. Of conditions, such like. Right after he handcuffed me to that tree."

The door on the truck is shot up pretty bad. Still drives good, has to give it that. In his mind, Whicher sees the figure kneeling on the road, by the yellow E-series. Deliberately drawing a line. A little high. A warning. Pulling the trigger.

"How'd he seem?"

McBride shrugs. "I don't know. On it, I guess."

"You didn't think he was going to snap? Shoot your ass?" Whicher looks at him, shivering in the wet night air. Thin hair plastered to his face.

"He seemed—pretty calm," says McBride.

Whicher nods.

"I was more afraid of her, tell the truth."

Above the hiss of rain, there's the sound of vehicles approaching. Tires slashing standing water on the dark highway.

"You made it out in one piece," says Whicher, "even if it took a while. There's a lot of country to cover."

"Do you think we'll find them, marshal?"

"Tonight?"

Three cars roll around a bend on the two-lane. They disappear into the black.

There's a beep on the radio, light flashing in the truck, another call.

Whicher steps out of the headlight beam. Climbs up in the cab.

"Whicher, go ahead."

"Marshal, this is Special Agent Cornell. Drew Cornell.

ATF out of Houston. We met Tuesday—down in Alpine."

Whicher pulls the door shut. Cranks the heat a notch. "You're working late."

"I was going to leave a message for you. I heard you nearly walked in on a hot one. That bunch of jar-heads you've been chasing? Out at San Angelo?"

"Yeah. Word gets around."

"You any closer to figuring out what's going on?"

Whicher stares at the rain running down the windshield.

"You have something for me, special agent?"

"Maybe I do."

The marshal rubs a hand across the stubble at his jaw. "Lay it on me."

"ATF are still dealing with that airport robbery. In Lafayette? Their first play…"

"Right."

"I called Lieutenant Rodgers earlier—he told me about a suspect truck registered to a Michael Tyler…"

"We know a little about him."

"Did you know he worked at that airport, part-time. Two years back."

"Okay. He's in."

"That's not why I'm calling. You remember me telling you about a suicide?"

"Yeah, Nathaniel Childress."

"I got a buddy in the division, following up the suicide, for the inquest. I saw him at the office tonight."

"Okay."

"I told him you nearly got aced trying to bust a heist out at some place called Jackson Fork. That right?"

"You heard right."

"He told me Childress was living out there. On a farm."

"Y'all sure on that?"

"It's in the inquest statements."

Whicher twists his mouth. Locks his arm out on the steering wheel. *A farm.*

"According to what I've seen, they got into problems, ended up losing the place. Some of the depositions point to loss of the farm being a contributing factor."

"In the suicide?"

"The farm was in the wife's family. A long time. Childress only took it on after they discharged him injured from the Corps."

"I know about the discharge…."

"Business was terrible, they hit a two-year drought. The short version is the loans they had got called in. They lost the place."

Whicher thinks of the fields at Jackson Fork. Dust dry soil. Steel booms above the dirty white cotton.

"The farm was swallowed up by some corporate agri-business head-quartered in Dallas. Guess what happened to the stock. The cattle from the farm?"

"How the hell should I know?"

"Sold off in lieu of debt. At Jackson Fork."

Whicher stares at the crack in his windshield.

A group of cars and trucks roll in across the hard ground. He recognizes the metallic gold and black livery on two of the vehicles; Tom Green County.

The lead car's unmarked. A black sedan. It signals, stops.

The rest of them pull out again, rolling on—in a spray of rain.

"Cornell?" says Whicher. "Can I call you back?"

"I won't be going anywhere."

From out of the sedan, the local chief of police gets out. Tall guy—six four. He steps across the wet ground. Plastic rain-cover on his wide brimmed hat.

He puts his gaunt face close to Whicher's window. "That's it," he says, "we're going to wrap."

"Don't want to lose 'em."

"It's set to worsen. We're not getting anywhere." The chief looks up into the night sky, rain glistening on his black and gray mustache. "We get flash floods, all kinds of kinks, it gets like this. Can't see. Can't move. There's not a whole lot we can do about it."

"Your call…"

"There's hundreds of square miles out there. They could be anywhere. But they can't stay out, not forever."

"Maybe these can."

"Come on down to town with us. They could already be gone. We'll get something to eat, keep a few on the road in case they show."

"You're sure?"

"We've got a few still up on the hill. I'm putting a

bunch of uniforms out to check overnight businesses—motels, garages, drug stores. They show up any place…"

"Alright, chief."

He jerks a thumb over his shoulder. "I'll take that little streak of a trooper…"

"McBride."

The chief nods. "You want to follow us down?"

"Is it far to run?"

"Eight miles."

"Only this damn windshield's starting to leak on me. Where you say we're headed?"

"Down into Kerrville."

South of I-10, Kerrville.

I got both hands on the pistol, I'm standing hidden from the glare of light on the lot.

A highway patrolman's talking with the clerk outside the motel office. They're looking to the far end of the row, towards the room. The desk clerk standing smoking. Rubbing at a tattooed forearm. The patrolman with a notebook open, looking at his watch.

I could just hear.

"I know it all ain't nothin'," the clerk talking.

"It's alright, sir. You did the right thing."

"Males under age forty. That's what we were told—any late arrival." The clerk takes another drag on the cigarette. "Anyhow, can't be them—the two you're after finding."

"Why's that, sir?"

"Well. It's a bunch of fellers, right? Two of 'em. Out there on the hill."

"Matter of fact, no. It's not. It's a man and a woman, sir. What car they all arrive in?"

"I don't know. It was raining so damn hard, I wasn't about to go stand in it. I didn't look."

"Well, I can't see the vehicle. I'm sure there's nothing to worry about."

The patrolman reaches on his belt. Pulls out a flashlight.

"I'll take a look around, all the same. Then I'd like to check those details."

The clerk flicks the cigarette butt in a puddle. He pulls up his bagged out jogging pants. "I'll get that registration card."

The patrolman starts walking under the steel balcony.

I moved from the shadows, gun arm hanging down beside me.

Outside the room, the patrolman paused. Flashlight beam on the door number.

I raised the SIG. Mouth dry. Looked down the sights.

The flashlight beam snapped off. He stepped back.

He turned from the door, started walking for the far-end of the building. He turned the corner. He was going around in back.

I ran, reached the room. Burst through the door.

Tennille's counting piles of cash. She looks up—at the gun.

"Move. Get the money."

She hesitates a split second. Then throws all the money in the flight cases—snapping them shut.

We ran outside, ran to the end of the row.

I stopped her. Told her; "Wait there."

I edged past the end of the building, down the ramp.

The patrolman's got his back to me. He's bent in over the Dakota, trying to peer in the window, gun out, resting on his hip. He's distracted; hand shielding the window glass from the motel lights. Rain coming harder, drowning out the sound.

I raced to him.

Feet away, he heard me.

He spun around, raised the pistol, fired a shot.

I smashed the butt of the SIG against his neck.

He dropped to the ground.

I stared down at myself; at my body, at my legs and arms. I wasn't hit.

Tennille was running out from the corner.

I grabbed the patrolman, dragged him away from the Dakota. Ripping the keys from my pocket. "*Get in…*"

She threw in both the flight cases. Snatched her shotgun out of the footwell.

"What'rc you doing?"

"*You drive.*" She ran to the passenger side. "You told me *speed…*"

A pistol shot cracked out from the motel office, a back door. The desk clerk, firing a revolver.

He fired a second shot, a third—the gun flying up with the muzzle-climb.

Tennille raised the 870. She fired it—lighting up the lot.

The clerk disappeared inside the office.

Both of us got into the Dakota, I jammed the keys in the ignition. I fired it up. Tore out of the rear lot. Flooring it out, up the concrete ramp.

The clerk runs out of the office front. He fires the revolver. A round strikes metal.

Tennille drops the window. She levels the shotgun.

I veered left.

She pulled the trigger.

Noise like a bomb exploding—inside the cab. My heart racing, sound ringing in my ears. "*Are you crazy?*"

I swung out on the highway, back down, back towards the town.

"Where the hell are you going?"

"We got to cross the bridge."

"Just go any way…"

"We got to get across…"

Coming up the road is a squad car, lights blazing, siren screaming. A black and white squad car, headed straight for us.

It closed us down. Snapped a right—trying to block the road.

I wrenched the wheel left, tires slipping, spinning on the wet road, the wheel light, turning into the skid.

The back of the Dakota smacked the side of the black and white.

We're out past it, trying to straighten up, hard on the gas.

A second police car's coming toward us. Metallic gold.

I hit the brakes, the truck locking up.

Tennille was pushing shotgun shells into the Remington.

Behind us, the black and white squad car's reversing—looking to block us in, get us pincered. I shifted into reverse. Yelled out; "*Hold on…*"

Tennille let go the shotgun, she grabbed the roof.

I backed the truck full-out—edge of the tailgate in line with the wheel of the black and white.

The truck piles into the car. It jumps on its axles; sick crack of metal on metal.

She shouts; "Am *I* crazy?"

I shifted gear, lurched forward.

The wheel was hanging off the black and white, its front tire burst.

Up ahead, the gold cruiser was almost on us. Fifty yards up, turning profile—readying to shoot.

I steered the truck onto the sidewalk, grabbed the SIG off the seat.

The driver ducks down below the line of the dash.

I fired on his windshield. Steered off the sidewalk—back onto the highway.

Behind us, the white cruiser's tearing out of the motel parking lot—the highway patrolman. Down the sidewalk, the desk clerk's running, revolver out in front of him, like a kid's toy.

I braked the Dakota to a dead stop. Raised the SIG, looked down its sights. And opened up—shooting, zoning, suppressing fire—till the whole magazine's emptied. Spent shells pinging off the road.

Tennille pinned me against the seat with the flat of the 870 barrel. "Sit back…"

She fired. The front light of the white cruiser exploding glass.

She pumped, fired, pumped, and fired again.

Till my head's reeling. And I'm halfway deaf. "*God damn*, Tennille."

She shouts, "*Get us out of here.*"

The white cruiser's in the middle of the highway—the cop in the gold car out of his vehicle, running behind the hood. All cars stationary. Light-bars flashing. Sirens wailing.

I floored the throttle, snapped the steering right, down a side road, unlit.

We barreled fifty yards, I snapped a left. Up a single lane, sparse trees lining the climb of a hill.

Windows down, the sound of sirens through the wet air.

We had to break visual. We passed a wrecker's yard. I made a right. "We got to bail. Ditch this."

"Then what?"

We're climbing still. The lane getting smaller, tighter. No telling where it goes. Past mail boxes to trailers on parcels of land, among the dripping trees. Topping out, passing down the other side of the hill. Coming to a bend in the lane—a logging road, headed left. Into dark woods.

I steered the Dakota up it, off the lane. Switched out the lights.

We're bumping up a track, already it's starting to give out—only two hundred yards and it stops.

There's a gate. Tube steel and wire. A padlock on it.

I revved the Dakota, headed straight at it. The fender hit the gate at full bore.

We smashed the lock, burst through.

Trees everywhere—no way forward. A voice. A man's voice shouting.

I wrenched the Dakota right, up an earth bank, along a ridge of dirt. Sirens, not far off.

"Get the money, we're getting out."

"How's that going to work?"

"We stay with this, we're screwed…"

The Dakota bottomed-out on the ridge, tires losing drive in the mud.

I braked. Killed the engine. "Let me get reloaded." I pulled a handful of bullets from my jacket. Dumped the magazine on the SIG. Filled it, ran a finger down. "Where's the shotgun slugs?"

Tennille pulls a ripped cardboard box of 12-gauge shells from under the seat.

I filled the tube of the Moss. She put the 870 across her lap.

We sat in the dark cab, fumbling ammo, like sitting in a scrape—with sweaty magazines, a combat helmet full of rounds. Loading everything max-out. Filling our pockets.

I pushed open the truck door. Took both the shotguns. "You take the money."

We ran from the truck, crashing through the undergrowth, into the trees. Tennille close behind me, deeper into pine woods.

In the sky above the trees an orange tinge showed.

"Is it clearing?"

"I don't know."

We were coming over some kind of high ridge, a line of rock, the trees thinning, then cut to stumps. A construction site overlooking the main part of town. Orange light. Bulldozers, stacks of block and lumber.

We crossed the edge of the site. Wet mud underfoot. To a new-built road, unfinished houses, the road curving; descending a long slope into town.

We ran down, into back streets, scarcely lit. Unsold plots between the few small houses.

A police truck rolls around the corner.

It's a Ford Ranger. County sheriff's truck. Painted gold, like the cruiser on the highway. Letters on the bodywork; *Tom Green County.*

I'm holding a shotgun in each hand. Tennille's got two flight cases. It takes a split second for him to make us.

I dropped the 870, raised the Moss.

He braked. Snatched up his radio.

"*Over here.*" Tennille shouts.

I grabbed up the 870, ran behind her, to another, smaller road.

There's a park, a baseball field. We ran across the soaking grass.

More sirens. Engines, howling, gunning down the tight lanes.

Across the baseball field we ran out onto another dark street.

A crossroad. A church.

Up ahead, another black and white squad car's tearing from a side road. It stops, skidding—two cops jump out, racing behind their open doors.

They open up, firing.

I rolled on the ground. Lined up the near-door with the 870—Tennille running in behind a tree.

I squeezed the trigger, elbow kicking off the wet road.

They fired back, rounds smacking out in the air, like firecrackers.

I raised the barrel for the range—fired again on the first door, then twice on the second—squinting at the mess of glass and scoured metal.

Tennille jumped a low fence. She disappeared into the back yard of a house.

I dumped the empty 870, ran after her.

We're crashing through a back yard, knocking down garbage cans, dodging laundry. Tennille pushed through a hedge. I followed her out onto an unlit street.

The gold Ford Ranger's blocking one end of it.

Coming up the other end—a Chevy Silverado.

"Gil…"

It's coming straight up the road.

The marshal.

There's a storm drain, a concrete-lined ditch we can get in. But they're too close. We'll be surrounded.

Across the street is a church. A cinder block wall around it—five feet high.

"Last stand," I says. "Take the shotgun…"

Chapter 27

We ran. Crossed the street. Got in behind the church yard wall. I pulled the SIG from my jacket—Tennille put the stock of the Moss to her shoulder.

"We've got to peel…"

"What?"

"Field maneuver. You got nine in the shotgun, I got fourteen in this."

I sneaked a look above the wall, the Ford Ranger still blocking an end—the Silverado pulled up somewhere—no seeing it for trees and houses on the dark lane.

Cops are shouting above the rain—close, not more than twenty or thirty yards.

"I'll take the money, make a run. If they spot me, they'll open up…"

"Then what?"

"Fire back. I find a position. You fall back, I cover."

"That's going to get us out of this?"

I picked a spot behind to run to. "You better hope."

There was a church bus parked in the yard at the back.

"Don't fire more than twice."

"Why not?"

"We need multiple overwatches."

I grabbed a flight case in my free hand, jammed the second case under my arm. I ran low, got behind a corner of the bus.

Nobody fired.

They hadn't seen. The marshal must be holding short; playing safe.

Tennille looked back, I signaled to run. She broke cover, cutting the line of sight.

She scrambled down by me at the bus.

"Move sideways—I can't fire if you're in the way…"

"So tell me."

Behind us there's a street running parallel—a bunch of agarito growing along a ditch, maybe linking up with the storm drain.

"Down there," I told her. "You go, I'll cover."

She ran, but too high, she had too much showing.

The Silverado rolled in line with the church wall. It braked to a stop.

I raised the SIG, staring at the shot-up door of the truck.

The marshal hit reverse, he pulled back.

I checked behind—Tennille was in the ditch.

I ran, I could hear shouting, now. I threw myself down beside her.

Behind us there's a restaurant lot, a few parked vehicles; the only cover left.

Other side of the cinder block wall around the church,

two uniform cops are taking position.

"See those cars? We got to use 'em. Get behind one."

She springs out of the ditch.

They open fire from behind the wall.

I put two bursts of three in—they ducked back.

I ran.

Tennille was in the restaurant lot, there's a guy; a black guy in a fishing hat—standing by a car, its door open.

I held the SIG outstretched; "*Hey, you.*"

"Don't shoot."

"Get in. Get in the car…"

Tennille ducked behind the hood of a panel van. She raised the shotgun.

I kept my pistol on the guy in the hat. "*Start it up…*"

He bent in to the driver's seat—started the motor.

I snatched open the rear door, threw the flight cases in back. Then jumped in the front passenger seat.

Tennille fired the Moss—twice, three times, back towards the church yard.

I shouted out, "*Get over here.*"

She ran, threw herself in back.

"*Go. Go.*"

"*Where, man?*"

"*Get us over the bridge.*"

He stuck it in drive, pulled out, swerving into the street.

We hit the junction with Main, he makes a left, east.

He's maybe forty years old. In a sweat top and fishing hat. Muscle working in the side of his face.

"Get us over the river," I says, "we'll let you go."

He stared straight ahead.

We passed two blocks—we could see the big hospital, by the bridge we came in on. Shut off; police cars line abreast.

"Shit, Gil…"

"There better be another way out of here."

The guy grips the steering wheel. "There's another bridge, downstream."

"How far?"

"About a mile."

"Go. *Get moving…*"

We drove straight across the main intersection.

"That *marshal?*" says Tennille.

"I know…"

"Where'd he come from?"

I rolled the window.

"Why didn't you shoot him?"

"Why didn't *you?*" I could hear sirens, but other cars were moving, other traffic not just us.

We crossed another block, another intersection. Then the road forked—we kicked a right.

"The river this way?"

"Yeah."

"Don't fuck with us."

"No, man."

We're driving down a wide boulevard. The car a ten-year-old Toyota, a Camry—nothing that was going to stick out.

I turned around in my seat, trying to get a look out the back. "You think anybody's following?"

"Let me look," says Tennille, "you make sure we don't get lost."

"You don't plan on getting us lost, right?"

The guy shakes his head. "I just want to go home. That's all, man."

"What's your name?"

"Darrel."

"You local?"

"No."

"Live here?"

"Kind of."

"What's 'kind of'?"

"I'm on a program."

"What?"

"VA program. Six months I been at the treatment center."

"There's a Veteran's Center out here?"

"They got me a job. That restaurant back there. Cleaning up."

"There's a bunch of cars behind us, Gil. I don't know what they are."

"You see lights. Police lights?"

"I don't know."

"Keep looking."

The guy turned towards me a fraction. "I guess they might've blocked this other bridge—but there's another way over. A ford. Across the river. Summertime, you can use it."

"How do *you* know?"

"Like to fish there."

He pointed to a turn, off the main road. A black lane, lined with trees.

"Down there?"

"It's along the river…"

"Do it," I says, "take it." Then, to Tennille, "Watch for anybody coming off when we make the turn."

He signaled. Steered into the smaller road.

"What service?" I says.

"Marine Corps."

"Semper Fi."

He throws a quick look. "You?"

"Somebody just turned off," Tennille says, "right behind us."

"How many?"

"One."

"You see what it is?"

"I can't tell."

"Keep looking."

We're running along the backs of houses, a single lane road, trees lining the edge of the river. The car wipers beating on the windshield, rain slamming in on gusts of wind.

"That's the parkway," the guy says, "up ahead."

I could see the river, now, through the trees. A main road bridge. Halfway over, a bunch of parked cars—red and blue light-bars showing through the tree line.

"Stop the car." I turned to Tennille; "Get the shotgun ready."

We pulled to the side of the lane, beneath the trees.

I popped the passenger door, hands wrapped around the SIG.

The headlights behind us drew level.

Then went by.

A Nissan sedan.

"Darrel?" I says. "I need you to get out, now."

I watched the Nissan as it rolled on, disappearing along the lane.

I reached back, took a flight case from the seat. Opened it. The cash inside bound in neat bunches.

"You count these?"

Tennille leans forward. "Each one's a thousand…"

I counted out a stack till I had a pile of thirty on my lap. "We need the car."

The guy just looked at me. I handed him the stack of money.

Tennille says, "What the hell are you doing?"

He held the money out in front of him, in front of his face.

I says, "Where's this ford?"

"Across the parkway. You go across, head down the other side. There's a track. Takes you right to the river. All you got to do."

"Alright. I need you to step out, now."

He opened the driver door, eased himself out.

I got out, walked around the hood.

He stood in the rain folding money. Folding it in the pockets of his pants.

"This hospital? It far?"

"No, man. A mile or so."

"Take your time."

He stood looking at me, rain dripping from his hat. "I'll have to report it…"

"Tell 'em we were headed north."

Tennille got out of the car—she jumped in the front.

I got behind the wheel.

She says, "Are we moving, now?"

I pulled out back into the lane.

Through the trees, we could see the parkway. I turned the headlights out, edged the car to the junction with the main road.

Two police cars were parked up on the bridge, three hundred yards out.

I drove across the parkway—back down the other side, towards the river, where the lane ran on.

I saw the track, straight off. Turned down it, towards the river bank.

Fifty yards and we were at its edge. Out in the river, a concrete strip ran off toward the far bank. The ford was just a few feet wide, the water rising in the rain; lapping up to it. Already over, in places.

"Gil?" she says. "You really think. Is this going to work?"

There was no way to see all the way to the far side.

The water was fast, the current strong.

The car lights were out; rain heavy against the windshield. I turned the Toyota out from the tree line.

Edged out—onto the disappearing strip.

Black water welled at both sides. But we were in it.

No turning back.

CHAPTER 28

The alarm clock sounds on a cell phone. An asphalt lot, off of Sam Houston Parkway.

Whicher opens his eyes to the upholstered ceiling of his Silverado. Outside, on the beltway north of the city of Houston, cars fly along a steel and concrete ramp beyond the window of his truck.

Eight-thirty a.m. His arms are numb. He lifts a big hand to his face, rubs his eyes, grabs the cell. And turns off the alarm.

A four-hour ride through the night from Kerrville. James and Labrea long gone.

Some guy staying at a veteran's hostel reports getting jumped in a restaurant lot, his car getting stolen. Whicher saw it happen—somehow it took the guy half the night to report anything. They'd knocked him down, he was confused; he'd had to walk back to his hostel. Police checked the last known location, it was down near a ford on the river—nobody covering. Writing on the wall.

Whicher'd driven to Houston. Then caught a fitful half-sleep in the truck. Seat cranked, like a bum.

In front of the truck is a five-story office building. Cream stone, smoke-effect glass. Two hundred thousand square feet of modern office block. Landscaped ground. Lake and fountain out front.

Whicher elbows the door of the truck open. Reaches for his tan Resistol hat.

The parking lot's already starting to fill up as he grabs the jacket of his suit and slips it on.

He clips across the asphalt, boots heavy on his feet.

He enters the building, reaches reception and pulls out his badge. More creases in his suit pants than there ought to be. The frosty looking sixty-year-old in a button-down and sweater looks him over.

"John Whicher. US Deputy Marshal. I have an appointment. Special Agent Cornell."

The reception clerk takes his badge. Checks it over. "ATF Field Division is on the third floor, Marshal."

"Cornell here?"

"He arrived at eight o clock sharp, sir. You'll find the elevator at the end of the lobby."

Whicher tips a finger to his hat. He crosses the polished, tiled floor.

The elevator's open. He marches in, hits three, leans back as the doors close. He thinks of Gilman James in the dead-air space. Of looking at him, not once, but twice down the barrel of his Ruger. He listens to the whine of gears in the elevator shaft.

Third floor, the doors slide open. Into a lobby, lit with floor-to-ceiling windows.

Standing in the doorway of an office is Cornell. Freshly shaved. Sunglasses in the pocket of a leisure shirt. "Marshal. You look like shit."

Whicher gives him a mean-eyed stare.

"Seriously." Cornell steps aside, into the room.

Whicher follows the ATF agent into a bright office, a view of the beltway, and the brand new sub-division, beyond.

"Take a seat, marshal. Watch your spurs on the wall outlets."

"Hey, Cornell?"

The ATF agent looks at him.

"Too early for that."

Cornell sits on the side of a wood-veneered desk. He clicks open a file on his computer monitor. "So, I got your message on my phone last night."

Whicher pulls out a chrome and black office chair.

"You had 'em in Kerrville and you let 'em get away."

Cornell watches the marshal staring blank out of the window. Big frame awkward in the office chair.

"We both work for the DOJ."

"So?" says Cornell.

"There's no conflict sharing evidence…"

"What do you want?"

"The suicide. Nathaniel Childress. Everything ATF have on it."

"I could have sent you the file."

"Tell me something? This business at Jackson Fork…"

"I looked it up," says Cornell. "That auction site—the bank that foreclosed the Childress farm own half—the Dallas agri-business that swallowed 'em up own the other."

Whicher shakes his head. He leans forward, propped on his elbows. "They robbed Jackson Fork in revenge…"

"Well put it another way," Cornell looks at him, "does it sound like a coincidence?"

He lets a moment pass, rolls a shoulder.

"Something bothering you, marshal?"

"Yeah. If you want to know. Yesterday, after that damn robbery, a local news crew showed up."

"So what?"

"I want this wrapped. Before they turn it into a story."

Whicher stands. Walks to the window, stares down at the traffic on the freeway. Beyond it, mile after mile of new-built houses, the kind of place, the kind of residential area a man might lose his soul. And call it a blessing.

He lets out a long breath. "Childress shot himself with his own military side-arm."

"Correct."

"How come his kid brother ends up with it?"

Cornell doesn't answer.

"This suicide inquest still ongoing? State's evidence, ain't it? How's his kid brother get a hold of it?"

Cornell picks up a pen from the desk. "I spoke to that friend of mine. At division. Covering the suicide. The family put in a request to have it. The investigating officer agreed."

"Alright," Whicher says.

"It was on compassionate grounds, the guy being a Vet, and a Purple Heart."

Whicher nods.

"The Childress family had moved, by the time of the suicide. They'd already lost the farm, they'd moved south to Rocksprings. It's out in Edwards County, some one-horse place."

"Then why go back to the farm at Jackson Fork?"

Cornell spreads his hands. "For some reason he got in his truck, drove a hundred miles to the farm. And blew his brains out. You tell me."

Whicher pulls at the collar of his shirt. "Damn television stick their nose in, before you know, they spin it into something every network across the country can run."

"Like what?"

"Like; how come they're doing what they're doing?"

The marshal watches the line of cars crawling off the freeway ramps.

"None of them had any previous criminal history. Gilman James was nominated for the Navy Cross."

"Muddy the story," says Cornell. "If it comes to it. What about the girl?"

"She's got a violent-ex. She's trying to protect her daughter. She's from a community that sees itself as ignored and discriminated against..." Whicher looks at Cornell. "What?"

"You put it like that..."

The marshal blows the air from his cheeks.

Outside, white clouds sail across the sweep of hard, flat land. Every soldier didn't claim an excuse. Every girl that married a bastard like Leon Varela. Third Armored Cavalry reunion nights it wasn't all stories of who made the latest trip to Huntsville. And Beaumont. And being owed.

"Twice, I had 'em. Looking down a gun barrel."

"Why didn't you shoot?"

"There were civilians…"

"Yeah," says Cornell, studying him. "But that's not it."

"I want to know what's going to happen next."

"Maybe there won't be any next. What did you really want from me, marshal?"

Whicher stands with his shoulder to the window. He taps a finger on the cool glass. "I'm looking to keep the lid on tight. No press. No feeds."

"I'm not getting on the wrong side of those people. Any chance they get to beat up on the Bureau…"

"I'm not asking you to lie."

"Look," says Cornell. "Don't get hung up on this. Who knows why he shot himself? Or why he shot himself on a farm?"

Whicher smooths the nap on the Resistol. He pushes it back on his head, settling it into place.

"This afternoon I have to be back up there. Jackson Fork. To meet with the sheriff of Tom Green County."

"You came all this way just to get me to keep my mouth shut?"

Whicher looks at Cornell. "Before I head up there, I have to go in to Brooke AMC, in San Antonio."

"Brooke? What for?"

"Unit CO wants to see me."

Cornell looks doubtful. "Their unit CO?"

"I talked to him already. Thursday. He wants to see me again. Left a message."

Cornell gathers together the papers on his desk. He turns to his office printer; "Let me run off a couple things before you go."

Whicher crosses his arms. He studies the bare walls; Cornell's work space detached, depersonalized—floating glass and concrete, a sixty mile view to the horizon. Nothing in it worth seeing, nothing outside, nothing within. He studies its numb anonymity. His own reluctance to leave it.

⚓

Graveyard Mountain, Rocksprings.

I lay on the caliche watching the sun inch across the hill to the east. Thinking on the fire. Fire that rolled down the hood of Michael's Humvee—blood orange; like the sun at the mountain. I never would've made it. Neither Nate nor me. If not for Michael.

A split second. All it took was a split second. An RPG hit him, leading the column down that Fallujah street.

When the smoke cleared, the turret was gone. Weld mounts sticking from the roof, the gunner vanished as if he never existed.

Fire. Rolling over that hood. A ball of flame turning against the windshield.

Five up-armored Humvees. A column. M2 machine guns, tearing up the left and right of the street. Michael leading. Fast, hard.

Nate would've died there. He never would've made it back to Orla. None of us would've lived.

I lay in the early light, heart quickening. Remembering the panic; heaving at the door of Michael's Humvee. Six hundred pounds weight, trying to get it open.

I blinked my eyes shut. Opened them. Sat and leaned against the wing of the stolen Camry.

Tennille was laying by the rear wheel, arms wrapped around her body, hunter's jacket pulled tight. The sun streaked along the seam of her jeans, knees drawn up. In the fall of her neck, her beating pulse.

Black smoke.

I could still remember the smell of it, the fear. Front end roiling. Michael, still alive, my gloves burning, smoke breaking in through the chassis.

He was breathing it, burning up his lungs.

I got the door of the Humvee open, pulled him out, dragged him on my knees. Down the rubble filled street. Four M2 heavy machine guns trying to cover us. A rifleman running out.

The first round hit my kevlar vest, right rib. The sweat turned to ice. I dragged Michael. With every ounce left.

If I closed my eyes, I could still see the blood on his vest, soaking the coyote brown.

A second round hit the center of my back, it knocked me forward, face down in the dirt, winded. Mind racing. Waiting for the whip of pain.

Nothing. Only moments stay clear in my mind.

Humvees backing up toward us. Three Marines, grabbing at Michael, at me. Things that must've happened are wiped away. I remember cover, the walled garden of a derelict house, everybody running in.

Minutes later; it must have been—I was throwing things out of the Humvees; med bags, ammo, a fire extinguisher—desperate to clear more space. Fifteen casualties. Seven of them dead. Michael beside the body of Nate's lead scout—shot in the face. The blood in Nate's ears already dried to black.

I put Nate and Michael in last. They'd be first out.

We took ammo, as much as we could carry. I ordered the Humvees out. They'd be trapped in the narrow streets, picked off with RPGs, like Michael. We'd get out on foot, we couldn't all fit.

I organized the remains of both squads. It was house to house, building by building on raw exhaustion, after that. A frenzy. Sick and sweet. Trying to keep ourselves alive.

The sun edged up another inch.

Across the ground, Tennille lay sleeping. Was Orla sleeping, like her?

Or thinking. On two kids to feed. Was she lying awake?

How many mornings would come in—sleepless, hollowed out. Jesse must've felt it, the same. What had changed, in a hundred years? Bare mountain, a sun with no warmth, an endless ride, no peace inside.

I watched Tennille sleeping. Soon she would be awake.

Everything she'd dragged from yesterday, and all the days in her life, a thousand moments of broken up fragments would fill her mind in a rush of memory. Tide of weight.

If only we could stand, and not be carried by it.

Soon we would both be gone.

⅄

We left the car half a mile outside the town of Rocksprings. West central Texas. Flat savanna, under a July sun.

We walked together, both of us carrying a flight case. Michael's 250 SIG in my jacket.

Rocksprings; maybe a thousand strong. The town stretched out ahead among thin oak and mesquite. Sparse housing on bone hard plots.

Inside the flight cases, the money was divided between us in equal halves. We'd counted it in the headlights of the Camry, eighty miles east of Kerrville, river water dripping from the engine bay.

Four hundred thousand. Money destined for a nameless account. Faceless owners of a dead man's farm. No more.

Tennille had called Connie.

Close on two in the morning she'd gotten hold of her.

She told her she'd pay her ten thousand dollars to find Joe, put him in her Chevy Tahoe, get Michael with him— and have the pair of them drive up to Rocksprings.

Connie told her no; the pair of 'em might be stopped.

Tennille said she could tell the cops they stole the car. It wouldn't happen; Joe knew the back routes, if any one could drive up, and not be seen, it was him.

I doubted Michael was strong enough to make it; two days sacked out on a drip.

Connie decided she wanted in after all—ten grand for letting Joe have her car keys; looking the other way. Joe'd drive up, take Tennille back down with him. She'd get Maria, cross the border with her, find her father in Mexico.

We walked along the highway into town, me and Tennille. Some twist of feeling between us, neither one speaking, just walking in the morning sun.

Two hundred thousand each. Half the money from Jackson Fork. A stolen Toyota, a twelve gauge Moss, a pistol.

Hunger; pulling deep in my stomach.

We passed a ranch front, grain silos at the side of the road. From behind a mesh of wire, a stick-ribbed dog followed us along the line of an old fence.

Tennille stared ahead. Past tin clad warehouses, a yard stacked with wheel hubs.

"How come you didn't leave before?"

She didn't answer.

"Maybe it would've been easier…"

"You can believe that," she said. "If you want."

The dog reached the end of the run of fence and turned away. To stare wall-eyed at an empty horse box.

"My father built that house," she says. "Him and Joe."

We kept on.

Small town Texas, waking up, Saturday. The temperature pushing ninety under the trees.

Past empty farm trailers, a scrap yard, an old school bus up on blocks.

"What did he do?" I asked her.

"Leon?"

I nodded.

"The truck business. Freight. Into Mexico and back."

"Doesn't sound so bad."

"He started taking risks. Carrying people. To make a little extra money."

I looked at her.

"He was hooked in long before I kicked him out of my life."

"How come he wants…"

She glanced at me. "For the disrespect."

I thought of the burn at the back of the house. The shotgun, never far from her reach. He couldn't come right out—but an accident, a fire, a break-in gone wrong.

"He can't have me," she says, "nobody will."

Underneath the power lines a dirt track stretched out off the highway, trailer homes under the Texas live oak, wash lines strung between the branches.

We passed a lean-to propped on rusting oil barrels.

"What about Joe?"

"Joe looks out for me."

Joe Tree. And his Marlin rifle. Living alone, the middle of no-place; the borderland, among those hills.

Wanting nothing. Asking nothing.

Talking with the dead.

✦

We found the main square. Sat on a bench seat, under shade trees. The grass burned brown in front of a two-story building, old stone—the County Courthouse.

Around the square was every business of any small town in the west. An auto shop, realtor, a grocery mart. A bank.

We sat on the bench and waited. Tennille smoking, under the trees.

"Tell me about Michael," she says.

I felt her gaze on the side of my face.

She blew out a long stream of smoke. Leaned into the bench, curving with it.

"He never made it. Back."

She watched me for a long minute. Smoking in silence.

"What about you?" she says. "What will you do?"

"Canada. Maybe."

I stared at the white stuccoed bank opposite. Thought of Jesse. Northfield, Minnesota. A disaster. Beginning to end.

Jesse and Frank were the only ones to make it out. They say it was revenge. One last thing that had to be done, the money in the bank Yankee money.

Tennille flicked a hair from her eye. "Is that it? Is that the place?"

Cars and trucks were parked up, angled in at the sides of the road. Townspeople, in ones and twos coming out of a building supply, a dollar discount, a liquor store. All the buildings lining the square must have dated back a hundred years. Frank James could've seen them in his old age, living in Texas. Selling shoes out of Dallas. Not Jesse. He was never going to make it that far.

"Don't," she said.

I didn't answer.

"What do you want, Gil?"

I looked at her, underneath the shade trees, face still, dappled light on her skin.

A rusted pick-up drove through the square, piled high with yellow straw. In its slipstream, a dust of gold. Light as air.

Michael should've never joined. He would've lived free.

Tennille stared down the street, beyond the square, searching for Joe.

"Don't," she said.

I just sat, one hand in my jacket wrapped around the SIG.

"You could walk away. Cross the river."

I didn't look at her.

"You could go south."

CHAPTER 29

Brooke AMC, San Antonio.

At the picture window in the neuro-care center, Captain Black stares at his writing in the little square of card.

The folds of a white T-shirt hang loose on him.

Whicher reads the logo; *Dallas Cowboys—America's Team.*

"I don't know if I spelled this right. Condo-lence…" The captain raises his burned face to Whicher. The grafted hairline stark in the window's light.

"It's fine."

"Yesterday I called Battalion. After what you told me…"

The marshal nods.

"I talked with my replacement. Nolan, his name is."

"All of this stuff. Everything that's been happening," Whicher says, "it's under civilian law. It's not a military matter."

The captain chews at the stump of a nail.

"Nolan told me he'd heard. About what happened to Sergeant Childress…"

"Childress and Tyler were invalided out on account of a patrol," says Whicher. "Whatever happened after that time, it's not your problem."

"They both went before a Medical Evaluation Board."

Whicher turns the Resistol between his hands.

"Tyler had respiratory problems. Burnt lungs. Childress was worse…"

The captain grabs the stick control of his motorized wheelchair.

He crosses the room to a corner worktop. The lone star on his shirt hangs limp.

"James kept up a lot of noise about Tyler. He wasn't getting all the help he should have. According to some…"

"He's on the permanent disability list," Whicher says. "I checked."

"They rejected him from a couple of programs…"

"Why was that?"

"Alcohol abuse."

Three hours on I-10. To listen to the worries of a wounded man. Reliving the past.

"Tell me something?" says Whicher. "Gilman James was nominated for the Navy Cross."

The captain's eyes dart in his mask-like face.

"The nomination was for actions on that patrol?"

"A full report was made. Nobody of equal rank was present…"

"But the men on the patrol—they wanted it?"

The captain takes the card he's written. He places it on the worktop, searching among the papers and pens. "Nolan told me the Childress family lost their house…"

Whicher nods. "The farm. Out at Jackson Fork. I know, sir. "

"No."

Whicher looks at him.

"Nolan said it was a house. A house they were living in. After that. After the farm."

"You sure on that?"

"Some little place. Out past the hill country, in Edwards County. They bought a house. You know? Some little house. In Rocksprings."

"No, sir. I didn't know."

"They lost it. About a month ago, to the bank."

Whicher stares at him.

"Will you see Mrs. Childress? The widow. Because of all this? I could mail this card to her, but it doesn't seem right…"

The marshal watches the trees, moving in the breeze beyond the window.

"They've got two children," the captain mouths.

A farm.

And then their house.

To a bank.

⋏

Rocksprings.

A Chevy Tahoe pulls in to the main square, same color as Connie's; right age, double-front grille.

Joe Tree's behind the wheel. Michael riding up front, beside him. They pull in at an angle to the road—Joe's mean face staring out of the windshield.

I stood. Swung the metal flight case up.

Joe rolled the window. He grunts at Tennille; "You okay?"

Michael stepped out, right arm in a sling, his leg stiff. Bandaged, it looked like—underneath his jeans.

He was clean-shaven. Faint color back in his face. "What's in the case, man?"

I yanked open the rear door. "Get in the back."

The two of us slid along the bench seat, Tennille climbing up in front.

"Swing around," she says to Joe, "make a right by the garage."

Joe jerked a thumb over his shoulder. "I want them out of here."

We pulled out, made a U-turn, took the first right.

I opened the top of the flight case, for Michael.

He sees the money, gives a low whistle.

I thought of the E-series. Four tires shot-out, pissing coolant.

Joe turns to Tennille. "Why can't we just kick them out here?"

"Take them to their car."

Michael broke off staring at the case. "What car?"

"We stole something."

Joe barked out an ugly laugh.

Tennille looked at him. "Did you make sure," she says,

"since Casa Piedra. Did you make sure you've been seen…"

"All day I spent working at Molly's place. The RV park. Fifty people must've seen me."

"You know we lost the Dakota?"

Joe shrugged.

"You can tell the police we stole it. I'll take care of everything, you know that."

He looks at her. "They found that F150 of his in your barn."

She stares out the window. "I wasn't planning going back."

Michael shifts his weight off his bad arm.

"I woke up Thursday night," he says, "I thought I was having a fuckin' nightmare. I'm crashed on this bed. Some bat-skin nurse smoking boom over me. A drip in my arm, like a horror movie."

"She's a doctor," says Tennille.

We drove out of Rocksprings down the back roads— Michael staring at the low-grown trees; high sun, kids playing in a backyard.

"Hell, it's good to be out," he says.

We were close to the main road south, I remembered. Two weeks, all it was. Driving around in my F150, working it through. Scoping every site, just like the service. Routes in, routes out. Steven still alive, itching to be started, to get to Alpine. He had to show us his bank, the damn bank that let him hang. Just like his brother went hang. How could he help Nate, after that? With no job. Burned up, he was. Ate to the bone.

We came to the junction with the highway. Not far from the stolen Toyota.

"Make a right at the end."

Joe waited for a truck to clear. He hit the gas.

One last thing, that's all there was. Then it would be over.

We reached the edge of town. Trailers, grain silos—half a mile on, the dead-end lane.

"Make a left up there."

Joe swings the big SUV across the highway. Powers the Tahoe up the lane.

The car's still there, beneath a stand of mesquite.

He hits the brakes. We skid to a stop in the loose gravel.

"Alright, get the hell out."

"We're leaving."

I stepped out.

Joe reached inside his jacket. He pulled out the snub-nose .38.

Michael steps out. "Put that thing the fuck away."

Joe held the revolver at me, waist high.

Tennille pushes open her door.

"Hey," Joe says to her. "You want to stay here? With them?"

She was out of the Tahoe, walking fast—to the far side of the lane.

"Gil," she says.

She stopped. Shoved her hands inside the hunter's jacket.

I followed her across the lane.

"It's too late," she said. "I have to get my daughter."

Joe shouted from the Tahoe; "*Get the hell back in here…*"

"Don't go near that bank," she says. "There's a crossing place. A canyon, at the river. Santa Elena, it's called."

I tried to imagine—for a split second, another life.

"Drive south." She stepped a pace closer. "Tonight, I'll be there."

I watched the shadows of the trees. Heat stacked above the hard ground. The border. An unguarded river.

"Then get to Canada," she says. "Or as far as you can. With Michael."

She walked away.

She climbed in the front seat.

I watched as Joe cranked it around, full lock. And floored it down the lane out on the highway.

She was gone.

Highway 41, TX.

Whicher steers his truck in the haze across the baked savanna. Inside an hour he can be there.

He listens to the sound his tires make running over tar strips in the roadway. A blunt rhythm—shudder, like rail cars in the night.

The flat highway stretches out ahead, lined with zinc wire fencing. Split wood posts. Nothing in any direction but bluestem and shrub mesquite. Dotted stands of live oak.

His radio lights up.

He checks the road in front; arrow straight. Lets his speed dip. Picks up the call.

"Did you go?"

"Cornell?"

"Did you go? To Brooke, marshal?"

"I went."

"You see that CO of theirs?"

"It's Rocksprings," says Whicher. "That's where this thing got started out."

"I told you," says Cornell, "Childress had been living there…"

"You didn't tell me he got his house repossessed."

There's a pause on the line. "I was calling with that."

At the side of the highway, twin stone pillars on a ranch flash by. Whicher eases back on the gas.

"Marshal?"

"Yeah."

"The bank that made the loan on their house is in Rocksprings."

"Actually *in* the town?"

"I know," says Cornell. "Maybe they thought they'd cut 'em some slack, going local. It's called Home Valley Bank."

"I'm running through Edwards County; I'm calling in there."

"Yeah, you do that."

Whicher pulls the shirt collar from his neck.

"Considering what happened with Jackson Fork," says Cornell, "you ought to give them fair warning."

"I'm hanging up," says Whicher. "I'm calling the county sheriff…"

Rocksprings.

Along the sidewalk, in the shade of the north facade, a farmer steps from the door of the bank. He tips back his hat, crosses the square, keeps walking past the auto shop, till he's out of sight.

Nobody else is inside.

Ten minutes have passed since the farmer went in, he's the last to enter.

I looked at Michael. "That's it."

We were parked among the cars and trucks in the square, just an ordinary sedan, nothing to look at. Michael behind the wheel. He could drive, just; with his arm in a sling. But nothing more, he couldn't handle a gun.

I slipped the SIG from my jacket, dumped the magazine, ran a finger over the top round.

"Last night," says Michael, "that doctor..."

"Connie?"

"She was drinking Lean." He grinned. Shook his head.

"What the hell's that?"

"Promethazine with Codeine. And Jolly Rancher candy."

"How do you know that shit?"

"Booze shark I know. Out of Houston."

I slapped the box magazine back in the grip. Put the pistol in my lap.

"I must've been pretty bad," he says. He grabbed the wheel, pulled himself upright in his seat. "We really doin' this?"

I nodded.

"Guess we're never going back to Lafayette."

I stared at the stone front of the bank.

"You think she'll even take the money?" he says.

"She'll take it."

"I keep thinking on Steven."

I'd tried to shut that out—what was the use? Steven was dead, in some cold room five days. When I thought of him a lick of anger flared in me. Michael took two bullets on account of him—rushing in a bank, not waiting, screwing up. He couldn't have been less like his brother.

"I'll do it now," I says, "while it's clear."

"Fuck, Gil…"

Michael pressed a hand against his brow.

I put the gun in my jacket, stepped out, crossed Main, no cars, not a living soul.

Tired as I was, run out, I felt Nate's spirit close to me— something like it. I felt him near me, clearer now.

I put a hand on the polished glass door of the bank. Pushed it open.

I knew in my heart what he would've said. From what he did, the life he led. But it was no good. I pushed the door wide. Stepped inside, into the dark interior.

Three staff.

All men in suits, no customers.

One man seated behind a counter—jacket off, white shirt, middle aged. A second guy at the left in a gray suit— older. The youngest of the three to the right. Black hair, gelled back off his face.

I reached in my jacket. Pulled out the gun. "This is a robbery…"

They all stared. Then raised their hands, slowly.

"I got fourteen rounds in this. But let's not do that."

The eldest, in the gray suit, clears his throat.

"We don't have any big cash deposits here, sir."

"You the manager?"

"I am."

"Where's the safe?"

"It's in the back."

"You two are coming with us."

The guy in the white shirt gets to his feet, the young guy with the gelled hair has to think about it.

I flicked the barrel of the SIG at him. "Don't fuckin' blow this."

He stood.

I marched all three of them on the point of the gun, into the back room.

The manager approached a steel door in an interior wall. He worked a code on a keypad.

I turned to the guy in the white shirt. "Get something to put the money in."

He opens up a desk drawer, starts to search through the stationery.

The young guy's starting to look real nervous.

The manager opens up the steel door, picks out a stack of wrapped money. He turns. "Mr Russell?"

The guy in the white shirt steps forward—a bunch of business envelopes in his hand.

"This is everything we're carrying, sir," the manager says. "It's Saturday. We don't carry much over a weekend."

"How much?"

"I believe it would be between twenty-five, to thirty five thousand dollars."

They stuffed the money in the envelopes.

The manager pushed the safe door wide, showing it empty.

I took the three envelopes he held out to me.

There's a noise behind, I span around the young guy's disappearing out the door.

I ran after him, he's already at the street door, grabbing for the handle.

He charges out, tearing into the road.

Across the square, a uniform cop's emerging from the County Courthouse—running between the trees, gun in hand.

From the side of the square, Michael's pulling out in the Toyota.

The cop gets down on one knee.

He shouts something—puts his arms out. Opens up— six shots, wild and fast.

I jumped behind the tailgate of a truck.

The bank clerk drops to the ground—to lay in the middle of the square, hands covering his head.

From the auto shop, a guy in greased-up coveralls runs out with a shotgun. He hoists it to his shoulder. Fires, twice.

Behind the kneeling cop, out the door of the Courthouse, a second officer's running out.

I put a round at the shotgun shooter—one at the kneeling cop.

The second cop's sprinting away left.

Michael's got the car facing up the main street, gunning the engine. "*Get in…*"

The grease monkey trains the barrel and fires—the rear window in the Camry shattering.

Then he turns, and runs back to the garage.

Michael's shouting, "*Get in here…*"

But the second cop's about to run down the side of the square and cut us off.

And a fourth guy's running from a storefront unit—three hundred pounds, a bright red T-shirt, carrying a handgun. He's on the left flank of the square, same flank as the second cop.

The grease monkey's back out from the garage.

The store owner in the T-shirt fires a square-looking semi-auto—a Glock.

Both cops are moving forward, shouting out; "*Drop your weapon. Get on the ground…*"

I fired at the red T-shirt, at the second cop, trying to push them back up the left.

I lunged for the Camry.

Michael hit the gas, tires screaming.

I snatched up the Moss from the back seat. The second cop's running forward, I stuck out the barrel—a warning.

He checked stride.

The guy in the red T-shirt turns to follow the movement of the car—snapping more rounds, loosing a second clip.

I pulled on the trigger of the Moss.

They both hit the ground, searching for cover.

But a sheriff's car is coming down the street from the back of the Courthouse building.

"*Jesus Christ, Gil...*"

"Get us out of the square."

Michael mashes the pedal—shots are spitting from all points.

The sheriff's car rams down the left of the square as we pass the end of the block.

And a green pick-up appears out of nowhere—from the next street back.

We T-bone the rear end of the pick-up, it spins, the driver flings open his door.

He jumps out, rolls on the ground.

The Camry's wrecked, front end buckled.

We're both dazed; winded. Michael scrambling out.

I grabbed the money, the flight case, the envelopes from the bank.

Michael shouting at me, "*Get in the truck…*"

He jumps behind the wheel of the pick-up, its engine still running. We're ten yards past the square, seconds left to get out.

The sheriff's car flashes out from the end of the square.

I fired on the engine block and the wheels.

I steadied myself at the pick-up side. Threw in the flight case, the cash-filled envelopes—and pulled myself up into the truck bed.

The grease monkey steps around the corner.

I hammered on the side, "*Go, go, go…*"

He aims his shotgun—fires.

He pumps another slug, fires again, pulling on the trigger, till he's out.

Michael floors it.

We're burning down Main, the west edge of town—the square receding faster and faster.

All the buildings in our wake, a red barn, a cattle yard.

We're clear.

"*Where Gil?*" Michael shouting, above the wind.

"*West,*" I shouted, heart racing. "*Any back road you can find…*" My own voice strange in my ears.

Chapter 30

Rocksprings.

The central hall of the County Courthouse is filled with people. There's Edwards County sheriff's men, civilian admin staff, a garage owner in oil-smeared coveralls, a guy in a red T-shirt; triple-X.

Plus three men in the center, dressed in suits.

Whicher eyes them all with the same unease.

A young deputy, name of Keane, stands closest to him. Gym-pumped arms. Neat trimmed goatee.

"We acted with proportionate force, marshal."

"Looks like you shot up half the town."

"It's not the Wild West."

"Y'all sure on that?"

Thirty minutes earlier, he could have stopped it. Whicher stares at an oak table to one side of the corridor. A shotgun on it. A Glock. Weapons used by two of the witnesses acting in support of police. Nothing the news boys liked better.

"No sightings? Nobody's seen 'em?"

"You haul out of here," says Deputy Keane, "there's a score of tracks any direction you can think of. East into the hills, west across the plains. North or south, who knows? They shot up the patrol car, it couldn't pursue."

Whicher nods.

"Once they're out of here, marshal, they could go anywhere."

"They can't just disappear."

A second officer takes a pace forward. "They're in Dale's pick-up." He points toward a shaken-looking guy in a denim shirt. "Dale Vance," he says. "Tried to block 'em in."

"Make? Model?"

"Green Ford pick-up. With a heavy side-impact. Anybody sees it…"

Whicher can already imagine the story they'll run.

In his hand, the marshal holds the photocopied picture of Gilman James. It's creased and battered, four days in his pocket. But the same defiant face stares back whenever he looks at it.

"Y'all are sure there was no sign of a girl? A young woman, Hispanic? Mid-twenties?"

Deputy Keane shakes his head. "I saw it all go down, I was first man out. I got out the courthouse, there was Brandon Wickes," he points up a young man with gelled back hair, standing with two suited, older men.

"He works in the bank?" says Whicher.

"Yessir. He was running out of there, followed by that guy." Deputy Keane points at the photocopied picture. "That's definitely your man, marshal."

"I know it's him. That Toyota out there with its front end stoved is the car they stole last night. In Kerrville."

Deputy Keane holds his wrist. Flexes the muscles in his forearm. "The guy driving that car looked like he was wearing something around his arm. A sling maybe."

"He have blond hair?"

"I think so."

The second deputy cuts in; "I was driving the patrol car, I got a look at him—I'll say he was blond."

Michael Tyler. Injured or no.

No sign of him at Jackson Fork. No sign of the girl, now.

"I need to speak with the manager of the bank."

Deputy Keane points to the elder of the three suited men talking with a female county sheriff's officer.

Whicher crosses the high-ceilinged hall.

The doors to both ends of the building are open, a hot Texas wind blows straight through. The courthouse is early nineteen-hundreds, according to the plaque on the wall. Whicher thinks of countless men in chains walking the floor.

The man in the gray suit turns at his approach. Thinning hair. A cold look in his eye.

"Deputy Marshal Whicher. Are you the manager?"

He nods. "Richardson."

"How much they get?"

"About thirty thousand." The manager purses his thin mouth. "We haven't had time to tally everything."

"Any chance tracing it?"

"It's not serialized. It's from small accounts here in town."

"No bait money?"

"No."

"Dye packs?"

"We're too small." Richardson shakes his head. "We don't have to trouble about all that."

"Y'all have cameras in there, right?"

"Of course."

Whicher shows him the photocopied picture.

"That's the man."

The marshal nods. Witnesses. Plenty of evidence. First, they'd have to find them.

"I need to ask about a former customer of yours at the bank. Name of Nathaniel Childress."

The manager bunches his small shoulders.

"It's part of a criminal investigation I'm running. Childress is now deceased."

Through the open doorway into the square, Whicher sees a group of vehicles arriving. New-looking Chevy express van. Mid-size Cadillac.

"Mr. Richardson, I need to know what happened to the Childress family? The widow and children? After they lost their house here."

"Oh." Richardson shifts his slight frame. "Good Lord. Yes. I remember, now. Childress…"

"That's right."

"I'd have to check. This was all very recent. And most unfortunate. They don't owe us any money…"

"Any address?"

"There may be some particulars. There's a process to be

gone through. In the circumstances, the bank thought a little time might be required."

"Y'all thought that now?"

Richardson clamps his mouth shut. The set of his small shoulders seems to harden under his suit.

The marshal glances through the open doors into the town square. Something happening. Something around the Chevy van. A young man, camo shorts and a polo shirt. Unloading a TV camera out the van door, lugging it onto his shoulder.

"Holy crap…"

"Excuse me?"

Whicher pinches the bridge of his busted nose. "You're telling me the bank have no current whereabouts for the Childress family? That it?"

"I'm afraid I can't be much help, marshal."

Whicher strides for the door of the courthouse building. Two sheriff's deputies are walking out into the square, thumbs hooked in their gun belts.

He follows them—stands alone, on the step.

Outside, a young woman in a tailored two-piece checks her hair fast, snapping away a compact mirror.

Whicher mutters under his breath. "Jesus wept…"

The camera guy is lining up a shot of the Home Valley Bank. There's a sound guy stepping from the Chevy van, now. Flip flops. A battery pack on his shorts.

Whicher takes out his cell phone. He dials the number for Agent Cornell.

It's ringing.

He watches the woman in the suit step towards the two

approaching deputies. A short exchange. Whicher watches her brash smile. Her eyes travel up the courthouse path to the single step where he's standing.

Cornell picks up.

"Hey, marshal."

"You heard yet?"

"I heard…"

"There's a goddamn camera crew here already."

Cornell's silent on the end of the line.

"I need you to find the widow. Orla Childress."

"What for?"

"Just find her. Anyway you can…"

⅄

"Suzanne Kaufman. For KENS 5 out of San Antonio."

"Deputy Marshal John Whicher."

She turns to the sound guy, "Alex, are we good?"

He nods, staring at a meter slung from his neck.

"Lee? Get a two shot of this…"

"Stand on the step," the camera guy calls. "Better yet, can the interview step down—and you step up?"

"Marshal?" The brash smile again.

Whicher screws the Resistol a notch further onto his head. "Ma'am, I'm going to have to make this quick."

"Okay, okay."

"Rolling," the camera guy calls.

"Marshal, can you comment on reports linking this robbery to a robbery in Tom Green County yesterday? A violent robbery at a cattle auction?"

"There's a possibility they're linked."

"Could this be the same Louisiana gang that attempted armed robbery at a bank in Alpine? Five days ago?"

"Ma'am, we're working on it…"

"According to some reports this is the same gang that also robbed a gas station on I-10 in West Texas on Wednesday?"

"No comment."

"What do you say to suggestions former service personnel may be involved?"

"Where did you get that?"

"Are you confirming that, marshal?"

Whicher clears his throat. He stares quickly across the square. "No," he says, "that's not confirmed."

"Many viewers may have concerns about their safety, marshal. How concerned are you—given four separate incidents in less than a week? What about the shoot-out in Kerrville last night? Was it the same gang?"

"Ma'am, I can't comment further…"

He steps out of shot and heads for the Silverado.

A hot wind scours across the square.

As Whicher dials the number for Division Marshal Reuben Scruggs.

Edwards County.

Ranch land, dust baked fields. A creek bed, between dirt tracks. I drove the Ford pick-up under a stand of prairie sumac. Scanning left and right on the horizon.

We dumped the route, bailed on it, straight off.

Rocksprings was a shooting gallery. We had to roll out hot. The route we planned on taking was fast; farm roads, county roads, but rule one evasion was no visual.

Michael watched out the windshield looking for any movement. Sweeping back and forth. "Whatever Connie gave me, it's wearing off…"

The GPS in the pick-up showed us on a blank space—heading west.

"Forty miles more," I says. "Hang tight."

I steered along the creek bank, the pick-up in shadow.

Rocksprings was barely behind us, we'd covered maybe twenty miles. The savanna spread in all directions—a farm truck, a ranch hand, that's all it would take—anybody saw us, it was over.

Michael was pale, weakening. Blue eyes hooded.

"What do you think made him do it?" he says.

I eased the pick-up out of the tree line. "What're you talking about?"

"Steven…"

Everything was meant to be different.

The moment he ran in that bank, in Alpine, the world turned, white to black. It shifted too far to catch. The Childress family lost both its sons.

Michael held his wounded arm. "I could use a drink…"

I looked at him. "Take it easy."

Tennille would be long gone.

Five hours, her and Joe, they would've made it. All the

back roads, the trails. All the way south.

She'd find her daughter, Maria. Make ready, wait for night to fall, cross the river. That was all she wanted.

Orla was no different.

She didn't pick up any gun but every other way they were the same. Both trying to hold on. In a landslide. Get through another day.

"Gil? You remember that day in Girard Park?"

I glanced at him. His head was flopped on the seat back.

"Steven was like, ten years old. We must've been fourteen. Fifteen…"

I shrugged. "I don't know."

"He had some Little League competition."

"Yeah?"

"We took a bat out in the park. You were throwing him a bunch of changeups, trying to get him to hit 'em."

A summer's day. Nate, Michael. And Orla. Steven tagging along. Family I never had. How many days had there been? I couldn't count 'em, they were the days of my life.

"He finally gets one," Michael says. "Hits a liner. Straight in the lake."

I remembered. It cracked, like a bullet. Steven's face, lit up under the trees.

"Nate ups and jumps in there, he actually swam in and got it."

I thought of him. Catching hold of it, raising it in the air.

"You believe they're both gone…"

I steered towards the light at the horizon.

"Orla said it should have been you."

⚔

Rocksprings.

Through the shot-up door of the truck, Whicher sees the black speck approaching—high in the air.

The truck's parked south of town, a DPS cruiser alongside it. The marshal thinks of the circus in the courthouse square.

The A-Star helicopter drifts off its course in the gathering southerly.

Reuben Scruggs' voice crackles on the radio; "It should be with y'all any minute."

"I'm looking at it, sir."

The trees around a four-legged water tower dip and sway in the prairie wind. In the yard of a one-floor house, plastic chairs tumble end over end.

Less than one hour. How far could they have got?

"Department of public safety just got through lighting up my phone," says Scruggs. "I told 'em if the state's so damn on fire, why don't they back it up?"

The helicopter starts its descent—tail rotor kicking up as the nose dips.

"DPS pulled a scheduled operation for us to have this."

The marshal stares into the sky at the north west. A flick of nerves in his stomach, watching the helo coming on.

The splinter in the Silverado windshield shines; a lightning fork caught in the sun.

"We're four-and-oh," Scruggs says. "I hear the TV

people are climbing on this? Don't be antagonizing them, John."

The helicopter's white and black livery is visible now. The noise of its engine reaches Whicher, despite the wind.

"You have any idea which way they could've went?"

"I'd guess west."

"You don't know?"

"No, sir. How would I?"

"You know why I put you on this?"

Whicher doesn't reply.

"You got a knack," says Scruggs. "Making the right call…"

Whicher thinks of Cornell in Houston. Captain Black at Brooke. Standing in the rain by a ford at the river in Kerrville, the night before. Always a step behind.

"If anybody on the ground sees 'em, you can be there faster than they can disappear."

"Alright, sir."

"There's one wrinkle in this. Weather conditions, later in the day."

"It's pretty windy here," says Whicher. "Visibility's okay."

"They say there's a dust storm coming up from the south."

The DPS trooper is out of his cruiser. He runs forward, waving the helicopter in.

"Grandaddy's time," says Scruggs, "they used to get 'em a bunch. Used to say the Lord sent 'em. Forever studying on the Good Book, he was."

"Sir, I've got to run…"

"Old Testament is my Bible, John, you know that. A vengeful God. Cut 'em down, to fall like ripe corn…"

Whicher stares at the flickering blades of the helo. Black-painted scythes.

The radio crackles; "You hear me?"

The marshal clicks it off.

He pushes the butt of the Ruger revolver down into the shoulder holster. Climbs from the truck.

The helicopter's touching down on a patch of scorched grass. Whicher clamps the Resistol to his head. He runs forward, the clatter of rotor blades pummeling the air.

The trooper leans in close to Whicher. "On board there's a Tactical Flight Officer…"

Whicher mouths the word, "Okay."

"He's going to give you his place—get you hooked in."

Whicher screws up his eyes as the rotor wash churns up a cloud of dust.

A man climbs from the helo, wearing an olive flight-suit. He signals Whicher forward, shows the marshal where to climb on the skid plate.

Whicher takes the rearward seat.

He straps himself in behind the pilot.

A flight helmet hangs from a ceiling rack, radio comm wires trailing from it. The TFO gestures at him to put it on.

Whicher snatches off the Resistol.

The TFO retreats.

The marshal breathes the scent of fuel as the rotor blades spin up. They lift into the air. Turning, climbing.

"Where to, sir?" The pilot's voice in his ear.

In the pit of his stomach he feels a wave of nausea. Not motion sickness, not the vertical climb.

Spread out on the land below is every available vehicle law enforcement have.

Less than one hour since they robbed the bank.

Nobody's seen them.

CHAPTER 31

Devil's River, Val Verde County.

The place Orla Childress took her children didn't exist on any map. It was down at the end of a sand track, eight miles from the nearest road.

Gray oak and soapbush. Salt grass stretching like a sea in all directions. A hundred years back, goats had walked it, before the owners gave it up and moved north to Jackson Fork—the chance of something better.

A shack. Rough-sawn board on iron hard stumps of footing. A front porch, an outhouse—barns of stone and battered tin. Jesse could've stabled a horse, not a thing would've been different.

It was off-grid, no connection of any kind. Hand-pumped spring, no running water. In all the generations that came and went, nothing changed. Shine on the handle of the pump was maybe deeper; duller. Grass longer. Shingle roof sagged on its beams.

It was primitive, unformed, clinging to the vast land. The

place she chose, in her grief.

Michael and I'd seen it only once before, two weeks after Nate died. After the funeral.

I told her she couldn't stay there, two kids, no facilities, no schooling. It being summer, she was safe for a while. She couldn't be around in Lafayette, what she told me, even if her family were there.

She upped and left. To a half-forgotten property by the Devil's River, south of Juno. A worthless piece of land, all it was. That stayed in the family, all that time.

She told me her and Nate spent a summer there, before the kids were born. A last summer.

I told her not to go.

She told me she'd been grieving for Nate for years—ever since the day he came back. She couldn't cry when folks expected her to cry, other times she couldn't stop, when she ought.

She held Nate's funeral, in Lafayette. The families and the friends all came; and tried to hide their shock, their despair. Somewhere running through it all, a feeling, something close to shame. Michael and Steven and me in a mute daze. Near as we could be to her.

Three nights later she packed the kids in a Jeep Cherokee, drove out of Lafayette, into Texas—where they'd tried to make it. Last place Nate was truly golden.

The kids ran wild in the day, king of the mountains, lords of the fields. Wondering when their daddy was coming back from going up to see God.

At night, she got 'em fed, got 'em falling down tired, put

'em to bed. And sat out on the rough porch under the sweep of stars. And talked to him, she told me. Until she felt like she'd lose her mind.

The night after the funeral, I drove around to her parents' house before she left the last time. To see her, me alone.

I faced a lot of things. But I couldn't look her in the eye, the girl I met in second grade. Freckles and the chestnut hair. If every bone in her body had gone, she couldn't have looked more broken. Crushed.

She told me she could sit on that porch, not a soul could see her—not a soul could hear her ask the world why it took everything. The boy she loved from eight years old.

The father she'd tried to save.

⅄

Orla stood in the door frame. She wore a snap-button shirt, white cotton, too big. One of Nate's. She squinted at the green Ford pick-up—an unfamiliar truck bouncing up the track across her land.

She recognized me, at the wheel. Touched the chestnut hair tied back off her face. Eyes turning to search for Michael—seeing him, searching for Steven in turn.

I steered away from the shack toward a tin-roofed barn.

She came forward to stand out on the porch. Eyes following us, lines in her brow.

I parked the truck inside the barn, cut the motor.

"I'll do it. Let me talk to her…"

Michael dragged himself straight. "We can't be here long."

"Get the kids. Take them outside."

Two miles east, we'd driven across a patch of melon and corn by a wood-frame farmhouse. Both of us with the same feeling; somebody'd seen us.

"Just give her the money," he says. "Don't explain."

We climbed out.

I took the flight case, grabbed the envelopes.

Michael hitched up his arm in the sling. He ran his good hand through his blond hair. Fixed a smile onto his face. "Make this fast."

We stepped from the barn and crossed to the shack. A fierce wind blowing from the south, sky yellow with the dust in the air.

Little Josh was standing on the porch, now. He stood by his mother, the image of Nate.

He waved, jumped down. Ran toward a twisted oak, a rope swing hanging from its branches.

Michael calls out; "Need a push?"

The boy grabbed at the rope, grinning back at us. Lifting his feet clear of the ground.

"Let's see what you got down there…" Michael walked toward him, under the tree.

Orla watched from the porch, a blank expression on her face. "Bonnie," she calls out. "Honey. Won't you come on out here?"

I reached the step.

In the open doorway, Bonnie appeared. She stood, arms

at either side, holding onto the door frame. Her mother's hair, same freckles.

"Uncle Gil and Uncle Michael are here."

She watched me, a quick, nervous smile at her mouth.

"Show Uncle Michael the swing you made."

Bonnie waited at her mother's skirts.

"Josh is showing him, I don't think he's doing it right."

She jumped from the porch and ran over to the trees, Michael kneeling to her, as she wind-milled her arms.

I caught Orla's eye, caught the rawness.

She turned.

I followed her inside.

She stood in the dark shack—a sole room, staring at the uneven floor. "What happened to Michael?"

"Nothing. He's alright."

"Whose is the pick-up? You get a new one?"

"No, I…"

"How come it's all smashed up on one side?"

I stared at the rough kitchen table. Kid's drawings, paste-board books. The remains of a meal scattered. I put the flight case and the envelopes on a corner of the table. By a plastic figure. A US Marine.

I walked to the window. It faced east, for the morning light.

I thought of the weight—that hung inside me. Was that where she stood at the start of each day? Behind me, I heard her footsteps on the floorboards. The scrape as she pulled out a chair.

I stared out the window, tried to imagine it; through Nate's eyes, a last time.

When he left the Corps, discharged injured, I thought it would be me. *I'd be first.* I'd stop a bullet one day. Set out down a garbage filled street, a patrol, some mud-brick town. I'd set out. Never come back.

I turned from the window, to face her. Laid a hand on the corner of the flight case.

"Put this somewhere. Where no one could find it. We have to leave."

I thought of never seeing her again. A feeling like a wave hit me. So long thinking on a moment.

She sat in the kitchen chair, staring up. Not really seeing. I hardly recognized the girl I used to know.

Through the open door of the shack, I heard the sound of Bonnie shrieking; Josh laughing, Michael calling out. At some feat of great prowess. On a rope swing above the tattered ground. The wind whipped away the sound.

Orla stared up at me. "How?" she says. "All this? How did we get here?"

I didn't answer.

We broke off looking at each other.

She sat at the kitchen table, hands together in her lap, rocking slightly.

"We can't stay," I said.

She nodded to herself. "You know we never blamed you. A doctor at Walter Reed told me." She stopped. "Even if you hadn't kept the patrol there. He said it wouldn't have made a difference…"

I blinked my eyes closed. Opened them. Felt the breath in my lungs.

"Nate said, you had to have been there…"

I ran a hand in my hair. Felt the grit and dirt. Thought of laying close to another human being. Tennille. On the hard ground. In the cold light of morning. What was there that I could tell her? What last wish, for Nate's woman. The children he'd never see.

"Keep everybody together…"

I pointed at the flight case, at the envelopes on the corner of the table.

She says, "What about Michael?"

I shook my head.

"He still doesn't know?"

"No," I told her.

Orla had the right, that night, after the funeral. The right to ask me anything.

I'd driven my truck across town, the streets I'd known all strange to me—Lafayette—my whole life, as if I'd never seen any of it before.

Nobody that knew Orla Childress would've denied her. Or cast the first stone.

We'd talked less than half an hour, no detail, no plan.

Nobody would ever know.

Steven was dead, better that Michael believe she never had a thing to do with any of it; that she was innocent. In the only way that mattered, she was.

We couldn't look each other in the eye no more. But we both agreed, me and her.

"Will you tell him?"

I shook my head. And stepped from the shack, out of her door.

My face stinging.

Under the strange yellow sky.

CHAPTER 32

Val Verde County.

The A-Star slides low across a swale of black and leonine grass. Whicher scans the burnt ground below the helicopter. From two hundred feet, it rushes at him as they sweep and turn.

"Bush fire," says the pilot through the headsets. "We've been getting more and more, since the drought."

A sighting—a vehicle reported trespassing on private property.

They'd listened to the radio traffic; a half-abandoned farm, some widow in her eighties. A green truck, she said, or it could've been blue—a truck that cut across the edge of her field of corn.

Nearest unit, a state trooper, had made his way up. Searched the place. Found nothing. Something went across the field, the trooper said. No telling what, or when it'd happened. DPS called up the grid reference for the helo.

"Shall I continue two-seven-zero, marshal?"

There's scarcely a feature worth the name. Abandoned farms. Homesteads with miles in between them.

The marshal searches the empty terrain—stands of oak, a score of dry creeks. A twisting river.

The cover's poor, the going bad—only thing in its favor, it's not running close to any road.

"What do you think, son?"

The pilot levels the helo. "This close to the border, that's what I'd be looking at…"

"The border?"

"Yes, sir."

"How far away is it?"

"Less than thirty miles from here."

The wind buffets the canopy as they hover in the air. The pilot puts the helo into a steady climb.

"You chase a lot of border jumpers?"

"Yes, sir, marshal. Mostly headed the opposite way, though. Running north."

"Catch many?"

"Hell, yeah. We get a bunch."

No sign. Nothing out there. If it had been them, they were in transit—they'd already be gone.

"Del Rio's only ten miles from here," the pilot says. "If they came through, maybe that's where they were headed…"

Del Rio.

What if everybody was tied up in the wrong spot?

What if they switched cars, right outside of Rocksprings?

One of them had to have been waiting. Tennille Labrea. It would've been her.

Whicher stares out the glass canopy. An eerie cast at the horizon—the sky turning orange in the distance.

"What do you make of that sky?"

"That's the dust storm, marshal. Doppler radar's picking it up. Strong pressure gradients over Mexico. Reminds me of the Middle East."

"You serve there?"

"Black Hawks. Out in Iraq."

Whicher thinks of Reuben Scruggs. His Good Book. "We stay airborne in that?"

"Negative. That could be carrying half the Chihuahuan desert."

Where to go, where to look? He thinks of the girl again; Tennille Labrea. Gilman James had his truck parked in her barn. Red paneled bodywork, shining like a fire truck when Sergeant Baker found it, two days back.

"How long before we'll have to land?"

"I can check…"

"Can you get me US Marshals Service, western division?"

"We can down-link to pretty much anywhere."

The pilot works on patching through the call.

Whicher tunes out the bursts of static on the radio.

Everybody tied up a hundred mile radius of Rocksprings. What if they're already gone? He watches a group of five horses, bolting in the shadow of the helo.

Gilman James left his truck inside her barn, the high desert hills at the border. Maybe they figured going back, all along. Nowhere more remote than that stretch.

A signal beeps in the headset.

"Press comm 2," the pilot tells him.

A familiar voice crackles in Whicher's ear phones.

"Marshal Reuben Scruggs."

"Sir, it's Whicher. I want to go after the girl—the Labrea girl."

"What?"

"I think they're gone. There's a storm coming in, I got one chance to get ahead of them."

"What's that on?"

"Gut call…"

"God Almighty, John, we need more than that."

"I want to head west. To Terlingua. I think they might be done."

Scruggs is silent a moment.

"I think Rocksprings could be the end of the line," says Whicher.

"You don't know that."

The marshal reaches in the pocket of his suit. He pulls out the lined notepad, his eyes skimming the handwritten notes. Looking for anything, checking, re-checking, his mind racing, clutching at threads.

"Lafayette was for Tyler," he says, "Michael Tyler."

"Say again?"

"We know he used to work there, at the airport—after he came out."

Scruggs doesn't answer.

"The bank at Alpine was Steven Childress."

"That's what you been thinking?"

"He worked there, he lost his job, he cut up rough…"

The cockpit of the helo is filled with noise; the turbo whine of the engine, the thrum of rotor blades. Whicher tries to push it all out.

"Jackson Fork was all about Nathaniel Childress. That killed himself. What the hell difference they thought it was going make, I don't know…"

"This the brother?"

"He was living on some farm, him and his wife, two kids."

Whicher stares down in the gulley of a limestone ridge, deep shadowed; barren. He wills himself to believe it. Lets his boss think it over.

"How about today?" says Scruggs.

"For the widow. Rocksprings was for the widow."

The house lost, finally. After the farm.

The helicopter lurches in a sudden gust of wind.

"Where's the damn girl fit?" says Scruggs.

"I don't know. Honest to God. But she's got a daughter in this somewhere, a little girl…"

"So?"

"I don't reckon she's going to leave her behind…"

So close to Mexico, that was where they had to be headed.

He could call Lieutenant Rodgers; get a search organized.

"Say they were going to try to cross the border?" says Whicher. "I think Terlingua's where they'd do it…"

"I don't know, John."

"She's unfinished business."

Whicher taps the pilot's shoulder. Points his finger to the west.

The pilot rotates the helo, pushes forward on the cyclic.

"You a praying man?" says Scruggs.

"Say again?"

"I know you ain't. But it's never too late."

Whicher stares into the sick-looking sky—dust gray, orange; yellowed at its edges.

"Y'all catch them birds down there, do me one thing?"

"I'll see that justice is served…"

"Amen to that."

South of Pandale.

We crossed the Pecos River through a country void of people, the land abandoned, only ghosts in the blistering heat.

Michael thought he saw a helicopter, running south along a ridge. It was just for a second—I looked but couldn't see. We stopped the truck in a gravel draw by a bank of desert willow. Waited. Then picked up again, heading west.

The course we made was parallel with the border, not more than thirty miles to the north, across the empty land.

We'd planned to head up country. Montana, it was going to be. Or maybe North Dakota. We'd live quiet, stay close to Canada. Cross if needed.

But Steven got himself killed, Michael was hurt bad—

now that it all came down there was only getting out, staying free. Running. Cutting off the past.

"Two thousand miles," I says, "to Alberta."

Michael shook his head.

"Or British Columbia."

"My blood's too thin for Canada, man."

"Thirty five hours. We could be there."

He held his arm in the sling.

Thirty five hours through Texas, Colorado, Wyoming. On into Montana. What were the odds? We'd never get to use an interstate, it could take us days.

I drove the Ford pick-up on through the trackless land. Brush scrub stretched out in every direction—the silhouettes of beaked yucca and ocotillo, clumps of tarbush, no end in sight.

"Coahuila," Michael says.

Coahuila, north eastern Mexico.

"That's the closest…"

"It's too flat," I says. "Too open."

They'd be looking for us there. We'd never get the truck across. Michael couldn't swim the river—if he did, they'd be waiting, they'd pick us up easy. On foot we were dead and gone.

"How about we boost a car?"

I looked at him.

"Steal something," he says.

"You even know how to do that?"

We were following a wash, dead wood and pieces of broken fence scattered in its path. Clouds of dust starting to gust now, in the tight valleys.

Thousands of miles to the border with Canada. I thought of Tennille, of Joe. The stretch of desert she came from, like the end of the earth.

She'd get out, at least, her and the kid.

I thought of standing up close with her—on the lane at Rocksprings.

"She's going across tonight…"

Michael raised his head off the seat back.

"Tennille."

"Tennille?"

"She's going to cross the border."

"Knock it off." He shook his head. "Forget it. That's a crock…"

Two hundred-odd miles. What would it take us? Three hours.

Farm roads, ranch roads. We could run in desert—if anyone could, we could. "She knows the land, she knows people…"

He didn't answer.

"She saved your life…"

He lay his head back. Searched the ceiling of the cab, mouth ajar.

"We're never going to make it," I says, "on our own."

The sky to the southwest was deepening amber. I felt a quickening in my gut.

"You thought about what you'll do?" he says.

I glanced across at him. In his blue eyes, the slightest of smiles.

"I mean, if we don't make it…"

I let the thought work, a thought already working the last few days.

The look in his eye was familiar, a look I knew. No self-pity.

It was a door we'd both looked in.

If it had to be, it had to be—no-one in this world I would've rather been with.

I didn't answer him.

But in my heart, I already knew.

Chapter 33

Lajitas.

Dust blows in choking clouds across the airfield strip. Whicher dials the number for Houston, ATF field division.

Behind him, in the dark hangar, the A-star pilot runs post-flight checks in the helicopter, sitting out of the storm.

Whicher listens to the ring-tone. It's picking up.

"Cornell? It's Whicher."

"Hey, cowboy. Where are you?"

"Lajitas. Right on the border."

"What the hell are you doing down there?"

"Category one severe weather event."

"You're doing what?"

"We got a major league dust storm. We've been searching by helo; we're grounded. Tell me you found Orla Childress?"

"No can do."

"You can't find any record?"

"I've been looking everywhere…"

"You try Lafayette police? What about the inquest?"

"Given address for Orla Childress is her father's house. I called there, he said she left, took the kids."

The marshal stares at his boots.

"The father doesn't know where she went. Or if he does, he isn't saying. They're not missing, she's not wanted by law enforcement…"

"Not yet she ain't."

Whicher thinks of a widow. Two young children.

"Listen. I'm going after James and Tyler. I think they could be with the Labrea girl, somewhere down here…"

"If you find them, you better watch your ass."

"Yeah. I'll do that."

Whicher rubs his eyes, clicks off the call.

In front of the airfield hangar, a black Ford Ranger truck reverses—backing up toward the hangar doors.

The driver leans over the passenger seat. Pops the door. Sergeant Baker.

Whicher steps forward. "You get my message?"

"Yes, sir. Looks like you only just made it in."

"Didn't plan on coming."

The marshal climbs into the cab. He pulls the door closed against the wind.

"Pilot told me he had to put down. No choice. Visibility dropped to less than three kilometers…"

Baker squints out the window. "It's more like fifty yards, now."

"Guy's an Iraq vet, used to dust storms," says Whicher.

"But the engines can't take it, what he told me."

"Lot of guys coming back from there."

The marshal takes out the Ruger revolver. "Rogue vets is the only ones make the news." He thumbs the cylinder release, opens it, pushes on the extractor. And dumps the six brass-jacketed rounds. "No sign of anyone up at the Labrea place, sergeant?"

"We sent a vehicle up again, after you radioed."

"You impound that F150?"

"The truck got towed away, Thursday."

"You don't think they'll be coming back here, do you?"

The sergeant blows the air from his cheeks.

Whicher spins the empty cylinder, feels its smooth rotation. Still empty, he closes the cylinder to the battery, points the six-inch barrel to the floor between his Western boots. And dry-fires the pistol. Three times in double-action. A long double. Three times in single, cocking the hammer. It clicks sharp and crisp.

From behind the wheel of the Ford Ranger, Sergeant Baker looks at him.

"Everything alright, marshal? Fixing on doing some shooting?"

Whicher reloads the .357 Magnum rounds. The feel of the rosewood grips smooth against his palm. He points at the dust storm through the windshield. "We step out in that, things is going to stop working on us. This better not be one of 'em." He hefts the big revolver back into the shoulder holster.

"Where do you want to go, marshal?"

"Head down to Lajitas."

Baker shifts into drive. He steers the truck down the link road to the highway.

In the mud gray light the visibility's right down. Whicher feels the strangeness of the desert—not a living soul, only looming shapes, the blunt mountains.

"You ever see a thing like that in your life?"

"Dust storm like that? Not so much."

"If any illegals were trying to jump the border today, how y'all going to stop 'em?"

Baker reaches the turn from the airfield to the highway. "It's the answer to a mule's prayer."

He swings the truck onto the deserted road, engine humming underneath the hood.

Whicher eyes the empty highway. Sand-blown—grit drifting across its edges. Road and land becoming one. Air and earth and light disappearing.

Lajitas. A border post. Where to look?

Labrea ranch checked out empty. "You had anyone take a look at Joe Tree's?"

"Same vehicle that went up to the Labrea ranch called in there. No sign at either location, marshal."

No sign, no word, no lead. Nothing but a feeling.

The Labrea girl had a daughter out there, somewhere. He thinks of the ranch, the burned up wall, signs of a break-in. Leon Varela. Standing in a freight yard. Telling him to get to hell.

"What about Varela?" says Whicher. "We could call in. At his yard?"

"What for?"

"I don't know. Yank his chain, see what happens."

Up ahead, among the clouds of dust, shapes of buildings are emerging.

"His haulage yard is off to the right, sir."

"Go ahead, make the turn."

There's not another vehicle, nothing moving as Baker drives toward the fenced-in yard, its gates closed up.

The sergeant stops the truck. Both men stare into the yard—a site office, empty step-deck, no rig. Chain and padlock on the gate.

"Nobody here, sir."

Maybe Varela was out on a job. He could've left before the storm blew in—he could be miles away, anywhere.

"That teacher friend of yours? Guy you had me meet in that bar…"

"Jed Reynolds?"

"Right. According to him, Tennille Labrea would never leave her daughter behind."

Whicher thinks of Lori, his own girl. He pushes the thought away.

"Anybody seen this kid? She has to be someplace."

Baker shakes his head.

Jed Reynolds. The bar, the beer-drinking goat. If anybody heard anything or knew anything, it'd be a place like that. Local bar. They may as well ask.

"Head on down to that little trading post, sergeant."

Baker turns the truck around. He steers away from the river, back onto the highway. Drives a hundred yards, both hands on the wheel, foot hovering above the brake.

Scattered buildings lie ahead—their outlines scarcely visible. How to find somebody in a dust storm a man could barely see in?

Whicher peers through the windshield. Block shapes of cars are parked in front of the trading post. He tries to make them out. A metallic SUV. A rusted truck. Panel van. A red Camaro.

"Varela drives a pony car, don't he?"

"That could be it."

The Camaro's lights are on. Dim red tail lights. It's backing out. It flicks round.

It's pulling out onto the road.

"That's him, marshal."

Already the Camaro's disappearing up the highway, a set of tail lights in the press of dust.

An estranged wife wanted for armed robbery. Hiding his daughter from him. The guy *must* be thinking on his daughter.

"You want to go after him?"

"Yeah. Do it."

They could rattle his cage.

Baker pushes down on the gas. "This truck's out of the unmarked pool," he says. "No light bar. I can't flash him down."

Twin red pinpricks show in the dirt gray light.

"Don't lose the son of a bitch…"

Baker accelerates harder. The pick-up lurches forward. Sand covers half the road—no horizon—only a broken yellow line marks the center of the highway.

"You got your lights on, sergeant?"

Baker checks. "No, sir."

"Keep 'em off."

Grit blasts against the pick-up sides. A raw sheen. A dust storm this bad, Varela couldn't be headed out anyplace—he had to be going home.

"Where's he live. Do you know?"

"Terlingua. Ten miles east."

The Camaro slows. It's stopping, turning from the highway. In profile, sleek and low.

"Keep back…" Whicher searches the highway's edge— flat scrub, rising to barren rock.

The Camaro's moving, heading north, into the desert.

"The hell's up there?"

Baker shakes his head. "Nothing. Just a track." He stops the pick-up. "That's the badlands…"

The Camaro's almost out of sight, the point of vanishing. Bare specks of red in the dirt-filled air.

"Keep following," says Whicher. "But stay right back."

Baker hits the gas again. The Ranger pick-up rumbles forward.

"Feel like a stranger," says Whicher. "In a strange land." He shifts his arm. Feels for the shoulder holster. "This all is their country. Not mine."

The Ranger bounces over the stony track in the lee of

the bare mountain. Burrograss dancing in the wind. They head north, deeper into desert.

"The hell is this going?"

"Old mining trail, marshal. Lone Star mine."

The track's running along a flat pass, the outline of the mountain hardly visible.

Up ahead, the tail lights glow a point brighter. The Camaro braking.

Baker stares. It's turning to the left. "Okay…"

"Okay what?"

"Up there's mountain country. Dry mountain…"

Whicher runs a hand over his face. Maybe it was a waste of time.

They could get back on the highway, forget Varela, turn around, head for Terlingua. James and Tyler—Labrea and her girl, they'd head for the border—south. Varela was headed north, whatever he was doing.

"Where's it end up? This trail?"

"There's a homestead. Esteban's place…"

"Say again?"

"Esteban. Segaro."

Whicher thinks of the name. Somewhere, he knows it, he's heard it before.

Baker drives slow, keeping distance. Only the lights show Varela's still up ahead.

"What are you thinking, sergeant?"

"I'm thinking I want to know where he's going…"

Esteban. Somewhere he's heard the name. Terlingua, was it? He thinks back to the afternoon he first came. He'd driven down to meet the guy that owned the diner. Big Lem Stinson.

Lem reported seeing Gilman James. Told him about a power outage, the day of the Alpine raid. And told him about an Indian finding the F150 truck. Joe Tree, Tennille Labrea's neighbor.

There was another guy that day. At the diner. Hispanic. Carpenter or a builder.

"This guy Esteban. He a carpenter feller?"

The sergeant rubs at his short khaki sleeve. "Yeah…"

"Buddy of Joe Tree's?"

Baker glances at him. "Matter of fact. I think he is." He turns back to peering out the windshield. Eyes trying to stay on the dim lights ahead.

"If he's buds with Joe, he's bound to know Tennille Labrea."

The sergeant doesn't answer.

"Hispanic community's tight. Everybody knows everybody. We know Joe Tree's been in helping her."

"How's that, sir?"

"It was his Dodge Dakota they took off in. To rob Jackson Fork."

"He can say they took it. Without him knowing."

Whicher looks at him.

"Joe goes walk-about for weeks at a time…"

"You and I both know he had to be helping 'em."

Baker stares straight ahead. "You think Esteban could be involved?"

"What if he were helping hide the daughter?"

They steer on in the worsening light.

"This place got a name, son?"

"It's called Casa Piedra."

Red Hill.

The dust storm was worsening, visibility right down. Signal on the GPS in and out.

We kept the pick-up headed west. Working the terrain, through gaps in the hills—across the flats, a score of tracks, mining trails. Somehow, there had to be a way.

A canyon on the river. That was what she said.

Nightfall. Santa Elena.

First, she'd have to wait it out, with her daughter, Maria. She had to be with her.

Her place, the ranch, would be no go. The law looking for her. A husband trying to get her kid.

The homestead was our best chance at finding them, that's what I told Michael—the place she'd shown me, after Connie'd taken him in.

We were crossing the last stretch of desert, my guess. I knew we had to be getting close, despite the storm. We'd watched it, towering in the southwest—fifteen hundred feet from sky to ground. Iraq, we'd seen them, back in the sandbox, dust storms that could stop an army.

By the time we hit it, it was too late to turn around or change our minds. We had to keep on going.

Supposing we couldn't find the place, we'd try to cross

the border on our own. We'd have a shot, we at least had cover. The storm was set.

We found a rail line, driving across a plateau—a disused line. *Texas Pacifico Transportation*. I remembered it passing nearby the homestead.

We followed it north bound, wheels barely on the outline of the track. Edging across the desert, slow. But there could only be one line.

Michael lay back in his seat, propped against the window. "You should've never brought the damn gun…"

I looked at him.

"That M9 Beretta of yours."

He stared unfocused at the swirling light through the windshield.

"Back at Connie's, tripping off that boom—I figured it out."

"You figured what?"

"How come you lost it. To Steven."

I nodded.

"It was after we hit the airport," he says. "Lafayette. We crossed the state line. Checked into that motel. Off of Bay Town."

I thought about the cheap room we stopped in. A post-hit high, the three of us pumped. The pain of Nate's death seemed to fade in those first few short hours.

"They were on a table," Michael said. "They looked the same. Steven must've picked up yours, you got his…"

"I never would've fired that gun."

Michael shook his head. He closed his eyes. Held his arm

in the sling, against his chest.

I stared out along the green hood of the truck. Debris whipping past, shreds of creosote bush. Thin branches, lumps of dirt.

We were running close to a creek bed. Switchgrass growing below a bank of crushed stone.

A group of buildings was up ahead.

I strained my eyes to make it out, in the failing light. I stopped the truck.

Michael looked at me. "That it? That the place?"

It was part stone built, part adobe. No vehicles, that I could see, no light showing.

"I think."

I cut the motor—wind battering us, the pick-up rocking side to side.

"I'll take a look. I'm leaving the headlights on."

The dust storm could worsen any moment. Once we got out, the lights could be the only way back.

I picked the SIG off the seat. Pushed it deep inside my jacket to shield it from the sand in the air. I opened up the door, the wind snatching at it.

I stepped out, eyes screwed into slits.

Michael climbed from the cab. He staggered in the wind.

No sense of space, no depth. Around us, just a dim hole—half lit.

We edged our way forward toward the buildings. Disoriented.

No sign of any life.

I felt the rip of sand biting against my skin. I put a hand over my eyes.

Through my fingers I could see the front face of the building. Wooden slat door, rough timber frame. Higher up in the wall, between adobe bricks, small windows. Square and black.

I felt a hand on my shoulder.

Michael gripped my jacket. Pulled me back toward him. "I don't like it…"

"Wait," I told him. "Wait here, if you want."

I took a few steps on toward the group of buildings. Thirty yards out. Searching, looking for any sign.

No cars. No vehicles.

The house gave nothing, it was blank, faceless, adrift—an ark in a sea of dust.

I stumbled on, choking, swamped. Eyes straining to make out detail; any movement.

There's a crack, in the air. Flat crack. A snapping sound.

I stopped.

Wind and sand. A swirling dust devil.

Another crack.

Something wrong. Strange and wrong.

I threw myself flat, rolled on the ground.

I scrambled to shout back to Michael—he was laying on the ground, ten yards back.

I ripped the SIG clear, raised it, sweeping for a target. Hands pressed together, wrists inching the barrel high.

Another crack.

A muzzle flash in a dim square of window.

Through the shifting light, a face was there. Long dark hair whipped by the wind.

"*Tennille…*"

The sound of my voice was gone, blown to nothing. I clamped my mouth against the suffocating air.

She had a rifle at her shoulder. Staring along its iron sights.

I turned to check for Michael—he was still down.

When I looked back to the house, she was gone.

I ran to Michael.

His scarred lungs were heaving, he was choking on the dust, he couldn't breathe.

I grabbed at him. He wasn't hit. I dragged him up off the ground, pistol in one hand, my free arm around him. Tripping, stumbling half-blind toward the house.

The wooden slat door juddered in the wind.

It was opening.

Chapter 34

Whicher leans all the way forward in his seat.

"Where the hell is this?"

Twenty yards. Twenty yards of dirt-brown desert and the next second, nothing, till the dust and sand clear again.

Varela's car is barely visible. Clouds of thick dust twist in every direction.

Sergeant Baker slows the Ford Ranger.

The Camaro's rolling down a hillside, slowing—steering between patches of guajalote. The car turning to left and right.

"That's the Alamito Creek," says Baker. "I think."

"We getting near this place?"

"Casa Piedra's just up ahead…"

Whicher draws the big frame revolver out of the shoulder holster. He feels his heart rate quicken.

The Camaro's slowed right down. It's stopping.

Baker hits the brakes.

"Stay back," says Whicher, "let's see if he's getting out."

Only strange shapes form beyond the windshield;

Varela's red Camaro a glowing ember. He steps out of his car, a dark slash, head down, hand covering his mouth.

He stoops in the dust storm, moves around to the trunk. Focused only on what's right in front of him. Not even glancing back up the hill.

He opens the flat-topped trunk of the Camaro.

He's reaching in. Pulling out something—four feet, black and brown.

"That's a gun he's breaking out."

Varela closes the trunk, his back still turned. He starts walking.

"Man makes a house call. With a long gun. In a dust storm…"

Baker nods. "It ain't going to be friendly."

Varela walks on—a streak in a spirit world, disappearing in a fog of choking sand.

Whicher glances down at the big steel Ruger between his hands. "Alright, then. Let's move down, son."

Baker shifts the truck into neutral.

They free-wheel down the slope toward the creek bed. Reach the Camaro. Both men still watching Varela swinging the gun in front of him.

He's climbing up a bank of scrub toward a broken wall of stone. An outlying enclosure. Edge of a homestead.

The sergeant stops the truck. He turns off the motor. Opens the holster at his side. And takes out a 229 SIG

Whicher pushes down his tan Resistol hat. "Stay with the vehicle."

"Really?"

"Anything happens, get on the radio…"

The marshal steps out.

Dust is everywhere, he screws his eyes tight against it. He holds his jacket across his mouth in the choking haze, sand scattering, the ground shifting.

Like smoke beneath his boots.

⅄

Tennille's in the open doorway, Joe's lever-action Marlin in her hands. She's wearing the green hunter's jacket, buttoned to the throat.

We're staggering in the thick gray air.

She steps back—we stumble inside, Michael clutching at the wall.

I pulled the rough door closed behind us; bolted it.

We're standing in an out-room, just enough light to see. Bare walls, a pile of cut lumber in a corner— toolboxes, a laundry rack, rebozo cloth hanging down in long strips.

"The power's out," she said. "The storm got it."

"Are you alone?"

She glared at me. "Esteban left with Elaina. They can't be any part of this."

"What about…"

"Maria's here. We're leaving, as soon as it's dark."

I glanced at Michael. And back at her.

"Leon knows," she says.

"He knows you're *here*?"

"I've got my truck. Out the back, inside a barn. It's ready to go."

A door opened further in, at the far end of the darkened room. "Mama…"

"It's alright, baby. Go back up."

I stashed the pistol out of sight in my jacket.

"I thought it was him." Tennille looked at me. "I saw headlights…"

"Is Joe here?"

She shook her head. "He left me his rifle."

She turned toward the doorway where Maria had been.

Michael leaned against the wall on his good arm— hacking; trying to clear his throat.

I followed after Tennille.

Beyond the outer room was a kitchen—dark, the power out, the room lit with candles on a table. Maria sat on a rope-backed chair, by a dresser, in the shadows. Long hair loose. Holding her knees, her face afraid.

Tennille knelt to her.

Maria turned the silver bracelets at her mother's wrist.

I watched from the shadows. Then turned back to Michael, still coughing in the outer room.

His right arm was out of the sling. He was trying to rub the dust from his eyes.

"You okay?"

"Fuck, no."

Tennille stepped through the doorway from the kitchen.

"Can you show us how to cross?"

She didn't answer.

"Did you do it?" she says.

I knew she meant the bank. In Rocksprings. I nodded.

"Jesus, Gil."

"I know, I know."

"Joe told me Leon's been up to the ranch…"

For the first time since I met her she looked afraid.

"You need to cut the lights on that truck," she said. "I don't want any sign out there."

Maria was in the kitchen doorway now.

Michael smiled at her. She stared back, silent.

I grabbed a strip of rebozo cloth, pulled it from the laundry rack. "I'll move the pick-up."

"Throw me one of them," Michael says.

"No," I told him. "Stay here."

"Come on," he says. "I'll watch your back."

He stepped forward, took off a piece of fabric from the rack. He winked at Maria.

"Watch this…"

He wound the long strip of cloth around his head, across his face, his mouth. Leaving only a slit for his eyes. The way we learned, desert fighting. He tied off the ends of the cloth.

He turned to Maria. "Like an Arab man."

She smiled.

I tied off my own scarf. Unbolted the outer door.

"Go on in the kitchen, baby," said Tennille.

Maria turned away in the flickering candle light.

"Can you show us?"

"You shouldn't have come here."

I pulled the SIG from my jacket.

She shook her head. "We have to just go…"

⚔

Varela's shotgun is feet away in the dirt. Whicher wrestles the younger man to the ground. He smashes the butt of the Ruger into his cheekbone.

Varela tries to roll, brings up a knee to strike at Whicher's kidney.

Pain whips through the marshal's side. He lashes out an elbow, feels the bone connect—anger starting to choke him, fast as the dust.

The young man's arms fly up, hands grabbing at Whicher's neck, fingers locking around his throat.

The marshal presses the barrel of the revolver to the side of Varela's head. He cocks the hammer, pain surging through his windpipe.

A boot cracks into Varela's skull, it snaps sideways— Sergeant Baker, out of the truck. The squared-off SIG between his hands.

Whicher rips Varela's grip from his throat. Rolls away. Gets to his knees.

He picks his service badge out of the dirt. Holds it out. "*Look at this*. You son of a bitch."

Varela's jaw is slack. He lays back in the dirt. Eyes the sergeant's 229 SIG inches from his face.

"I'm going say it again." Whicher coughs. Spitting out dirt. "My name is Deputy Marshal John Whicher. US Marshals Service. You have the right to remain silent…"

"Cabrón…"

"Anything you say or do may be used against you in a court of law…"

"Hey, pendejo," Varela juts his chin. "What do you want? What's the fucking charge?"

"Open-carry of a firearm, the state of Texas. Felony intimidation. Resisting arrest…"

"I'm out shooting coyote…"

Sergeant Baker leans in closer, steadying the black barreled pistol.

Whicher gets to his feet. "We find your ex-wife or your daughter up there in that house yonder—you're going on the goddamn yard."

Varela pushes himself up. He sits in the churning dust.

"I saw what happened," says Baker. "You fired on a federal law enforcement agent."

"Cuff him."

Whicher holds a hand to his side. The pain from the knee-strike is deep inside his body. Too deep, his age.

He spits more sand from out of his mouth.

"Get him back to the truck. Call it in."

He picks his battered Resistol from out of a creosote bush.

Baker reaches for the cuffs at his duty belt.

The marshal clutches the Ruger. He moves forward, wind lashing over the rough ground.

His throat is raw—from Varela's grip. The blood up, fighting like some bust-head in the dirt. Too old, all that shit. Makes him want to reach for the trigger.

He walks on, pulls the lapel of his jacket across his mouth.

Ahead, at the far-edge of visibility is the outline of a group of buildings. Oblique shapes. Blurred out.

A homestead. Dark blocks in the half light.

He picks his way, spines of cactus catching at his knees. He pulls his boot free from a clump of snakeweed.

He looks up. Stops in his tracks.

Through a cloud of dust, there's two columns of mud yellow light.

A shape, in profile. Twin beams of a vehicle's headlights, boring out in the swirling grit.

Whicher checks behind.

Baker's nowhere. He's lost already in the sand-filled air.

He should go back. Find him.

He holds out the Ruger revolver.

The pick-up's stationary, side on. Whicher stares at the cab. No sign of any occupant.

He can run back, find the sergeant.

It could be the stolen Ford pick-up.

Rear lights show dim on the license plate. He can check the tailgate, he'll recognize the plate, from the calls in the helo.

If it *is* them—then what?

From the left-hand edge of his vision, he sees a figure, walking.

His pulse races.

A man's walking toward the pick-up.

Sergeant Baker's too far back. He can't call out.

The man stumbles, swaying through the storm of dust. His head is wrapped, like a desert Arab.

Gilman James. Making for the pick-up. The Ford pick-up stolen six hours back, outside the bank.

Whicher feels the adrenaline. He pushes himself forward, gun raised.

He shouts out; "*US Marshal…*"

The wind whips away the sound—before it's out of his mouth.

But James stops. He pulls at a corner of the headscarf. Then turns to stare through the billowing dust. He puts a hand to a pocket.

Whicher fires once.

James staggers. Collapsing, backwards. Left hand clutching at his chest.

He hits the ground. Lays still. Then drags himself towards the front end of the pick-up.

Whicher re-cocks the hammer. He runs forward.

James has stopped moving. He's lying in the wind-whipped dust.

The marshal reaches him, he squats on his heels, pulls off the headscarf.

A face stares back at him—fighting for air. Blue eyes, panicked, as the dust curls about him. His blond hair is dull against the dirt. *Michael Tyler.*

Whicher stares at him, helpless as he starts to writhe. He takes his shoulder, turns him on his side, coughing, gagging—limbs starting to thrash in the dust.

Michael Tyler. Marine Corps vet.

Choking to death, blood filling up his lungs.

In a dirt gray desert.

Under no star.

⋏

Michael had the keys, no gun—he was moving the truck—
if it *was* a shot, it couldn't have been him.

My breath caught in my throat. I turned back, ran
towards the outline of the house.

He couldn't hold a gun, he could move a truck.

I left him to do it—headed out to sweep the ground,
clear it; make sure.

I ran, choking, to the house, on past the end wall.

I could just see—the green pick-up, its headlights on.

Michael laying on the ground.

I ran as fast as I could.

The scarf was gone from around his head, his blond hair
caught in the truck lights.

I reached him, knelt to him, stared in his face. Saw the
blood in his mouth.

I put a hand to his neck, to the artery. No beating pulse.

A bullet wound.

The middle of his chest. A single blood-stained hole.

Shock held me rigid. Flashes, snapping inside. A desert
war rushing in my head.

I turned to stare at the house—smoke of dust curling,
like buildings in my memory.

I crouched low, SIG in my clenched fist. Ran at the
rough-framed empty doorway.

In there somewhere, he must be—*Leon*; a dead man.

I strained to listen. The house was silent. Just the wind. Open door rattling against the wall.

I moved through the outer room, ripping off the wound rebozo scarf. Adrenaline tight in me. Light flickering from the kitchen.

I stepped in—no one was in there. The rope-backed chair was empty. The far side of the kitchen dresser, a door opened into a darkened hallway.

Wind was racing through the house. The candle flame on the table snuffed out.

I pitched forward in the dark, into the hallway, running down it. A door was open at the end. I rushed it, stepping out into a yard—choking on dust, fighting to see.

Across the yard there's a stone barn—black opening beneath an iron lintel. I ran to it, sand flaying my skin—almost tripping through the opening in the wall.

A dark interior. I could just make out a truck. Red and black, Tennille's F350.

She was in the barn, leaning into the cab, trying to start the engine. The motor caught, the noise of it booming off the stone walls.

She turned, saw me. Gripped the Marlin rifle. Maria already climbing in through the passenger door.

"*He's here*," I shouted.

She swung the barrel of the Marlin up.

"Go," I told her.

She stared back at me.

"*Just get out. Go…*"

She held my look a split second. Then ran to the far end of the barn—to a set of wide double-doors.

She loosed the bolt, tried to open up, the wind pushing back against her.

I ran forward, grabbed the first door. Dragged it open—lashing it back on a rope stay.

She stepped closer.

For a moment, something showed in her eye.

I grabbed the second door, banged the butt of the SIG against the bolt to get it free. Unlatched it. Hauled it back. "Get as far as you can…"

She turned. Ran for the truck.

I watched her climb inside.

Let her go.

I'd finish it. Find Leon, wherever he was.

No after; nothing in my mind.

I'd get Michael, get him in the pick-up, cross the border. I rammed the door back against the wall of the barn.

Tennille snaps on the headlights.

Whicher.

Twenty yards from the barn's open doors.

Whicher. Standing out in the dark. Wide-legged. Dust whipping at him.

He held his gun arm out in the wind. A strip of fabric, Michael's headscarf, trailing from his left hand. It curled around the leg of his suit.

I felt the air rush from my lungs.

I raised both arms in front of me. Iron-sights of the pistol centered with the middle of his body.

Not high, not fast.

Whicher. Not Leon.

He was standing just off the headlight beam—blocking in the 350 truck.

I made myself walk slow. Toward him. One foot in front of the other. Jaw tight. Thinking of the snap from the gun—double-action into single, the recoil, the way it would feel, the sudden noise.

Michael.

Last thing he saw was that bastard's eyes.

A wave rising up inside, heart blood. Sweep of heat.

I stared at him. Walked—on my last breath. To shoot him, let him shoot me, to never leave that sea of dust.

I thought of four kids. Nate and Michael. Eight years old. Orla. A schoolyard in Lafayette; ablaze in light.

I stopped.

From nowhere, I could see Maria, Tennille's girl, in my mind.

Fear in her face.

Watching two men. Flat out kill each other.

I lowered the gun.

I stared in the marshal's eyes. He held my look.

For a second, he broke off—to stare at the truck still inside the barn.

I put a thumb down on the hammer-drop. Released it. Tossed the SIG in the dirt.

His eyes shone. He lowered his revolver; staring at me a long moment.

He de-cocked the gun, held it loose.

And then he turned.
And walked away.
A ghost in the dust.

Epilogue

The Old Cemetery, Terlingua, TX.

The wind rakes the old stones and broken down crosses. Graveyard weeds push up through the scoured earth. By a small headstone of granite, a red plastic rose buffets on a weathered length of twine.

Whicher steps along a path lined with ocotillo and mariposa. Past piled up stones, twisted wooden grave-markers, so many crooked; fallen. The wind has had its way.

He walks to the cemetery gate, two drystone pillars; squared off. Ornamental crosses are set at their tops. He stares at the scrolling black iron, against the sky. Stops. And puts some money in the little glass jar.

His eyes drift to the horizon, a ridge of hills, the Chisos mountains. An emptiness is all he feels.

No trace, no sign. And in his heart, he hopes there never will be.

He walks to the Chevy Silverado—the door replaced, and the windshield. He takes off his tan Resistol hat.

Nobody was there. Nobody ever would be. Everybody lost, in the end.

He climbs back into the truck cab, out of the wind.

Too late. That was what he told them. Sergeant Baker. Alpine police. His own boss, Division Marshal Scruggs.

They'd been at the homestead—Casa Piedra, but they'd run, before he could stop them.

He'd found Michael Tyler. Shot him, resisting arrest.

Whoever else had been there, they'd fled as the dust storm raged, no chance stopping them. They'd likely made for the border.

Sergeant Baker's testimony confirmed it—he'd been occupied detaining Leon Varela. And couldn't assist.

Varela was charged. Two counts relating to his former wife, a third count, attempted murder of a US Marshal. Awaiting trial, the county jail, in Alpine.

ATF left the file open on the suicide of Nathaniel Childress. No record could be found of the whereabouts of Orla Childress. Somewhere, she'd taken her young family. Whicher stopped looking. Told Cornell, in so many words—let it slide.

He thinks of Lori. His wife, Leanne. The borderline.

Somehow, Terlingua drew him—he could find an excuse to check the Labrea ranch. The adobe house. Find it shut up, like the last time. The land at Joe Tree's place, deserted. Nobody knowing when he'd be back. Or if.

He thinks of Gilman James—lowering his outstretched arms. A black gun between his hands. The moment.

Looking in that barn. Maria. About the age of his own girl.

But maybe there'd never be an answer.

In his mind he can see it all. The 350 truck, rear door open, James climbing in.

Seconds later, they were gone.

On the seat of the Silverado is an open briefcase; preliminary report, almost finished. Whicher reaches over. He picks it out, opens it, eyes skimming the lines written; bare sentences.

> *US Marshals Service Criminal Investigation*
> *…concludes that Gilman Francis James, of Lafayette, Louisiana remains the sole suspect still at large in connection with the serial armed robberies of Lafayette Regional Airport, attempted armed robbery of the Farmers Bank at Alpine TX, and armed robbery of the Home Valley Bank at Rocksprings, TX – all other known perpetrators and associates being now deceased.*

He turns the stapled pages. The wind rocks against the truck side.

> *…subsequent investigation into armed robbery of the Exxon Service Station at Interstate 10, in Reeves County, and the Jackson Fork Livestock Auction, near San Angelo, remains ongoing…*

> *…Tennille Maria Labrea, and Maria Lucita Varela, of Terlingua, TX, remain missing—it is the opinion of this officer that Labrea and her daughter are*

now in Mexico, where the suspect is known to have
family…

Whicher's eyes search the horizon, once again. He closes
the report, places it back on the seat. Through the truck's
open door, the wind catches at its edges, lifting the pages, to
flutter like wings.

He thinks of the teacher, Jed Reynolds. Maria's teacher,
in Lajitas.

'If she ends up losing her mother, whatever chance she
had gets snuffed out pretty early…'

Above the cemetery, three buzzards wheel in the
towering sky. Weightless. Through an unending circle.

Michael Tyler saved a doomed patrol. Gilman James
tried to keep everybody alive.

What man, so much the product of his life and times,
could be entirely condemned? Except by his own hand. And
by the hand of God.

He stares at the cover of the printed pages.

John Joseph Whicher,
US Deputy Marshal, Western Division

⚓

We crossed on a summer rock slide. In an unnamed
ravine. Truck wheels in the shallow water. The storm
blinding.

But Joe had shown her, he'd made her learn it by heart.

If anyone tried to stop us—at the last—we never knew.

Where we are now, I won't say. Nor do I know how things will be.

The mountain is high. Wild burro graze in the shadow of a canyon. Stones mark the old ejido land.

Maria sits and talks with me now. White-tailed deer come in the mornings. They drink from a water hole, with their young.

I had a better chance than some. Better than Jesse.

Each generation has something. We hardly see it, and time won't wait.

Tennille watches the twisted trail from the village.

Sometimes she places her hand on mine.

I don't move it away.

Made in the USA
Las Vegas, NV
14 October 2021

32338574R00236